2 Dirty
Wedding
Nights

# 2 Dirty Wedding Nights

## JAINE DIAMOND

Dream Warp
Publications LLC

2 *Dirty Wedding Nights*
Jaine Diamond

*Dirty Like Us* First Edition December 2016
*A Dirty Wedding Night* First Edition May 2018

ISBN 978-1-989273-77-7

Cover and interior design by Jaine Diamond / DreamWarp Publishing Ltd.

Published by DreamWarp Publishing Ltd.
www.jainediamond.com

# CONTENTS

# Dirty Like Us

*For my man;*
*you're more of a romantic than you think.*

# AUTHOR'S NOTE

This book is a prequel novella for the Dirty series. It takes place in the timeline before *Dirty Like Me*.

As a prequel, *Dirty Like Us* is a cliffhanger novella; this is Zane and Maggie's story, but it's only a slice of their story. These two have a complicated relationship; this is not an easy love, and it's bound to go so very wrong before it goes right... All of which means that Zane and Maggie's story won't be continued and resolved until later in the series, when they get their own full-length novel (*Dirty Like Zane*).

In the meantime, *Dirty Like Us* gives us a delicious taste of what's been going on between these two!

With love from the beautiful west coast of Canada
(the home of Dirty!),
Jaine

# DIRTY LIKE US

# Maggie

THE RED CARPET was worn beneath our feet. The altar was a single step, also carpeted in red, on which we stood, along with the officiant.

The officiant wore a black leather motorcycle jacket, a faded Steppenwolf T-shirt, ratty jeans and biker boots. A black leather bible decorated with silver studs lay open on his hands.

I wore a pink dress.

The room was small, and there were no windows. The ceiling was arched and the walls were black, strewn with neon beer signs and replica platinum albums.

There was a row of eight gunmetal chairs, four to the right of the aisle and four to the left, two of which were occupied. A woman I didn't know stood at the back of the room with a polite smile on her face. A man with a gun stood guard at the door.

Outside, traffic rumbled by, occasionally vibrating the kitschy junk on the walls.

In the next room, an awful song played faintly on repeat. A cheesy, sleazy rock song about a schoolgirl.

Near me, someone was talking.

But all I could hear was that old Steppenwolf song, "Magic Carpet Ride," playing in my head. I heard it the way Zane once sang it, as we sat around a campfire drinking Jäger from a bottle someone passed around, his voice so raw and smoky and beautiful it gave me goosebumps. I heard it the way my mom used to play it, loud, on her wonky old turntable, as she danced in the kitchen in one of her flowy blouses and a pair of cut-offs.

I could see her now, dancing in her bare feet, and looking so, so young.

And I wished she was here.

I was holding hands with him, and my knees were quivering. I could feel his heartbeat in his fingers wrapped tight around mine. His thumb smoothed back and forth across my knuckles, over the new ring on my finger, as I breathed, shallow and slow.

He was looking at me. I knew he was. I could feel the heat of his gaze moving over my face.

"Maggie."

I took a breath and felt his heartbeat, once... twice... Then I looked up into that gorgeous face. His arctic blue eyes held mine. He squeezed my hands slightly.

*Zane.*

Me.

Holding hands at the altar.

*Holy shit.*

"That's your cue, babe," Zane said, and I realized the man in the leather jacket had been the one speaking. To me. Everyone was looking at me and waiting.

And I just stared at Zane.

The corners of his eyes twitched. He smiled slightly and I couldn't stop myself. I never could, when it came to him.

I smiled back.

"Yeah," I said, in response to the man's question, but the word cracked and came out a whisper. I cleared my throat and found my voice. "I do."

# CHAPTER ONE

# *Maggie*

*Two hours earlier...*

I STOOD in the middle of the massive, glittering bathroom, trying not to imagine how much this hotel suite would've cost if we had to pay for it. And trying not to think about why we didn't.

I'd told Coop to go ahead and help himself to the complimentary champagne, because no way I was drinking it. Instead I grabbed one of the little glasses by the sink and fixed myself a vodka cran, pouring from the bottle of Stoli I'd paid for myself. Then I lay my travel case open on the floor and took a breath.

The last hour of my life had been a total gong show, the conversation with my father pretty much the furthest thing from an aphrodisiac. I just needed a few minutes to get my head together and switch gears.

I took a swig of my drink and assessed myself in the mirrored wall. I was still wearing the jeans and midriff-baring jacket I'd worn to dinner with the crew, but I'd already decided the occasion called for something a *lot* sexier.

I dug through my stuff, unearthing the new lingerie and snapping off the tags. Then I went over my mental checklist as I got undressed.

The band was all settled into the hotel, finished with the promotional interviews I'd set up for them earlier in the day, and they were officially set loose for the night. In Las Vegas. The last I'd seen of each of them, they were off in various directions in search of sex (Zane), booze (Dylan), and/or solitude (Jesse and Elle). Tomorrow night was the final show of the tour and everyone was jacked up on a hazardous cocktail of anticipation, adrenaline and hormones. Not the kind of hazard I could do much about, other than stay out of the way and be on hand for cleanup later. My boss, Brody, and I were band management, which meant we booked gigs, made sure everyone got paid, and generally kept the money flowing in. But it also meant we took it upon ourselves to make sure everyone stayed relatively sane, so the reality was, if anything fell apart between now and tomorrow's show, my phone was gonna blow up like the Freemont Street light show, and not like I could ignore it.

Story of my life, but at least everything was as it should be on that front.

Security, crew, and gear were all accounted for and everything was set for Dirty, hottest rock band on the planet and my kickass employers—fuck, yeah—to rock the hell out of the new arena on the Vegas Strip. And while I was excited about tomorrow's show in that bittersweet way that marked the end of each tour, I was really looking forward to a momentary diversion from the madness.

A diversion of the sexual variety. Because the Penny Pushers were also in town for the show, and that meant I was hooking up.

I slipped into the skimpy lace babydoll and matching thong, both a vibrant lime-green that looked amazing against my complexion. Thanks to my mom, I had flawless light-brown skin, which I'd always considered my best feature. Admittedly, because it made me look less like my dad.

Usually when people found out who he was, they assumed I'd *want* to be associated with him. He was rich and famous, after all.

But those were the people who'd never met him.

I took a couple more swigs of my drink, hiked up my cleavage with the stiff demi cups of the babydoll, and touched up my makeup, letting the liquor and the bizarre, hyper-reality of this moment soak in.

I, Maggie Omura, was about to fuck a rock star.

*What would you think of that one, Mom?*

She'd laugh, I figured. Hard. Since this went completely against The Rule.

I'd made up The Rule myself when I first came to work for Dirty six years ago. Actually, I'd made up many rules. What the hell did I know? I was a nerdy, idealistic nineteen-year-old with stars in my eyes. But as I'd discovered, in the total shit storm of rock 'n' roll chaos that soon became my life, there was only one rule that warranted keeping.

No Screwing The Talent.

When I first met Dirty, their debut album had just incinerated the charts and they were coming off their first world tour. I was naive and inexperienced, but I had a head for business and all I'd ever wanted to do was work in the music industry. I managed to get an incredibly tenuous foot in the door merely because of a lucky-horseshoe-up-the-ass situation—I happened to have a class with Dirty guitarist Jesse Mayes's sister in college, and she and I had become friends. I also had the hugest, stupidest puppy-love crush on Zane Traynor, blond bad boy and lunatic lead singer... and when he set his ice-blue eyes on me, I knew the only way I wouldn't fuck everything up was by eating, sleeping and breathing The Rule.

Over the years, The Rule had kept me out of trouble. A *lot* of trouble. However. Sometimes rules became outdated. Needed a little revising. Or strategic bending.

And since I wasn't about to screw a member of the band I worked for, it didn't totally count, right?

"Maggie?" Coop tapped on the frosted-glass bathroom door, amusement and a touch of concern in his voice. "You ever coming out?" He also sounded horny, his voice low and a little huskier than usual.

Perfect.

I stood back to check my work and felt ridiculously sexy for about five seconds, knowing he was gonna love it... until it really dawned on me that I'd bought the lingerie for that reason. Because Andy Cooper had mentioned, months ago, that I looked hot in this color. Which meant... yeah. I was putting way too much effort into this.

Kinda like I did with every-fucking-thing.

But this was weird, right? Crossing a line?

Coop was just a hookup, and no sane woman bought hot, expensive lingerie just for some guy she was hooking up with unless she was looking to turn that hookup sex into hang-out-afterward-and-do-it-again sex, followed by wake-up-together-the-next-morning-and-do-it-yet-again sex.

And I definitely wasn't looking for that.

Was I?

I smoothed my long, dark hair and chewed my lip at my reflection. Hot. But yeah, weird.

"Maggie?" Coop knocked again.

I pounded back the rest of my drink. "Coming."

Lingerie or no? I could take it off, walk out there naked.

Veto.

Put the jeans back on?

I made an executive decision to go with the lingerie, took a deep breath, and opened the door. Despite the fact that I didn't feel quite as special about Coop as the lingerie implied, my night had just gone to hell and I *really* needed this distraction.

I just hoped he had time to help me blow off all this steam; it could take a while.

Coop stood back, his eyebrows raising as he drank me in. He wore a vintage Sex Pistols T-shirt with the sleeves cut off, showing off his incredibly decent arms, with gray jeans and a studded belt. His blond hair was tousled to shit, like it always was, and an impish smile broke out on his face. "Whoa. Maggie... shit." He scrubbed his hand through his hair. "I feel kinda underdressed."

"Then let's get you undressed," I said, letting my inner slut take over as I grabbed him by his shirt and pulled him over to the giant bed. I'd claimed the smaller of the two bedrooms in the penthouse suite, yet the bed was king size, which made me wonder what was in the master bedroom. Harem size?

Fitting, given who'd be sleeping in it.

*Don't even go there.*

I yanked Coop against me and we came together in a hungry, slightly awkward kiss. He pushed me back onto the bed, his warm weight settling over me. Despite the offer of free champagne, he tasted vaguely like beer, which reminded me of finding him in the hotel bar half an hour ago... which reminded me of running into Zane about half an hour before that—

*Do. NOT. Go. There.*

Coop's body was lean and hard as he ground himself against me, his hips dragging over mine, the hard ridge of the unmistakable erection in his jeans setting off sparks of pleasure between my legs, and I gasped.

Oh, *hell* yes... this was exactly what I needed.

He kissed his way down my neck and I groaned, arching my back, getting into it as he sucked on my throat—

*Holy. Shit.* I stiffened as joyful screaming and laughter erupted in the room next door—the main room of the penthouse suite.

The voices of multiple women.

Coop didn't seem to notice. Or care. He just ground his hard dick against me and kissed me again. I shut my eyes as his weight pressed me down, his hips moving faster against me, his body heating up. He grabbed my breast, squeezing hard, and sank his tongue deep in my mouth.

Then I heard it. I heard *him.* My "roommate" for the night. His smoky voice so close outside the bedroom door I cringed.

My eyes flew open. I ripped away, stopping Coop with a hand on his chest, so suddenly I startled us both.

He looked down at my hand as I panted beneath him. "You okay?" he asked, disoriented. "Did I hurt you?"

"No," I managed to choke out, clearing my throat.

*Fuck. Me.*

My head was spinning, and I could still hear his voice in the other room. I couldn't tell what he was saying, but I knew that cocky timber. I knew the sound of Zane Traynor working his magic on a bunch of women.

"Just... don't..." I gasped out, shaking my head, "... don't stop." Then I grabbed Coop by his neck and smashed my mouth to his as a ridiculous wave of guilt crashed through me.

I didn't feel guilty about breaking The Rule. I'd been breaking it with Coop on a casual but semi-regular basis for a while now.

I felt guilty I wasn't breaking it with *him*.

Yeah. That was the messed-up truth of it. Because I'd always secretly fantasized that if I was ever going to break The Rule I'd do it balls to the wall, in a total blaze of glory, me and the ice-blue-eyed reigning god of rock—and cock—swinging from chandeliers and breaking furniture.

But thank God my mother didn't raise that kind of fool.

I, Maggie Omura, was never going to let my incredibly misguided lady parts lead me to Zane Traynor's bed. No matter how much they might want me to.

*That way lies madness.*

On the other hand, Andy Cooper, wickedly talented bass player for the Penny Pushers and genuinely nice guy, was worth breaking a rule for, right? Besides that, Coop was exactly my type. Which was tall, blond, and rock 'n' roll.

Also, he'd just torn off his shirt and tossed it on the floor, and the sight of his bare chest helped me to focus.

He yanked the babydoll over my head and tossed it somewhere across the room as I tried really, really hard to block out the sounds of screeches and giggles from next door. I was pretty sure Coop said a bunch of nice things about how sexy I was as he kissed his way down my body, but I didn't really hear it.

Instead, I heard Zane's laugh. That potent, sexy-ass, full-on Viking laugh I would know anywhere, had creamed my panties to enough times that I'd never be able to hear it and not get wet. It was like a goddamn Pavlovian response.

I wriggled uncomfortably as Coop ran his fingers down between my legs, skimming the lace of my thong, hyper-aware of the fact that I was more turned on by that laugh than the feel of Coop's touch on my body. He rubbed me up and down, his hand moving in small, eager circles as he kissed his way down my stomach... and I tried to enjoy it, I really did.

But then the music kicked in.

Loud.

It was Guns N' Roses, "You're Crazy," at top fucking volume. Not the acoustic version. The heavy version, hard and fast, thumping through the wall.

Coop looked up in a lust daze, the corner of his mouth hooking in a slight smile. "Who's out there?"

"Just... ah... one of the guys..." I said, my brain split between the pleasure of what he was doing to me and the party going on next door. "And... about... half a chorus line... from the sound of it..."

Coop laughed. "Should I go tell them to turn it down?"

Sweet. But no way I would do that to Coop.

"No," I said, "just keep..." and then my head dropped back on the bed as he increased the urgency of his touch. He swirled his tongue around my navel, letting out a low groan, then kissed his way down. I took a breath and struggled to focus on the sensations of his tongue licking its way along the lacy edge of my thong, his fingers slipping inside to peel back the fabric. Then I felt the caress of his hot breath, just as laughter exploded on the other side of the wall.

*His* laughter, loud and cocksure.

A chorus of female giggles followed, and a surge of raw jealousy scorched through me.

Worst. Roommate. *Ever.*

Would it totally kill the mood if I put in earplugs before Coop fucked me?

Yes. Yes, it would.

Maybe we could put on some music of our own? I had a laptop here somewhere... but no way my laptop speakers could compete with the sound system from hell next door.

Zane laughed again, and my nipples pricked.

I clenched my teeth and squirmed in frustration.

Maybe my father was right.

Maybe I was just some glorified groupie.

God knew I'd had it bad for Zane since long before I'd met him in the flesh. And ever since... yeah, I still lusted after him—in secret. Physically speaking, Zane Traynor was a god among men, and I was only human.

But that didn't mean I'd ever, ever act on it.

*Screw him*, said the voice of reason in my head, the one that sounded suspiciously like my mom's. Because what the hell did my dad know about it anyway?

No mere groupie would've worked as hard as I had, for as long as I had, and put up with the shit that I had—much less stuck to The Rule for as many years as I did.

And now that I'd chosen to break The Rule? So what? I was a single woman. It was my prerogative if I wanted to screw every rock star I'd ever met. Besides, I was having a great time with Coop, I was ignoring Zane's inconvenient presence, and I wasn't at all imagining that it was his face between my legs right now.

Yeah.

I totally was.

Good news, though: I'd completely tensed up and my hand was on Coop's forehead. I was tongue-blocking him.

Sexy.

He stopped, obviously, and looked up at me. "Uh... are you sure—?"

"Hang on a sec, while I commit a super quick murder."

He backed off, letting me up.

"You sure you don't want me to—?"

"Nope." I rolled over and off the bed in one angry lunge, righting my lime-green thong. "I've got this." I scooped up the first thing I saw—his giant T-shirt—and thrust my almost-naked self into it as I stalked over to the bedroom door.

When I threw it open, the scene that greeted me was pretty much what it sounded like.

The main room of the penthouse suite had been overrun with groupies, bits of their skimpy clothing flung across the gaudy, oversized furniture. There were five of them, and while I doubted they were actual strippers—Zane didn't tend to hang with women who expected to get more attention than they gave, since he preferred to be the center of attention in any given room—I'd definitely walked in on some kind of amateur revue for their one-man audience.

Two blonds were dancing together on the coffee table, the one with the big fake breasts, already topless, undressing the other.

A chick with jet-black hair, in a metallic shrink-wrap dress, was bent over in the kitchen snorting what I could only assume was cocaine off the glossy countertop, showing off her matching metallic thong while she did it.

The other two were pawing each other on one of the big, plush couches. And there was Zane, front row center. Sprawled back on that same couch, legs spread wide. The girls were kneeling over him, and I really could've sworn he looked kinda bored as he watched them make out.

I was already bored, but then again, I didn't have a penis.

One of the girls in his lap was a redhead. The other looked suspiciously Filipina, and even though she didn't look much like *me*, it really fucking irritated me. The man had a serious talent for irritating me—and for sniffing out exactly when he was doing it, like some sadistic bloodhound. I was pretty sure he got off on it. It didn't surprise me at all when his ice-blue eyes met mine, though none of the girls even noticed I was there.

He stared at me, his eyes flaring. He looked pretty blown away to see me, actually. Well, no shit.

Not like I *wanted* to be stuck in the room adjoining his latest orgy.

I pointed one finger at him and rolled it back, in the universal gesture for *Get your ass over here*. Which he could've ignored. He could've told me where to go with a finger gesture of his own.

Technically, the man was my employer.

Instead he dumped the girls off his lap, eyes still locked on mine, and adjusted himself in his low-slung jeans. That's when I made the mistake of glancing down.

The top button of his jeans was undone, showing a triangle of sun-kissed skin and a hint of his golden treasure trail, not to mention the perfect, tight abs that disappeared under his shirt.

The girls kept going at it, oblivious to his departure, as he rose and stalked toward me.

Tall. Blond. And *very* rock 'n' roll.

I just watched him, my features carefully arranged in a look of cool, unruffled displeasure as I forced myself to keep breathing so my heart wouldn't explode in an epic cataclysm of rage and repressed lust. Luckily, I had a *lot* of practice with this. Still, my traitorous gaze wandered down the thin black T-shirt stretched over his broad, hard chest and the badass black leather vest, the muscles bunching in his sleek, California-tanned arms... the unbuttoned jeans just barely clinging to his hips... and *fuck*... did it make me a total weirdo that I had a crazy weakness for the man's bare feet?

It didn't exactly escape my notice that his dick looked pretty hard, either. Kinda like it was about to punch through his jeans, but Zane's package pretty much always looked that way.

It wasn't exactly an industry secret that Zane Traynor was well-hung.

In fact, I'd seen his naked cock with my own eyes, multiple times. Not that that meant anything. Pretty sure everyone and their dog had seen it. Since the man was Adonis incarnate, you couldn't even blame him for showing it off, though his habit of walking around naked in mixed company—irritating for a multitude of reasons—was the main reason everyone in the band refused to share a suite with him.

Well that, and all the groupies.

Really, you'd think a decade would be plenty of time for your average man to tire, or bore, of the groupie thing and move on. Zane, though?

Nothing was average about Zane.

He stopped a few inches from me, all up in my space, but I stood my ground. I looked straight up into his beautiful face and met his unholy blue eyes.

His blond hair, shaved short on the sides but long on top, slid over his eye as he looked down at me. He raked it slowly back with one ring-laden hand and I caught a breath of him... that crazy-delicious man scent of his that always made my ovaries skip a beat.

"Maggie May," he said, and the devil was in his slow, easy smile. Yeah. The son of a bitch smiled, like he was happy to see me. "Just thinking about you."

*Fuck me.* He totally said that.

He eyed the oversized T-shirt I was wearing, the diabolical gears turning in his head. "The hell are you doing here?"

I wasn't gonna touch that. Not the point. Though I *was* glad to hear that he didn't know I was in the next room when he decided to throw this little party.

Then the song changed, and Marvin Gaye's "Let's Get It On" started playing... and the bottom completely fell out of my anger. Because seriously.

"Classy, Zane."

"I'm all class, sweetheart," he said, and the smile lit up his gorgeous face.

I couldn't even help smiling back as I rolled my eyes. *Shit,* though. I was supposed to be mad.

How the hell did he always do this to me?

Oh, right. Because the man was evil.

He was also charming as hell, and while I wanted to hate him, a lot, sometimes I failed at that. Big time.

Sometimes—well, most of the time—I liked Zane Traynor far too much for my own good.

# CHAPTER TWO

## Zane

MAGGIE CROSSED her arms and glared up at me, like she was trying really hard to stay pissed. Which was cool with me. When Maggie got pissed, I got hard. Which meant I was already a helluva lot harder than I was a minute ago watching a couple of random chicks suck face. Especially when her nipples popped out against her shirt.

I did kinda feel like a jackass though. Had no clue she was in there.

My gaze skimmed down the oversized Sex Pistols shirt she was wearing, obviously a dude's. Not Maggie's usual look. Her lips were swollen and her compulsively-smooth hair was mussed up like she'd just gotten something on her back besides sleep.

What the hell did I interrupt in there?

I glanced over her shoulder but I couldn't see shit, just the door to a bathroom. I shifted closer until we almost touched, leaning a shoulder on the door frame.

"Who the fuck's been sucking on your neck?" My gaze had snagged on the mark I was pretty sure was a hickey.

She made an exasperated, frustrated noise in her throat that made my balls pull up tight.

It was no secret, at least to my dick, that I wanted this woman. Unfortunately for me and my dick, I'd never gotten my hands on her for more than a hug.

Maggie and I were "coworkers" and "friends" and not supposed to "go there."

According to her.

"Zane," she said extra-politely, "please take this in the nicest way possible, but you need to fuck off right now."

I ignored that. Maggie told me to fuck off at least once a day. Justifiably.

We had that kind of relationship. I was comfortable enough to piss her off, she was comfortable enough to tell me to fuck off, and at the end of the day none of it mattered. Maggie and I *were* friends. The kind that occasionally wanted to kill each other, but still.

What kind of friend would I be if I didn't at least make sure she wasn't in there with some loser?

I tried to get a look behind her again but she closed the door as far as she could, wedging herself in the narrow opening. I wedged myself right in with her, shouldering the door a little farther open. I drew the line at forcing my way past her, but fuck yeah. I was gonna check up on this asshole whether she liked it or not.

"Come on, Maggs. I wanna meet him." I gave her my wickedest smile, the one that made most girls soak their panties.

Maggie? Maggie wasn't most girls.

"Don't be an asshole, Zane. And would you please mind banging your new lady friends in your own room? You've got the master bedroom. See, over there. Behind those nice big solid doors."

"Oh, they're not for me."

She rolled her eyes. "Right."

"I brought them for Jesse," I said, which was true, even if she didn't believe it. "Hear he and Elle are fighting."

Yeah, so I was a shit disturber. But when weren't those two fighting?

Fuck if getting together wasn't the worst mistake my two

dumbass bandmates ever made. I'd put money on a breakup at the end of this tour. Better for the band. Better for everyone.

Loved Elle, she was a great girl, but my band brother needed an epic cocksuck, badly, to remind him life was too short for one pussy. Especially one that drove him up the fucking wall.

"Well," Maggie said, "I'm sure Jesse *and Elle* would appreciate the gesture, but Jesse isn't here. I am."

"Cool. And why is that?"

She sighed. "Let's just say... things got screwed up with the rooms, okay?" Then she started chewing on her lip.

"Uh-huh," I said, distracted at the sight of her teeth gnawing on that full bottom lip. Fuck, but Maggie had a hot mouth. "Screwed up how?"

What the fuck happened to this girl's mood since I saw her in the lobby an hour ago, looking all flushed and fucking cheerful? It was a great look on her, and I wanted some of it. I'd gotten a little carried away, putting her up against the wall, and for a nanosecond as those gorgeous gray eyes blinked up at me I thought she might actually accept my invitation to come party, which she never did. I always asked. She always said no.

It was kind of a ritual.

Maybe for once I shouldn't have taken it like a gentleman.

"Look, it sucks we have to share a suite," she said, ignoring my question. "But we're both gonna do what we're gonna do." She cocked her head a little, glancing past me. "Seriously though, can we draw the line at the coke?"

I waited until her gray eyes lifted to mine again. I didn't love seeing the worry in them... but Maggie *always* worried about me falling off the wagon into a vat of whiskey. I got that. Cocaine was never my thing, but Jack Daniels wasn't exactly a hard man to find in a Vegas hotel.

Then I gave her what she wanted, because yeah. It was Maggie. And I was pussy-whipped like that.

"Yo, Snow White," I called over to the black-haired chick in the kitchen. "Time to go, sweetheart."

She was dancing by herself to Marvin Gaye, but Natalie jumped down off the coffee table, dragging the other blond with her to form a protective wall of bitch. "What!" Nat squawked, then threw me a theatrical pout. "If she goes then so do we."

"Then go," I said.

"Zane! What the fuck! Who the fuck is *she*?" Nat stood there in her panties, totally fucking indignant, looking at Maggie like she'd just stepped in shit.

Which really cranked up my stone cold.

"Get your skank ass outta here, Nat."

Natalie's mouth fell open. It was a good mouth to have around if you wanted your cock sucked, but other than that, she could keep it shut as far as I was concerned. She was the only one of them I'd met before half an hour ago, and that wasn't exactly a ringing endorsement for the rest.

"You're a real asshole," she snapped, yanking on her skirt.

"So they keep telling me."

Nat huffed, grabbed the rest of her clothes and stalked out with her coked-up friend. The other blond yanked a top over her fake tits, kissed me on the cheek, gave Maggie a catty once-over and left.

"Don't let the door smack your ass on the way out!" Maggie called after her, then grumbled, "Wouldn't wanna give it chlamydia."

I stared at Maggie and she gave me a fake-ass smile right back.

So fucking interesting.

Six years I'd known her, and I'd never seen her in this particular mood. Normally she kept her shit under wraps. Cool, controlled Maggie; it wasn't easy, even for me, to faze the woman. But right now, she was definitely pissed the fuck off, and frustrated.

Sexually frustrated?

If I didn't know better, I might've even said she was jealous.

Whatever it was, it was giving me a raging hard-on.

She made an irritated noise in her throat and I followed her gaze; the other two chicks were still at it on the couch, but now they were horizontal and kinda scissoring.

"Good night, Zane."

Maggie tried to shut the door, but I stopped it with my foot.

"Aren't we in a mood."

"Hey." Some shirtless dickwit appeared behind Maggie, running a hand through his scraggly hair, and a flash of kill-crazy jealousy went off like a firecracker in my gut. "Everything okay?" He met my eyes and flicked his chin at me in greeting.

Fucking *Coop.*

I blinked, 'cause I couldn't quite believe it.

*Maggie* was fucking *Coop?*

Shit, no.

I was all for fucking, in general. Was even pretty sure on a rare occasion or two some fuckwad had probably slipped under my nose and snaked his way up Maggie's skirt. I was no idiot. Chick as hot as Maggie had gotten cock somewhere, at some point in history, even if she was too fucking discreet, not to mention uptight, to ever let on about it.

But this? Not happening.

So fucking not happening.

"Give us a minute," she said to him sweetly, like really fucking sweetly, in a tone I'd sure as fuck never heard her use on me. "You know, band business."

"Oh. Sure." Coop disappeared, reluctantly. No shit. I'd get impatient too if Maggie was talking to some asshole at the door instead of riding my dick.

"You're not fucking Coop," I said, low enough he wouldn't hear it, leaning in to make sure she did, my face tipped down to hers.

She didn't back down. She just glowered at me, her eyes narrowing and her sweet mouth puckering, all pissed off and petite.

Which was why I loved fighting with Maggie. She was so fucking hot when she was mad. Hot, and cute as all fuck. Adorable. Like a feral kitten.

Also, if I really hit the sweet spot and she lost her temper, made it a lot harder for her to ignore me like she usually tried to do when I jabbed her buttons.

"Are you fucking Coop?" I pressed.

"News flash, Zane," she bit out. "You're not the only one who might want to do it in this stupid-fancy hotel suite, okay?"

"Jesus, though. *Coop?*"

She glared up at me, a storm brewing in her gray eyes. Then she growled. She actually *growled*, low in her throat, and I swear to Christ I almost came in my pants. "What the hell is wrong with Coop?"

"Where do you want me to start? For one, he's not me."

"Nuh-uh," she said, pinching the bridge of her nose. "Not doing this. Not getting into this with you."

"Let's get into it," I said, pushing another inch into the room, my pulse beating in my dick, spurring me on.

"Nope." She put her hand in the middle of my chest, holding me off. "It's been a really bad night, I have not been laid since Christmas, and you are *not* going to ruin this for me."

Then she shut the door in my face.

Christmas?

Christmas was four months ago.

As I stood there, my back to the bedroom door, I racked my fucking brain to figure out who the hell Maggie'd fucked at Christmas.

Coop?

Some other fuckwit?

As far as I knew she wasn't seeing anyone regular. Maggie'd never had a boyfriend in the years I'd known her. I'd seen Coop checking her out. I'd seen him flirt with her, but big fucking deal. Who didn't flirt with Maggie? Half the crew was hard up for her, but the girl was so fucking proper and all-business she hardly seemed to notice. She so rarely partied with anyone, I'd gotten pretty comfortable telling myself if she wasn't sucking my cock, at least she wasn't sucking anyone else's.

Now I had a visual. Sweet Maggie, down on her knees sucking off Andy Cooper—*fuuuck*. The murderous surge of testosterone and adrenalin made my dick so hard it felt like it might split in half.

*Shit.*

Maybe I *was* a fucking idiot.

Two hot chicks, horny and willing, were going at it right in front of me, and my head was in the next room.

But no fucking wonder. I'd been hot for Maggie, one of a very few woman I'd ever spent more than an hour with who wouldn't spread her legs for me, for years. *Years.* And now she was giving it up to Coop?

Fuck. That.

Who the hell did he think he was?

Asshole had pretty much fucked his band's sweet ride on Dirty's coattails the second he breathed on Maggie. I said the word, the Pushers were off the next tour, and that gave me a grim fucking sense of satisfaction.

Would I actually do it? Maybe.

Depending how things went down tonight.

I grabbed the remote to lower the volume on the music. Too bad. It was Wolfmother's "Woman," a decent song to fuck to.

I liked sex the way I liked my music: loud and hard.

No idea how Marvin Gaye got in the mix. Probably my wise-ass drummer, fucking with me.

I listened, but I couldn't hear shit from next door. What kind of awkwardly quiet, polite sex were those two planning on having? What were they doing in there, right now?

And how long was I gonna let this slide?

According to my phone, three fucking minutes had passed since Maggie shut the door. Felt like a goddamn hour.

But the longer I let this go, the worse it would be for Coop when I kicked his ass out. Yeah, so I was a sadistic prick. Didn't bother me in the slightest that I was about to cockblock a brother.

Not when he was in there right now with Maggie, getting ready to stick his dick in her.

Right. That was about far enough.

I hammered my fist on the bedroom door. Hard.

Half a minute later, Coop opened it.

"Maggie!" I thundered over him. "Get your ass out here."

"Don't let him in!" Maggie called from inside. "He's like a goddamn vampire. You invite him in, you give him power."

Coop's eyes narrowed a little as he looked me over and every muscle in my body coiled tight. Pretty sure he could smell the lust and aggravation rolling off me, but he just shrugged. "Sorry, man."

He started to close the door but I stopped it with my hand.

"Coming in to talk to Maggie," I said evenly. "You can step aside or I can take this shit right through you."

He sized me up again and I flexed my other hand at my side, a couple of knuckles cracking as I made a fist. Adrenalin surged through me. Never woulda thought Coop had it in him, but shit. Was he actually considering fighting me for Maggie?

I'd spent years as a kid getting the shit kicked outta me by dudes way tougher and way meaner than Coop, and you got a clue, you lose enough fights, eventually you learn how to win. Which meant Coop took me on, he was so gonna lose this fight.

He knew it, too.

"Whatever," he muttered and opened the door.

"For fuck's sake, Zane!" Maggie scrambled off the bed, yanking her shirt down to cover herself. She was still wearing Coop's T-shirt. "What do you want?"

"Want?" I met her in the middle of the room and once I was in her face, I leveled her with a hard, simmering eye-fuck, seeing as that was the only way I ever got to fuck her. "You really want an answer to that, babe?"

"You two got some shit to sort out?" Coop asked, standing off to the side, scrubbing a hand through his hair.

"Yup," I said, in the exact same breath that she said, "No."

We stood there a foot apart, me eye-fucking her and vibrating with adrenalin, my dick standing at attention, her glaring up at me with her chest heaving and not blinking.

"Yeah, I'm just gonna go."

"Cool," I said, as Coop headed for the door. "Coupla girls in the other room. They're yours if you want. Just take 'em with you when you go."

"Alright, brother."

Maggie's jaw dropped.

"Andy." She looked from me to him as he paused in the doorway. Then she walked over to him. "I have your *shirt*," she said, clearly unable to process what the fuck was going on.

"Keep it," he said. Then he gave her a chaste little kiss on the forehead and left, shutting the door behind himself.

Maggie drew a deep, ragged breath, then let it out between her clenched teeth. Her shoulders dropped as she turned to me.

"Are you kidding me?"

I shrugged. "He scares easy, Maggs. And he was pretty quick to replace you. Better you find that out now."

She stood there raging, kinda like a baby bull about to charge. Then she took a few slow, measured breaths. She walked over and stood in front of me. Her gray eyes met mine, so fucking stunning against her honey-toned skin.

"I hope that amused you. Because it really fucking sucked for me."

"Maggie—"

"Don't. Coop's a nice guy, and you just treated him like—"

"Coop's a fucking pussy," I ground out. "He just *walked out on you*. While you're wearing his shirt. And why don't you take that shit off? Take a shower while you're at it, 'cause you stink like smarmy bass player."

Yup.

Shit disturber.

But some things just needed to be said.

Maggie stared at me and an ugly, loaded, fucking terrible silence landed in the wake of my words. Her lips parted... then she shut her mouth. Her jaw spasmed, her eyelashes trembled, and for a horrible minute I thought she might cry.

Then she scowled instead and something raw flashed in her eyes, between hurt and rage.

"Yeah?" She whipped the shirt off over her head and flung it across the room. "Well, the shirt's not the only thing he touched." She stood there in her tiny, neon-green panties and nothing else, and my jaw went slack.

I had no words.

No. Fucking. Words.

I'd never seen so much of Maggie before. Couldn't believe how much better the flesh was than my imagination, and I'd spent a helluva lot of time imagining her.

I drank in her petite curves, the soft swell of her breasts, her hard nipples a dark, dusky pink as her chest rose and fell with the force of her uneven breaths.

Then I swallowed, hard, and ground my teeth. I shoved my hands in the pockets of my jeans.

Had to, or I was gonna grab her, slam her down on the bed and devour every inch of that gorgeous smooth skin.

"Guess I should take this off too." She plucked at the see-through lace of her panties and my dick achieved a new level of hard, kinda like reinforced steel. Then her finger touched my chin, guiding my eyes up. "Go fuck yourself, Zane."

"Okay," I said. "If you're into that, I can show you a few things."

She made a little choked noise, shaking her head in disbelief. Her eyes never left mine and it was still there, the raw and the rage, her jaw hardening like she was fighting the urge to literally bite my head off.

"Oh, for fuck's sake," she hissed. "Is that all you *ever* want? Seriously. What. The. *Fuck.*"

Then she launched herself at me.

Maggie was a small woman, but it took me so off-guard, it brought me to my knees as she smashed her mouth to mine. I caught her in my arms, just barely, and her legs went around my hips as she kissed me with a fucking vengeance, all angry lips and teeth, her hands clawing at my neck, her fingernails digging in.

Holy mother of fuck.

*Maggie was kissing me.*

I gripped her tight and kissed her back like my life, my very next breath, depended on it, my heart slamming a fucking dent in the wall of my chest as my brain completely spun out.

All I could think was, if I fucked her right here on the floor, would she hate me for it?

Because my gut was telling me to put her down... to let her go, to back the fuck off... that this wasn't right, that Maggie wasn't gonna be happy about this even *if* she started it... but my dick just wanted to make her scream and figure the rest out later, and my dick was a bull-headed prick.

I caught my teeth on her bottom lip and when she gave up a ragged gasp, my tongue plunged into her like a heat-seeking missile. I tasted her like I'd wanted to do for fucking years, desperate to have her, any way I could get her, angry, clawing at me, I didn't care.

Then it hit me, and I almost gagged.

The taste of liquor. Pungent and sour... revolting... and totally fucking intoxicating.

And I dove right into it.

I screwed my tongue into her mouth like I was tongue-fucking the neck of a bottle, sucking hard, the bliss of that taste and a brutal crush of memories smashing me in the back of the skull.

Then I caught myself. I almost gagged, again.

I ripped myself away with such force I shoved her off.

I spit out that bittersweet taste on the carpet and mashed the back of my hand to my mouth.

Yeah... not the best thing to do after kissing a woman. Kinda ranked right up there with laughing at her and throwing up.

I saw it in her gray eyes... the exact moment she started hating me. Or at least, hating me more than she already did.

Her face shut down and she wrapped her arms around her chest as she sat there on the floor staring up at me, next-to-naked in her lace panties, looking small and so fucking vulnerable it gutted me.

"You're so full of shit," she whispered.

"Maggie—"

"Get out."

And for once, there was no arguing the point. I was the world's biggest asshole, and now she had proof.

I got the fuck out.

# CHAPTER THREE

# Maggie

THERE WERE FUCK UPS, and then there were Fuck Ups.

And I had just Fucked Up.

Despite how I might look, given that I was on the petite side and my tastes ran to pretty makeup, manicures and four-inch-heels—in which I was still petite—I was a tough chick. Had to be, given the life I lived and the job I had to do. Which meant that Fucking Up the way I just did hurt in a way I didn't often feel hurt, because my night had already gone bad, I'd already been hurt bad, and now I'd taken that hurt from bad to worse.

And now I, Maggie Omura, the tough girl, the "on it" girl, the organized-as-fuck girl, the girl *always* armed with a plan, was at a loss for what to do about it.

For once, I had no plan.

I didn't even have the first clue.

Freshly showered and wrapped in a hotel bathrobe, I leaned against the low wall of the giant rooftop patio, gazing out over the shimmering lights of the Strip below, as if they might have answers. I had my sunglasses on, dimming the night around me, because my eyes felt suspiciously tingly and *no one* was gonna see me cry.

Not that anyone was around.

I'd already checked to make sure Coop and the groupies were

gone; the main room of the suite was empty, the music turned off, and Zane was nowhere to be seen. The only thing out of place was a random lacy stocking, which I'd deposited in the trash before heading outside for some air.

The patio ran the full length of the penthouse, but I stuck to my own end. The last thing I needed was to wander past the glass doors that opened onto the master bedroom and glimpse Zane in there naked and doing God-knew-what.

I'd had enough of that man and his dick for one night.

*You're just mad because he shoved you away before you got to the really good part.*

*Jesus, but you can be a perv, Mom.*

God, why'd she have to butt into this? Not as if she'd never made any questionable decisions when it came to a charming, slutty rock star.

Guess this particular strain of masochism ran in the family.

I tore the foil from the top of the champagne bottle and untwisted the wire that secured the cork. To hell with my dad and his stupid free shit with all the strings attached. I was gonna drink his champagne, because fuck him.

And fuck Zane, too. Whatever his problem was, it was so not my problem. I just needed to remember that.

"Managing" the members of this band only went so fucking far.

I popped the cork and sucked off the gush of bubbly that erupted, hoping maybe I could lose the last hour-and-a-half of my life to champagne-induced bliss... because I couldn't even wrap my head around it.

I kissed Zane.

*And he shoved me away.*

Oh, and then there was that really fun part where he spat on the carpet.

Thank God for that, because it was just the punch in the face I needed. A reminder that throwing myself at Zane Traynor was a *complete and utter* Fuck Up.

I'd let him get under my skin, when I'd made it a policy, long ago, *never* to let that man anywhere near my skin. And now I was gonna pay for it in crazy.

*Shit.*

I got more than enough crazy from my dad.

I could not afford to let Zane's crazy overflow the professional bounds of our relationship just because I was hurt and angry—most of this hurt and anger misplaced, since it was my dad I was truly pissed at—not to mention horny, humiliated and vulnerable, and I lost my temper, snapped, and did something totally ridiculous.

It was my own fault, too. As much as I'd like to blame Zane, it wasn't exactly his fault I threw myself at him, no matter how big a dick he was being and how much that unfortunately, annoyingly messed with the signals between my clit and my brain. Acting on it —the anger and the messed up signals—was all me, and it was totally out of character.

Zane, for his part, was just being Zane.

Years ago, he and I had reached a kind of stalemate in our relationship. He wanted to sleep with me. I wasn't going to sleep with him. Neither one of us was about to budge, and as much as we butted heads over it, we kinda respected each other for it too. We were who we were, and that was just the way it was. He kept trying to get in my pants, because that's what Zane did. And I kept turning him down.

Simple. And the system worked for us.

Until it didn't.

Tonight the system totally crashed and burned. Thanks to me hurling myself, half-naked and angry, over that crucial line I'd never let *him* cross.

In the cold shower that followed, all I'd concluded about that was that for such a smart girl I could, on occasion, be really fucking stupid.

What the fuck was I thinking?

Like I was gonna teach Zane a lesson by shoving what he wanted in his face, once and for all? Like angry-kissing him for cock-blocking my hookup was some kind of punishment?

And then what? What did I expect him to do?

Grope me, definitely.

Try to fuck me, probably.

And then I'd laugh in his face and shove *him* away?

Right. Really fucking mature.

More likely, at the rate I was going, I would've hate-fucked him into next Tuesday.

Great plan. Like that was gonna help anything.

*Couldn't be any worse than being rejected by him, Maggie May.*

*Yeah, thanks, Mom. I kinda got that.*

I flopped onto one of the cushioned lounge chairs and put my feet up, taking another few swigs straight from the champagne bottle. Yeah, so I was drinking alone and that was kind of pathetic. Plus, I was having a two-way chat with my dead mom in my head. Nothing new, but it might be a good idea to bring another living person into this for a sanity check.

I pulled my phone out of the robe pocket. There were a couple of work-related texts awaiting reply; nothing urgent, but I responded. Then I thumbed through my contacts. Under *Favorites* I had the members of the band—Zane, Jesse, Elle and Dylan—as well as my boss, Brody, our head of security, Jude... and yeah, my dad. Not that I ever called him. The only other person on the list was Jessa, Jesse's sister, my girlfriend who'd introduced me to the band and to Brody in the beginning.

I stared at the very short list, stunned.

How the hell had my personal life come down to this?

It was no big secret that over the years I'd grown apart from, drifted away from, or just plain alienated all my girlfriends back home. Not on purpose, but life with the band, on and off the road, and working twenty-four-seven had taken its toll. I couldn't remember the last time I'd had a meaningful conversation with anyone outside this fucked up little rock 'n' roll bubble I called a life.

Mom. But she'd died three years ago.

I might've called Jessa, but I knew she was in New York for work, which meant she was probably asleep right now. That, or getting laid. And I didn't really want to interrupt either of those activities.

Didn't really feel like hanging with anyone in the band, either. The way my luck was going tonight, far too good a chance of running into Coop, and I was not having that.

Zane was right about one thing. Coop was a pussy.

I was totally gonna burn his shirt along with my expensive hookup lingerie. I didn't need any souvenirs from the worst sexual disaster of my life. Rejected by two hot guys in the span of five minutes? Might've set a new land speed record on that one.

Way to go.

If my future sex life was gonna end up as barren as my list of friends, it wasn't looking good.

I tossed my useless phone aside and that's when it hit me, hard. I'd broken my own biggest rule by pouncing on Zane, who had all but vomited in response, and I had no one to talk to about it. No one to call up on a Friday night and vent to.

No one who loved me enough to snap me out of my funk and tell me I was better than this.

*You are better than this.*

*Thanks, Mom.*

I drank to that.

Then I heard a door open behind me and I cringed.

*Please, please be anyone but Zane. The cleaning crew. Coop? A half-naked groupie looking for her lost stocking?*

No such luck.

Zane swaggered onto the patio, followed by room service. I refused to look at him, focusing instead on the giant room service tray the dude brought out and laid on the low table next to my lounge chair. It had a bowl of vanilla ice cream and a little glass pitcher of what had to be chocolate syrup, a stack of trashy magazines, and a martini glass filled with jellybeans—red, orange and purple only.

All my favorite shitty-mood fodder.

Zane tipped the room service guy and as soon as the guy was

gone, he took the champagne bottle from my hand. His fingers brushed mine and I caught his scent, again... my guts clenching as the memory of our kiss slammed into me. I could still feel it. Could still *taste* it. And lucky me, I now knew Zane smelled almost as good as he tasted... like raw, clean man, pure sex and total fucking trouble. I could never quite put my finger on that crazy-delicious scent of his. A hint of cool steel and warm leather... and some kind of spice? Fresh ground cardamom and cloves?

Who the hell smelled that amazing all the time?

I watched as he crossed the patio and set the bottle on one of the weird pseudo-ancient-Greek-motif mosaic tables, out of my reach.

"Whoever decorated this place, it's tacky as shit," he muttered.

Yeah. It was.

I considered protesting about the champagne, but I'd already sank half the bottle anyway, and truth be told I didn't like drinking in front of Zane. Seemed kinda wrong. Like eating a giant piece of chocolate cake in front of someone on a diet... only so much worse.

Maybe if the person was deathly allergic to cocoa and one bite could end their life. Because that's what booze could do to Zane. I didn't even like seeing him touch the bottle, but shit, you had to have some faith in the man's ability not to self-destruct. Couldn't babysit him all the time.

God knew I'd tried.

I watched him pull up a chair on the other side of the table, an upright one, not a recliner like mine. He sat with his thighs spread wide, the top button of his jeans undone, and leaned way back. His leather vest was gone and he'd changed his T-shirt to a white one.

Guess I'd gotten "smarmy bass player" on the other one.

He'd showered, too. His hair was kinda damp, smoothed back from his face. It made him look harder and somehow more gorgeous than he usually did—which was really fucking gorgeous—as he looked at me with his ice-sharp blue eyes.

God, he was beautiful.

The man was born to be a star; anyone could see that.

But beauty aside, if Zane Traynor was shriveled and hunchbacked and covered in warts, I was pretty fucking sure he'd still find a way to get under my skin.

It was the king-of-cool way he spoke, the king-of-the-jungle way he took up space, the god's-gift-to-rock-'n'-roll way he sang; hell, the way he *breathed*; even the way his twisted mind worked... the way he looked at me like he'd eat me alive if I ever so much as gave him the chance, exactly like he was doing right now... yeah. The list of things about Zane that screwed with my mind and body on a moment-to-moment basis went ever on.

I never knew quite how he was gonna floor me next. I just knew he was going to.

Always.

I watched as he pulled a Zippo, a baggie of weed and a pack of rolling papers from his pocket and said, "You wanna tell me what's got your panties all in a twist?"

Yeah. Just like that.

King of cool.

The man just shoved me on the floor and then *spat* on that floor, all because I kissed him, and now I was the one with the problem. Made perfect sense, really, that level of crazy being just an average moment in the life of Zane Traynor.

Not so much in the life of me, and since my head was feeling a little fuzzy from all the champagne, I actually let myself *hope* I hadn't heard him right.

"*Excuse* me?"

"Dig in," he said, eyes narrowing as he flicked his chin at the ice cream. "Know a fellow junkie when I see one."

He wasn't wrong about that. I was definitely addicted to the sweet stuff, and no matter how ticked I was at him, there was no sense wasting good ice cream. So I dumped the warm, fudgy syrup over it and dove in while he fingered weed into the crease of one of the little papers. If this was a peace offering, it was incredibly effective. As the ice cream sank in, I could definitely admit I was more ticked at myself than I was at him. No matter how much his supreme coolness irritated me.

I watched as he ran the tip of his tongue along the edge of the paper and sealed up the joint. He sparked up the Zippo and lit it, then tucked the lighter away. He offered the joint to me, but I shook my head. Last thing I needed was anything else clouding my judgment tonight. Probably shouldn't have opened the champagne, but I didn't actually think I'd be seeing him again when I did.

He took a few short drags, exhaling a wisp of smoke as he studied me. Even though I rarely smoked it, I loved the smell of good grass. I didn't love it when Zane smoked up, though. Over time, I was afraid he'd just replace one addiction with another. I wasn't shy about voicing it, either. We'd debated it, ad nauseam, and it was Brody, not Zane, who'd finally convinced me to let it go. *Let the man have his weed. He's battled back a large-size demon, and you don't do that without earning some scars.*

That was some straight-up Brody-style man logic, but since he was usually right about anything and everything to do with the band and their business—professional and otherwise—not to mention he was the hands-down master of diffusing situations that were bound to otherwise end in me throttling Zane, I let it go.

Didn't mean I liked doing it.

Zane cocked his wicked eyebrow at me, the double-pierced one, as I watched him smoke. He took another slow drag, his eyes never leaving mine. "Your panties," he said, his blue eyes narrowing as he exhaled smoke. "They're all up in a fucking twist tonight, Maggs. Gonna tell me what that's about?"

My spoon froze halfway to my mouth, and it took a *lot* to get between me and ice cream.

I set my bowl down, my appetite leaving me, and tossed the spoon in so it clattered loudly. Then I drew in a breath, digging deep for the strength, the patience, and the will to resist committing murder that I was sensing this conversation was gonna take.

"I don't know, Zane. Maybe you could tell me why you've gotta crank the crazy on up to eleven. I mean, everyone knows you're pretty fucking crazy all on your own... but get you and me alone in a room together, and *Je-sus.*"

He considered this a moment, looking completely unvexed. Then his gaze skimmed down to the gap in my robe where my thighs were on display, lingering a moment on my naked skin.

"Because I can't fucking think like a sane person when you're around and my dick is up."

Yeah. We'd kind of established that already.

But as much as I tried to pretend it didn't happen, my pussy clenched at his words.

Admittedly, it was a stupid pussy. Which was why it didn't call the shots.

Unlike Zane's dick, which definitely did.

"Nothing was gonna happen, Maggie," he added, as if reading my thoughts, his voice low, quiet. "You were hurting. I could see that."

Hurting? Yeah, I was hurting. But not so much about Coop, which was probably what he thought.

"Whatever you think of me and my track record with women, I'd never do you like that."

Well, that made me soften.

"I know that," I said.

I did kinda know. Was really nice to know it for sure, though.

"Anyway," he added, "I don't fuck women who've been drinking."

He looked so fucking serious I almost held back the laugh. "Right. Smoke pot much?"

"Totally different. Doesn't bother me the same."

"*Bother?*"

That's what we were calling it?

I'd seen the man drunk, pretty much constantly, for the first few months I knew him, and *bother* didn't even begin to touch the state he got into after a few.

"It's hard to explain," he said, breaking eye contact. "Temptation isn't the right word, but since I don't have a better one... booze and women together... that's a temptation I just can't hack."

Shit.

*Shit.*

My incredulous laughter died as I suddenly sobered. And now I felt even worse for jumping on him... and shoving my pickled tongue down his throat.

Okay, not like I was drunk or anything, but still.

It wasn't as if I knew when I drank that vodka that Zane was gonna show up and cockblock Coop, much less that I was gonna throw myself at him and attack his face. If I'd known that, I would've left the booze alone.

But *still.*

It was extremely impressive that Zane hadn't taken a drink in almost six years, especially when you considered the world in which he lived, and I was proud of him for that, but we both knew those six hard-fought years of sobriety could come screaming to an end with a single sip. Which was why I wasn't letting him off that easy, either.

"No? How about women who snort coke off the kitchen counter?"

He stared at me, unfazed. "I got rid of them, Maggie. What more do you want me to say? If I knew you were here, I wouldn't have brought them up." It was decent of him to say, and I knew he meant it.

And therein lay the most dangerous thing about Zane Traynor.

That being, that I was just masochistic enough to care about his ass, which made him and everything he did a threat to my well-being... especially when he looked at me like he was doing right now; like he cared about me, even more than he cared about getting laid. And Zane cared about getting laid a *lot.*

"Look, we can't have shit between us, Maggs. So let's just get this out." He took a final hit off his joint and mashed out the little roach in one of the big tacky planters shaped like a smiling sun. "Take your fucking sunglasses off."

I took them off, casually, like I'd been meaning to do it anyway. Actually, I'd forgotten I was wearing them.

It wasn't as dark out on the patio as I thought. The twinkly lights dangling along the walls really lit it up. It was kinda magical, really.

Romantic.

Too bad I wasn't gonna get to enjoy it like that.

"Didn't mean to push you away, Maggie," he said, his tone soft and sincere. "Really fucking sorry about that." He stared at me a long, long moment, unflinching, his cool blue eyes burning into mine. "You feel me on that?"

"Yeah, Zane," I said softly. "I feel you."

Maybe a little too much.

# CHAPTER FOUR

# Maggie

"SO, you ever gonna tell me why we're shacking up tonight?"

Zane was still staring at me and I was staring right back, as he asked the one question I was really hoping he wouldn't ask.

Did he actually think I *wanted* to share this ridiculous hotel suite with him?

Yeah, not so much. Zane and I sharing a hotel suite could only end in disaster. Maybe I didn't picture him cockblocking my hookup and spitting on my floor, but Zane and I had never shared walls before. I'd always been really, really careful about that.

Because when Zane and I got alone in a room—which was not often—he got crazy and I got... weak. As in, my tough girl, smart girl self dove right out the window and my resistance to his diabolical charms got low.

Like dangerous low.

I'd just never let him glimpse how low before tonight.

And now the damage was done.

I'd kissed him, I'd lost my cool, and there was no taking it back. Really, all I could do now was try to salvage what was left of my dignity by making it clear I didn't *plan* for that to happen. It just wasn't gonna be easy or without any pain.

So I took a deep breath and accepted the fact that I wasn't

getting out of this conversation. If Zane wanted to have it, we'd have it. Tonight, tomorrow, for the rest of the fucking year if that's how long it took for him to get it out of me.

Might as well rip off the bandage and begin the slow bleed.

"Because things got messed up," I started to explain, wondering how much I could edit out and still satisfy him. "We weren't supposed to share a suite. No one was. Except Jesse and Elle, but you know how that goes."

He grunted, and I knew he did.

"About two seconds after I saw you in the lobby, I ran into Elle," I said. "She looked upset, so I tried to help."

"Big fucking mistake."

"Yeah. But not exactly my job to walk away." Seriously. Elle had tears in her eyes when I'd seen her, and that was rare. "She said she and Jesse had a fight and we needed to get him his own room. Didn't really sound like a kiss-and-make-up situation. Which would've been fine, except the hotel's fully booked, so I couldn't even get us an extra room. The ones we have were booked months ago." Not that that was my problem, exactly. The tour coordinator usually handled such things, but since the rooms were booked through my dad, I insisted on handling it myself.

Last thing I needed was that man coming into unnecessary contact with anyone I worked with.

To that end, I'd given up my room to Jesse, so at least I was the only one out a room, and Jesse Fucking Mayes, hottest guitar player in the universe, wouldn't be slumming it on someone's couch—which he probably would without complaint, he was that cool, but no fucking way was I having *that*. So, problem half-solved.

Zane was shaking his head. "Those two aren't gonna last."

Yeah. I knew that. I saw it. Wasn't my place to say anything about it, though.

I wasn't close enough to Jesse, in that way, to say anything to him. Elle I could talk to, but when it came to shit within the band, I tread carefully. I wasn't in the band; she was. And I sure as hell wasn't in her relationship with Jesse.

Besides that... the woman was totally gone for that guy. She'd break herself to hell and back for him if she had to. I could understand, in a way. Jesse was gorgeous and talented; tall, dark and elusive. Elle was beautiful and talented, too. But Jesse wasn't the one who was head over heels in love; anyone could see that. He'd have to be the one to end it, and when he did, it would be bad.

I felt for Elle, but the band had to come first. That was the unspoken agreement we'd all made when we came on board this crazy train.

"What happens to the band when they don't last?" I asked, wishing I didn't have to. But this was the first time anyone had even talked to me about it. Brody and I hadn't even discussed it yet.

"Fuck all," Zane said. "They go to their separate corners a while, lick their wounds. And we keep doing what we do. Nothing's gonna break this band. Not ever. We'll be eighty and still doing our thing."

I cracked a smile, hoping he was right about that. Would be pretty interesting, to say the least, booking gigs for eighty-year-old rock stars.

"Think we could still get Coachella?" I asked.

He tipped his head back and gave a sexy laugh, and I tried to laugh with him. But his blue eyes were on me, and among his many talents—unfortunately, for me—Zane had the incredibly inconvenient talent of being able to read me better than anyone else I'd ever met. Including my mom, and I was *tight* with my mom.

Hence, why it was a terrible idea for the two of us to share walls.

"Give it up, Maggs," he said, his expression darkening as the laughter died.

"Give what up?"

"Maggie." He leveled me with his ice-blues. "Whatever it is you're trying not to say, but we both know you're gonna tell me eventually."

Right.

I cleared my throat, got brave, and let it bleed. "I talked to him tonight."

"Who?"

"My dad."

"Shit." Zane tensed like he'd been punched in the gut, pitching forward in his chair and leaning on his knees. "*Fuck.* I shoulda known. You should've told me, Maggs."

I shrugged.

Yeah, I should've known too. I should've known better than to drop my dad's name at the front desk when I was hoping to score an extra room. I'd considered just getting a room elsewhere, but I really didn't have the time if I wanted to hook up with Coop, and I totally did. Besides that, I needed to be close if anyone needed me. It nauseated me to do it, but I was desperate... as one of the owners of this tacky-ass hotel, he was my only hope. But I'd coughed that shit up for nothing. The hotel was still fully booked, and by the time the woman at the desk confirmed that with him via text, I heard his gravelly voice. I turned around to find a tall, blond, aging rock star standing behind me—my dad.

I'd hoped I could avoid him while we were in town, even though we were staying in his hotel.

No such fucking luck.

"What the fuck did he do this time?" Zane demanded, his voice going scary-low, stone cold murder flashing in his eyes as he read my face.

"Oh, you know," I said vaguely. "Dizzy has a way of making me feel extra special about myself."

"You really gotta stop talking to him."

"Yeah," I agreed, and I meant it. But I'd never do it. Totally cut off my dad.

He was my *dad*.

Even though he was a royal douche.

"I'm so gonna kill that dude one day," Zane muttered, almost to himself, as he flexed his fist and cracked his knuckles.

"I really wish you would."

He grinned at me, that heart-stopping, swoon-inducing grin, all beautiful, badass Viking with a side of cocky rock star, and I reached over and poked his knee.

"Seriously. Don't go all stabby on me, okay? I don't wanna have to explain that shit to Dolly."

Just what we all needed.

I'd already had to spring the man from jail enough times in my life. Not that he'd ever done anything *that* bad. No, Zane Traynor's rap sheet was a colorful list of minor offenses with descriptive words like "indecency," "disorderly" and "lewd." But the mention of his grandma, Dolly, the sweetest woman on Earth and the one who'd raised him after his parents checked out, made him soften.

"Okay." He settled back in his chair. "No violence. For now. Tell me what the world's greatest dad had to say."

Oh, *shit.*

Here I was complaining about my dad for being a douche, but at least my dad had been *somewhat* present in my life. Unlike Zane's, who'd been a raging alcoholic, ditched out on him when he was a toddler, and then gone ahead and died.

"Shit, Zane. Never mind. Let's just forget it. He's not worth talking about anyway."

"Maggie," he said, his eyes locked on mine with a casual air of command. "You can tell me what happened with your dad, or I can come over there and fuck you senseless, and then you can tell me what happened with your dad. Either way, you're telling me what happened with your dad."

Holy Jesus. Were those my options?

No. Definitely not the come-over-there-and-fuck-you thing.

"Fine. He insisted I have a drink with him and steered me into one of the lounges," I said, trying to pretend he didn't mean that little threat, because I was pretty fucking sure he did. "I figured I should just hurry up and get it over with, because—"

"Because you had a date with Coop," he said, his eyes frosting over.

"Well... yeah. But also," I added quickly, "because I didn't want to hang out and have cocktails with Dizzy. Every time we're in one room for too long, like over five minutes, you know how he gets. He starts talking about my mom, and how things should've been, and blah blah fucking blah, and I want to kill him."

Yeah, Zane knew. He'd heard all about the crazy stories my dad would weave, and his warped sense of reality. It was Zane who'd pointed out that after all the years of partying my dad had done, he might've actually believed the way he remembered things was the way they'd happened. Which was probably accurate, and about the craziest thing I'd ever heard.

But how do you get someone to own up to their part in a reality they never knew existed, because they were too wasted and self-absorbed to notice it happening in the first place?

"I never should've had that drink with him. I knew he wanted something. He gave us these hotel rooms for free, but no way they were really free, you know? Nothing with my dad ever is." That was a sad fact, because the man was insanely loaded. He just didn't like to share.

Zane nodded, taking this in. "So what did he want?"

"You," I said, forcing it out. "He wants to record a song with you."

Zane burst out laughing, that full-on, sexy-ass laugh that sent tingles down my spine... and if I dared to acknowledge it, straight to my clit.

"I'm fucking serious," I said.

"I know you are. That's why it's so fucking funny."

"*He's* serious. And it's not funny. He expects me to set up a meeting with you. He wants to do a full album, actually, but he thought you could start with a song. He's already written one and he wants you to lay down the vocals."

It was embarrassing to say it out loud, because it was pathetic. My dad had to know Zane would never do it; I was pretty sure that's why he was trying to go through me. To see if I had that kind of sway over the man—which had led to the ugliest part of our conversation... But my dad was so split with reality, I couldn't even guess what he really believed was gonna happen.

Did he actually think Zane Traynor, one of the hottest rock stars on the planet for the last decade, would want to record an album with his washed-up, one-hit wonder ass?

Possibly.

All I knew for sure was that Derek "Dizzy" Bowman was not a generous man, and he wasn't selfless either. There was no way he would've offered us free hotel suites while Dirty played Vegas if he didn't believe he could get something out of it.

I just hoped he didn't plan to accost Zane in an elevator.

"I can't believe he fucking asked you that," he said.

"Yeah." I could, absolutely.

This was exactly my dad. He only showed up in my life when he wanted something.

Last time, he wanted to talk to Brody about working with Dirty on a re-recording of his biggest hit song, "Schoolgirl." When I refused to set that up, I guess it pissed him off enough that he decided to try harder this time. He'd called Brody directly to offer the free rooms. Not like Dirty couldn't afford their own hotel rooms, but it was a luxury hotel and Brody had no real reason to turn down the offer. He also had no idea the extent of the shit I'd been through with my dad.

Not like Zane did.

I'd told Zane about Dizzy wanting the band to cover "Schoolgirl," and we'd had a laugh. Then he'd put his arm around me and held me close, and I'd so needed that at the time. *We'll never record that song*, he'd promised me. *I will never, ever sing that fucking song.*

I still didn't know if he knew how much that meant to me, but he did know I hated that song. And why.

My dad was thirty-one when he wrote and released that song, about a seventeen-year-old schoolgirl. Maybe not a big deal in itself, since adult male musicians had been writing songs about their infatuations with underage girls since pretty much the beginning of time. But in the case of my dad's song, the schoolgirl in question was a real person.

She was my mom.

And yes, she was underage when they met. She was seventeen

when he knocked her up, yet somehow it was her fault they never rode off into the sunset together. Dizzy went on to become even more rich and famous than he was before he met her, thanks to that stupid song, while my mom raised me alone. My dad only ever paid the bare minimum of what he was made to pay in child support over the years, even though he was loaded, and now, after she'd died, he had the fucking balls to sit there and weave stories to me about how much he loved her and how they should've been together. Maybe he did love her, in his own warped way, but my mom never took Dizzy seriously. I never understood why she didn't get more upset about the way he ignored us, but I knew for a fact she never wanted to marry him.

"What did you tell him?" Zane asked.

"I told him I couldn't help him."

"And what did he say?"

"He said, 'You're management, you can steer him in the right direction.' I told him I don't make those kinds of decisions, or give that kind of career advice to Zane Fucking Traynor. But I did tell him you were pretty busy with Dirty and your other commitments."

Zane tipped his chin at me, a little proudly, I think. "Good for you, Maggs." He considered me sidelong, his head cocked in a dangerously sexy way that made my guts clench.

No, not my guts. A little lower than that.

"I gotta say, though," he added slowly, "even if you begged me, with my cock in your mouth, I don't think I'd ever record a song with that fuck."

"If I begged you with your cock in my mouth," I replied dryly, "I don't think you'd hear me."

His gaze held mine, something dark and twisted at work behind those ice-blues, but I refused to look away.

"Maggie," he said. "You know you deserve so much better than he ever did for you, right?"

"Well... yes," I said. And I did know it. Deep down.

Of course I did.

But holy hell, did I ever need someone to say that to me right now.

Okay. Not just someone. *Him.*

Hearing those words out of Zane's mouth and knowing he meant them made everything go kinda blurry around the edges. And as his gaze held mine, a familiar chaos began to unfurl inside me.

The thing about this was, I did not do chaos.

I did neat and orderly.

Zane Traynor was the last thing from neat and orderly, and I knew this. Zane Traynor was messy. Hence, why I did not do Zane Traynor.

Still, I'd tried my best over the years to keep our relationship neat and orderly. No matter how I tried that, my feelings for Zane were not neat and orderly; they were, in fact, a complete and total mess.

They were not rational.

They were complicated and, at times, utterly confusing.

Most of the time, they were not in my best interest.

Which was why I usually pretended they didn't exist.

What I'd learned from that? Denial was a powerful survival mechanism.

Until it wasn't.

"So how did you two leave things?" he asked, still studying me. "And don't tell me you ate more of Dizzy's shit, or I really will have to kill him."

I blinked at that, feeling kinda blindsided by this clusterfuck of emotion I had no idea what to do with.

One giant downside to being a tough girl who generally avoided getting the feels over every little thing? Kinda made it hard to process the feels when they showed up, and when they showed up large... yeah.

Cluster. *Fuck.*

But it was hard not to get the feels just now. Because, in a neat and orderly and even objective sort of way, the fact of the matter was that when Zane wasn't acting like a total madman and trying to get in my panties, and I wasn't avoiding him because I secretly wanted him in my panties but knew it was a very, very bad idea to let him go there, he was a great friend to me. Yes, Zane Traynor was without a doubt the most frustrating, perplexing, and maddening person I'd ever known. He was also hilarious, patient, steadfast and smart, and he always had my back. He always nailed the one thing that truly mattered.

Zane was always there for me.

Always.

And I'd been there for him, too. At least, I'd tried like hell to be, no matter how many sleepless nights it cost me. I'd lied for him, against my better judgment, to countless women, covering for him so he didn't have to reject them in person. I'd picked him up, literally, when he fell down drunk. I'd bailed him out of jail when he got himself in trouble. I'd held Dolly's hand in the hospital waiting room when he got himself in worse trouble.

I'd been at the front of the line to kick his ass when he got out, too.

And if that was true, if we had that kind of friendship, I should be able to tell him everything, right?

All of it.

Right down to the honest and the ugly.

"Well... I, uh, told him politely yet firmly, again, that I couldn't help." I paused to clear my throat. I really didn't do so well with the heartfelt, emotional stuff, and this was getting dangerously close to a Hallmark moment. Time for a cold, hard bitch slap in the face, courtesy of my dad. "At which point he looked me in the eye and asked me what the hell I was managing for you guys if I wasn't actually managing your careers, which is when I told him he was out of line, and he told me I was a slut."

Zane's face hardened. "The fuck he did."

"He did. So then I told him he was a washed-up has-been with no real talent, and he told me I was nothing but a glorified groupie, of no more use to him than my mom, and I was a, quote, 'lousy fucking daughter.'"

Did I just say that out loud? God, it sounded so much worse coming out of my own mouth.

How could he say those things to me?

I mean, I'd said some harsh things too... but shit.

A whole world of crazy was going on behind Zane's blue eyes, and I looked away. It was more than I could handle just now, with my dad's words hanging between us. I felt utterly exposed, admitting all that shit to him. *My dad thinks I'm a loser and he hates me, and I have no idea why. I still fucking love his crazy, mean old ass.*

Life's a bitch, right?

I helped myself to some jellybeans, scooping up a handful and tossing several in my mouth. "Sweet family reunion, huh?"

It didn't end there, though.

Nope. My dad Dizzy was a class act. As I'd gotten up to leave, he'd tossed another pretty little nugget my way. He'd offered me his suite. The penthouse suite.

He'd been checked into it, but said he'd clear out, thus solving my room problem. It was two bedroom and two bath, and he'd take one of our single suites in exchange. So now we had the two bedrooms we needed, and all I needed to do was figure out who would room with Zane. Because Zane was the only one who'd bitch if he didn't get the penthouse... and everyone else would bitch if they had to room with Zane.

Hence, my ending up here, in this beautiful mess.

I'd ended up thanking my dad for it, hating myself for needing to thank him for anything, but I really needed the suite. And how did he top things off? By reminding me to tell Zane what we'd discussed.

*If I call him cold and you haven't talked to him, how would that make me look?*

Right. Because God forbid I did anything to make the infamous Dizzy Bowman look bad.

At that point, I'd gotten the hell out of there, collected Coop from the bar, and dragged him up here for a please-help-me-salvage-my-night fuck.

Good thing that turned out so well.

Might as well start laughing. I did that, and Zane just watched me lose it for a minute, his eyes narrowing.

"The fuck is so funny?"

"Nothing," I half-snorted. "Was just thinking how this night panned out exactly like I planned it."

"Right," he said. "You'd be in there getting drilled by Coop right now, that it?"

"Please," I said, popping another jellybean in my mouth. "Coop would never last this long."

# CHAPTER FIVE

## Zane

JESUS. How did Maggie put that smile on her face?

She was so fucking pretty when she laughed, it made the vise around my chest squeeze tighter at the thought of the shit that useless fuck of a father said to her.

"Babe," I said, "maybe you should slow down on the jellybeans." I watched as she shoveled a handful of them into her mouth. She seemed a little blitzed from the champagne, probably more than she realized. The sugar rush wasn't gonna help.

"It's okay," she said. "I'm not driving anywhere." Then she laughed, her soft, husky laugh, and I fucking melted.

Christ, but I was whipped for this girl.

I pushed the room service tray aside and moved to sit on the edge of the low table, facing her, leaning my elbows on my knees to look her straight in the eye.

"Don't punish yourself because your old man's an asshole," I told her. "You're better than that."

Her eyes locked on mine, and she sobered for a second. "Yeah," she said softly. Then she sat up, dropped the rest of the jellybeans back in the martini glass and stared at her hand. She sat there with her elbows on her knees, facing me, picking at the jelly-bean colors that had stained her palm. "You know if I don't laugh about it though, it just hurts?" She looked up at me with those gorgeous gray eyes, and I knew for fucking sure I could murder that man. Sleep like a baby afterward knowing he'd never hurt her again.

"I know, babe."

"He really, actually thinks I'm useless," she said, her voice wavering a little. "I swear he thinks you guys just keep me around as some kind of party favor. You know, like, 'Hey, I didn't have time to pick up some chicks tonight, here, just pass Maggie around.'" She shook her head and laughed, but there was no humor in it. "What an ass."

"Not your fault," I told her. "That's his fault, Maggs. His failing. Nothing you can do about it. Just how he views women."

Her eyes met mine, and there was a world of hurt in them. "Guess you would know," she whispered. She stared at me, and I stared right back. Then her gray eyes went wide. "I'm sorry," she breathed. "That came out all wrong..."

But we both knew it didn't.

"It's okay, Maggie," I said, my voice soft. "I'm gonna let you have that one, because you're right. I don't give a fuck about women. The only woman I've ever kissed and actually gave a shit about was you."

She stared at me, shaking her head a little. "That's pathetic."

"It is what it is. And you know why?"

"Why?" she asked warily.

I leaned toward her, like we were sharing a secret. A secret that meant fucking everything. "Because we're friends."

Her mouth curled in the whisper of a smile. "Yeah," she said. "We are."

"We are. And you know what else?"

"What else?" she asked, her tone still cautious.

"I think we should get married."

It took about five minutes for Maggie to stop laughing.

I sat back in my seat, ate a few jellybeans, even flipped through one of her shitty magazines.

Then I'd had enough. She was still laughing her ass off, sprawled back on her lounge chair, tears shining at the corners of her eyes. Clearly, she'd keep right on going if I let her.

I tossed the magazine on the table and stalked over.

"Oh, God, thanks," she said, wiping the tears from her eyes as I stood over her. "I really needed a good laugh."

I leaned down, set my hands on the arms of her chair, swung a leg over and lowered myself on top of her.

"What are you doing?" She started to jackknife up, but I was on her too fast. I got my knees on either side of her and dropped my hips to hers. She fell back against the cushion and lay staring up at me. The feel of her, soft and warm beneath me, delicate and strong, sent a rush of blood straight to my dick. I was already getting hard again. It was starting to piss me off.

"I'm asking you to marry me. You could take it fucking seriously."

And maybe I wasn't thinking straight, with all the blood hammering to my cock, but I never said shit I didn't mean.

Maggie knew that much.

I lowered myself down on my elbows, my chest to hers. I could feel her breathing, feel the swell of her tits, her nipples hardening against me through the plush robe as she squirmed.

"Okaaay," she said, like I'd gone stone cold crazy. "Do you have to do it right on top of me?"

"Yup. Got you to stop laughing. Looking good so far."

"What's looking good?" she asked cautiously.

"The odds you're gonna see the brilliance in this and say yes."

"Okay. Now you're kinda scaring me 'cause I think you're serious."

"I am serious."

She squirmed again, putting her hands on my chest and pushing lightly, like she was testing the likelihood of being able to push me off.

Not fucking likely at all.

I let my hips take more of my weight, looking for a comfy place to put my hard dick... like between her legs. Maggie's eyelashes fluttered as she struggled to hold my gaze. "Is this... ah... some crazy thing about getting in my pants?" she gasped out as I got comfortable.

"It's not about getting your pants. We don't even have to have sex. We're just gonna get married. One thing at a time, babe."

She laughed, but the sound was forced. "Right. Because married people never have sex."

"I'm sure some don't."

"Get off, Zane." She shoved at my chest.

"Would love to," I told her. "Not getting up, though. Not until you say yes."

"To marrying you?" She laughed again. "Come on. What the hell kind of grass did you just smoke?"

"I think you're failing to see the genius in this plan."

She went still and her eyebrows pinched together. "What plan?"

Yeah. I knew the p-word would get her attention.

Maggie never could resist a good plan.

"The one where you marry me, tonight, in Vegas, and Dizzy shuts his fucking mouth and keeps it that way for the rest of his life."

She blinked, processing this. "Right. Until the second we get 'divorced' and he tells me he always knew it would happen because I'm nothing but a groupie slut."

"Fuck that. Who says we're getting divorced?"

She gaped at me. "You mean we wouldn't tell him?"

"We're not gonna tell him jack shit. Far as he knows, he came to witness our union and that's all the fuck he has to know. Beyond that, it's between a man and his wife. He's got a problem with you from that moment on, I've got a problem with him. He calls my wife a slut again and I break his face."

"Zane," she said softly, shaking her head. "That's not gonna work..."

"He never got married, never married your mom, right? So I

marry you, he sees what I really think of you, he knocks off the disparaging comments, or I make him knock them off." I lay my hand on the side of her face, resting my thumb, lightly, on her soft bottom lip. "I fucking mean it, Maggs."

She shook her head, slowly, in disbelief. "You're fucking crazy."

"I'm a fucking great friend. And I'd make a great husband."

She laughed, hard, which cut me in a way I didn't care to acknowledge. "And how's that, do you imagine?"

"Let's see. I've got a great cock, I'm giving as fuck in bed, I'm loyal to a fucking fault, and I'd kill for you." Her expression got serious, quick. "Pretty sure I'd kill Dizzy if you asked me to. Pretty sure Jude would help me do it, no questions asked. Instead, I thought I'd marry you, which seems less complicated."

"It's really fucking complicated, Zane. If you think it's not, you've got no business asking me to do it. And where do you get off using the word 'loyal' when you go through women like toilet paper?"

"It's fucking simple, Maggie," I said, tugging gently on that juicy bottom lip with my thumb. "You're the one who always has to complicate things with your overthinking and shit. I told you, I've never given a fuck about another woman."

She rolled her eyes in extreme disbelief. "It's not that simple," she protested.

"It's simple as fuck. All you have to do is say yes."

She scoffed. "I say yes, and we get married? Tonight?"

"Tonight."

"Such bullshit. You don't even have a ring."

I ripped the big skull ring with devil horns off my index finger and shoved it on her thumb.

She rolled her eyes again. "An engagement ring, jackass. It usually has a sparkly thing called a diamond?" She pulled the ring off and stuck it back on my finger.

I locked on her gray eyes, daring her to look away or bullshit me. "I get a ring, you saying you'll marry me?"

"God... it sounds so fucking weird when you just say it like that..."

Yeah. I knew she was stalling. I could see her mind at work as she calculated the odds that I could find a diamond ring at this time of night, in Vegas... and then she got really scared.

"Weird or not," I said, "I'll marry you."

She stared at me, looking totally fucking bewildered. "Why would you wanna do that?" she whispered.

"To see the fucking look on Dizzy's face," I said.

*Because I want you,* I could have said. *Because I've always wanted you and I'd do fucking anything to have you.*

Probably should've said it, since it was true.

But she was still giving me that look that said she didn't trust my ass, and I didn't fucking like it.

It's not like I actually believed she didn't want me back. As much as Maggie pretended the fuck out of that being a fact, it was a bunch of bullshit. Straight up, I'd been with enough women to know when a woman was into me. *Deep* into me. Physically, at least.

More than that, I really couldn't say how deep things went between us. Not like we'd ever had a chance to explore it, since what Maggie wanted and what she was willing to do were two vastly fucking different things. I'd had six long, frustrating-as-fuck years to learn that much about the woman.

"We can't," she said.

"This is Vegas," I told her. "We sure as fuck can."

She just stared at me. We'd both gone still. My dick was still throbbing between us, her heart pounding against mine. But she wasn't shoving me away.

I wasn't getting up, either.

In my defense, it was *Maggie.*

Underneath me.

And she wasn't wearing any pants.

Shit like this didn't happen everyday. Shit like this *never* happened, actually.

Not too fucking sure why it was happening now, but as long as she was letting me get away with it, I wasn't gonna be the one to end it.

"If we do this," she said slowly, swallowing, "you can't tell anyone. It's just you and me and Dizzy. No one else."

"No one else."

"And you have to make the arrangements *yourself*." Her tone said there was no way in hell she thought I would.

"No problem."

"Right," she said.

Zero faith in me.

*Jesus*. When, exactly, had I fucked things up so royally with this girl?

No secret she'd been keeping my shit together for years, but that's because I *liked* her keeping my shit together. Didn't mean I was a fucking moron.

"I make the arrangements," I said carefully, slowly, so she couldn't pretend she'd misheard me. "We go do this. No excuses, no backing out. No Maggie May overthinking things bullshit. No blaming me if they don't have an Elvis impersonator available to offi- ciate our shit or whatever. You say yes, you own it. You follow through with it. And I promise you, we'll make that prick of a father of yours eat his fucking words."

She narrowed her gray eyes at me, but I saw the sparkle in them. Tears. The idea of sticking it to Dizzy was just too sweet to resist.

And maybe it wasn't the best marriage proposal in the history of man, but it would have to fucking do. Not like I planned this shit.

Planning was for Maggie. I was more of a fly-by-the-seat-of-my- pants type of guy. Hadn't failed me yet. I was still alive. Plus, I had Maggie beneath me, her heart pounding against mine.

"Either that, or I kill him," I told her casually, running my thumb across her lip. "Your call, Maggie May."

"You don't have to kill him," she said, sniffing just a bit. "He's a douche but he doesn't deserve to die. I already lost my mom and my stepdad. I don't need to lose him, too."

Shit. That prick didn't come close to deserving this girl's love or forgiveness.

"Have it your way," I said. "But that's not a yes. I've gotta hear it from your lips."

She rolled her eyes. "Yes."

"Fucking finally."

I took my time getting up, re-arranging my throbbing dick in my jeans. Yeah... probably shouldn't have told her we could do this without sex.

Not sure what I was thinking on that one.

I looked down at her, lying there in her robe all askew. Her dark hair spread out around her face. Her wide gray eyes looking up at me, a little hazy from champagne... so fucking pretty.

I shook my head.

"Now get your ass up, woman, and go put on the best dress you've got."

Ten minutes later I had a car service booked and I was almost ready to go.

It took all of one phone call to the concierge to make the arrangements. So maybe I didn't do it *all* myself, but I didn't give them my name, just our room, which was in Maggie's name. If she didn't want me to tell anyone, I could do this shit incognito.

Felt a little strange not bringing my boys into it, though. Jesse, Jude and Brody had been like brothers to me since we were kids, and getting married was one of those things I would've thought they'd be here for, either to have my back, or to talk me out of it.

No fucking way I wanted to be talked out of this thing with Maggie, though.

If she couldn't talk me out of it, no one could.

I walked into the master bathroom, shaking my head. Maggie. Fucking ball-buster.

And that's when it really hit me.

Holy *fuck*. I was marrying Maggie.

Maggie was marrying *me*.

I stopped short as I felt that fucking *thing* overtake me, gripping me so tight I could barely breathe—my heart jackhammering like it did in that final moment just before I stepped onstage... when I always had a brief, private attack of self-doubt, never quite knowing how I'd be received.

Would they love me, or would they turn away?

I knew this was some screwed-up subconscious shit about my parents fucking off on me at such a young age. Also knew this was why, deep down, I wasn't good enough for a girl like Maggie. And maybe I'd never be. Because there was something wrong with me. Something missing.

Something gone, lost, that might never come back.

I started to sweat, just like I did in that moment backstage, the roar of the crowd loud in my ears.

How many times had I dreamed it?

Stepping out onto an empty stage, to find the venue empty, the sound of the crowd still thundering in my head and not a single person in the place. No one backstage, either. Even my band was gone. I was alone, but I could hear the concert rocking on the other side of some wall I could never get to.

The show had gone on without me.

Shit.

Just *shit*.

I splashed cold water on my face and just stood there leaning over the sink for a long, long minute, gripping the counter and letting the water drip down.

Did Maggie love me?

Would she?

I had no idea. No. Fucking. Clue.

I looked at myself in the mirror, right into my own eyes, and maybe it was wrong but I knew I didn't care. Didn't care at all what her reasons were for marrying me. As long as she did.

My eyelashes were wet, clumped together and dark, making my

eyes look like ice. When I was a kid and I got over hating myself, I'd learned it was a good face. I'd never had a problem with women. Sometimes they had a problem with me...

Didn't care.

But Maggie? Maggie was different.

She'd always been different.

Ever since I met that girl, other women had been nothing but placeholders. Since that night, so many years ago now, when I cornered her and told her what I wanted... and she shot me down for the first time of many. Yeah. Just bed warmers, in the place of the one girl I really wanted.

And maybe I didn't plan to propose to her tonight, but it sure as fuck wasn't the first time I'd ever thought about making her mine. Far fucking from it. I just never figured out how to do it before—goddamn bane of my existence.

I dried off and took a giant, belly-deep breath.

*Maggie.*

Holy fucking shit.

What happened when you got everything you'd ever wanted? The one thing that truly mattered?

Did shit like that actually happen?

To someone like me?

*No. Because she's not in love with you, asshole.*

Fuck. Whatever.

Even if she was *only* marrying me because of Dizzy... by the time she woke up tomorrow, I'd make sure she knew she'd done the right thing. Hell, I'd spend the rest of my life convincing her of it.

Damn.

Motherfucking *Dizzy.*

I stood up tall and got my shit the fuck together.

My shoulders went back, my jaw hardened, I cracked my neck, and just like that, the adrenaline started building again. Just like it did as I forced myself to take the stage. To claim what was mine. To *make* it mine. My pulse took on the steady, solid thump of the bass drum, the don't-give-a-fuck self-assurance and the familiar confidence taking over.

No time for amateur hour stage fright bullshit. I had shit to take care of.

I'd found Maggie's phone on her patio chair and I used it to call her dad. Told him to be ready in ten. Just tried to keep the disgust out of my voice. Not easy. But the man was so eager to talk shop with me, pretty sure he didn't notice.

Head way too far up his own ass. Probably stoned, too.

How that loser made an angel like Maggie, I'd never know. Met her mom a few times though, so I could kinda see how it played out.

Maggie would be sad she wasn't here for this. We'd have to mention her during the ceremony.

I put on something marginally respectable, which meant a leather vest and jeans that weren't as ripped to shit as my other ones. I grabbed a cap to wear later; probably gonna need it. I thought about jacking off again, but I didn't do it. That one time in the shower would just have to get me through the next few hours. Easier said than done if Maggie turned up in a white dress anything half as slutty as what I'd been picturing her wearing ever since I proposed.

When I knocked on her bedroom door, it took her a few minutes to answer and the adrenaline buzz started to fade. She opened the door looking stunned, and not just a little bit confused.

No slutty white dress either.

"Holy ssshit," she slurred through her mouth guard. "You were fucking ssherioush." She had one of those blindfolds people wore to sleep pushed up on her hair, and silk jammies on.

Fucking hell.

"You were fucking sleeping?"

She pulled out the mouth guard, wiping slobber on the back of her hand. "Well, I—"

"Not cool, Maggie," I said, stalking past her into the room. "We had a deal."

I looked in the closet. Empty. Guess she didn't have time to go all neat freak on her clothes yet and hang them up in order of color. I dug through her travel case, ignoring her protests. I found some lingerie, hot pink lace, and tossed it at her. The closest I could find to a white dress was a baby-pink thing in a soft, clingy knit, which would totally fucking do.

When I turned to her she was holding the lingerie out with her fingertips like it was someone else's dirty laundry. "Zane, I can't get married in this!"

"Not my problem. You've had like twenty minutes to pick something out. We need a marriage license before we hit the chapel and the office closes in fifty minutes." I tossed the pink dress at her and she stared at me, still looking stunned. "Put this the fuck on and let's go."

"WE'RE GOING *WHERE*?"

I stared at Zane, my mouth gaping open. Pretty sure it was a super-hot look, combined with my bed-hair-and-pajamas ensemble. At the moment, I couldn't give one fuck.

"Wedding chapel," he said, playing with his phone, completely unconcerned with the fact that *we were going to a wedding chapel.* "Don't worry, Vegas is lousy with 'em."

When I just stood there, his blue eyes flicked up to meet mine, a spark of challenge in their icy depths. It was at that exact moment that the situation really slapped me in the face.

This was happening.

If anyone could pull off a stunt this insane, it was Zane.

The man had zero impulse control. I knew this. So why the hell was I surprised?

Yes, I told him I'd do this if he pulled it off. I just didn't think he'd actually do it, to the point that I'd brushed and flossed my teeth, put in earplugs and crawled into bed.

Basically, I figured once the high of acting on his impulse started to fade and I was out of sight, out of mind, his ADHD would kick in and he'd be on to something else... like finding himself another orgy.

Apparently, I was wrong.

"Get the fuck moving," he said, a wicked-crazy gleam in his eyes I didn't even want to look directly at. What happened when you looked pure evil in the eye anyway?

Nothing good.

"Zane. We are not just going out and... and... getting *married*," I sputtered, "you know... without security." And yes, I was stalling. Desperately. The wheels in my head were turning way too fucking slowly. "I mean... I am not getting trampled in a stampede of drunk chicks on my... *Jesus*..." I stopped to swallow and work up the will to say it. "On my... *fucking wedding night*... you know, when they start recognizing you... and..."

I was starting to sweat. My silk pj's were sticking to my breasts. And leave it to my soon-to-be-husband—*holy shit,* that sounded weird—to notice it. His gaze raked down over my chest, zeroing in on my nipples, which pricked a little too eagerly at the attention.

I crossed my arms over my chest and looked at him pointedly. "Security, Zane. You take care of that little detail?"

"On it." He thumbed his phone and I tackled him. Because apparently jumping on Zane was now my thing. He didn't go down this time, though. He just stood there looking surprised and suspiciously turned on as I clung to him like a monkey, the phone I'd just ripped from his hand in my grasp.

I let go, dropping to my feet and backing away... the phone was already dialing Jude. Oh, no. No, no, no.

I hung up. "You are not calling Jude."

"You just said we need security," he said casually, studying my nipples through the silk pajama top again. Fuck it, let him look. I didn't have time to ward off his eyes and the full force of his crazy at once.

"Yes, and I told you when you 'proposed' that you can't tell anyone, and if you make Jude come with us, everyone in the universe will know by the time the sun comes up."

"Why'd you say 'proposed' like that?" he asked, and if I didn't know better I could've sworn I hurt his feelings. "It was a legit proposal, Maggs."

"A legit proposal usually climaxes with the presentation of a ring, Zane."

"Offered you a ring. And you ask me—"

"I didn't ask you."

"—a legit proposal climaxes with celebration sex."

And there it was.

"You *said* no sex."

He shrugged, like it was the world's most unimportant detail. "I said we didn't have to have sex. But let's stay on focus here, Maggie. Dizzy's waiting."

Right. Almost forgot about that ass, I was so busy dealing with the one in front of me.

At least the mention of my dad's name served to remind me why the hell we were even considering this crazy shit in the first place.

"Whatever," I said, shoving his phone into his washboard abs. "You're not calling Jude."

"Jude's discreet, Maggs," he said. "It's his job."

Great. We hadn't even gotten to the ceremony and we were already arguing. Again.

*Ceremony...* Jesus, that sounded official. Even though it would only be a *fake* ceremony, to screw with my dad... still. Jesus.

"Listen to me carefully," I said. "You can't tell Jude. Jude's best friend in the entire universe is Jesse, and he's going to tell Jesse, even if we tell him not to. It's a given. You and me getting married tonight —even just for Dizzy's sake—is too juicy a tidbit to expect people to keep it to themselves. Do you get that? Jesse will tell Elle, and Elle is too close to Dylan not to tell him. Dylan will tell his best buddy, Ash. Ash is the Pusher's lead singer. Odds are he tells his buddies, too." Including Coop. Ugh. "Which means Pepper finds out, and Pepper will tell the whole fucking world." It was true. The Penny Pushers' drummer had a big fucking mouth. "Do you see the path of destruction?"

"Guess I can kinda see how that would go down," he said slowly, following my logic. "Pepper does have a big mouth."

"The biggest."

He eyeballed me thoughtfully. "You put that together quick."

"It's kinda my *job*," I said.

"So when you said we're not telling anyone... you meant literally anyone."

"That's right."

"For how long?"

"For-fucking-ever."

He stared me down for the longest few seconds in history, shaking his head like I'd truly fucking stumped him. Too bad. We were doing this my way—in secret—or not at all.

Finally he cracked a bemused smile. "You know, you're a strange one, Maggs."

"Trust me, my friend, you are way the fuck stranger."

He shrugged. Then he was back to his phone, all business. "I won't call Jude. We'll get someone else."

"But—"

"Trust me."

I bristled, and he caught it.

"If I'm gonna be your husband, you're gonna have to learn to trust me," he said.

"Don't start that shit."

"What shit?"

"Calling yourself my husband. There's still plenty of time for me to ditch your ass before we get to the altar."

He just smiled his crazy-hot Viking smile and stood there, staring at me, like he was waiting for me to go ahead and ditch.

Yeah. The bastard was calling my bluff.

I rolled my eyes. But I made no move to disappear.

"Go put that sexy dress on," he ordered, "or I'm marrying you in your jammies. You've got... six minutes."

I gave him my coolest, most unhurried look. "Sure. After you get out of my room."

"No problem. Meet you out there." He flicked his chin toward the main room and sauntered out.

I shut the bedroom door behind him. Then I tossed those slutty pink undies across the room in a frustrated snit and started digging through my travel case in search of something else. I wasn't sure what the right underwear to get married to Zane Traynor in was, but it wasn't those. If only I had some granny panties to put on. Serve him right if he tried to get up under my skirt. Knowing Zane though, it'd probably just turn him on.

Fucking perv.

I knew I'd found just the right panties and bra when I saw them, though. I grabbed my makeup bag and took everything into the bathroom to get ready.

I put on the lingerie, really fucking glad I'd had a hot date tonight—yeah, right—so I was all neatly shaved and moisturized. No marrying Zane with shin stubble. I pulled on the dress, made up my face with the basics—quick dash of mineral makeup, lip gloss and mascara—and smoothed out my hair, with a couple minutes to spare. With all the travel and the crazy pace of my work life, I'd become pro at doing this top speed, able to get ready for any given situation at a moment's notice.

Never thought I'd be doing it for my own wedding, though. Probably would've thought I'd be paying a professional to do this when I got married. And maybe I'd have some friends here, getting ready with me?

*Like who? Your good pal, Zane?*

Fuck.

Whatever. This didn't really mean anything, right?

*You'll get married for real, to someone kind and handsome and sane, when you're ready.*

*Thanks, Mom.*

*And by the way, you look beautiful.*

For a moment as I stood back and looked at myself in the mirror, I felt proud and so intensely sad it nearly tore me open. I had to drop down to a crouch and take a few deep breaths to keep myself from crying.

God, she would've been so proud of me. Even like this. Even

though it was a stupid pretend wedding and I was just doing it to stick it to my dad... she would've stood by me.

Hell, she would've laughed her ass off when I told her about it.

*This isn't like you, Maggie May. But that's okay, too.*

And she'd be right.

So I was about to do something dead-crazy and totally out of character tonight. This was Vegas.

Why not go all in?

So hitting up a wedding chapel with Zane Traynor wasn't exactly the least self-destructive thing a girl could do on a Friday night. It's not like I didn't know that.

In fact, I'd be the first girl to tell any other girl who cared to ask that Zane Traynor was exactly the kind of guy you screwed in the bathroom at some off-the-hook party after a few too many drinks; afterward, maybe you told your girlfriends about his otherworldly body, his giant dick and how many times he made you come with his demonic tongue. Maybe you masturbated to the memory a few times or a thousand. Then you moved on. You met that handsome, sane, regular guy who might also have an otherworldly body, if you were lucky, but who hadn't fucked half the continent.

Zane was *not* the guy you took home to your father, so to speak; even a father like mine.

He was most definitely not the guy you married.

No matter how much the idea might be sparking some misguided yearning deep in my gut, setting off a stupid thrill that was permeating my body and making me sweat just a little. No; Zane Traynor was *not* that guy.

Which was why I was not letting myself get carried away with what this wasn't.

This was not Zane suddenly doing a one-eighty and becoming the man of my dreams. As in, the hottest rock god I'd ever laid eyes on, talented, charming, *and* committed, suddenly willing to give up his legions of adoring groupies to throw down and love me—and only me—for the rest of his life.

This was Zane pulling a classic Zane stunt, and me, for the first time ever, going along for the ride. Willingly. A little recklessly, but with good reason.

And my dad was that reason.

Tomorrow we'd laugh about the whole thing and go on with our lives. Down the road, we'd have one hell of an inside joke. *Hey, remember that time we got pretend-married in Vegas to fuck with Dizzy?*

Hilarious.

I stood up, taking a few calming breaths. The tears still sparkled in my eyes but I blinked them back.

Not a real wedding. No crying allowed.

I checked myself in the mirror one last time for signs of distress. Nope. Shit totally together. And damn... the dress *was* sexy. Slinky, clingy and tiny, I usually wore it as more of a long shirt with leggings and a little jacket.

But when I stepped out of the bedroom a moment later and I saw the look Zane gave me, and the look Flynn gave me, too... I knew I could do it. I could rock this suddenly-a-bride thing.

"Flynn," I said, nodding my approval at Zane. "Good choice."

Flynn had been a member of Dirty's security team for three years, and he was solid as they came. And definitely discreet. The guy had barely spoken more than a few dozen words in my presence in the years I'd known him.

Zane grabbed a sweet little bouquet of pink flowers off the entranceway table.

"We're getting married," he said bluntly, answering the look of mild confusion on Flynn's face as he handed the bouquet to me.

I rolled my eyes. *"For now,"* I muttered under my breath as I took the bouquet. The stems were cut short and it was tied with a white satin bow. It fit perfectly in my hand.

Nice touch.

Still, this whole thing felt hella ludicrous when I glimpsed the silent question in Flynn's eyes. I was pretty sure he wouldn't tell a soul what he'd seen, but I had to be certain.

I drew my shoulders back and held his gaze, undaunted by his size, the fact that he had a gun, or the cool, professional detachment that had settled over his features again. Yes, I was a small woman, but I ate rough-and-ready dudes for breakfast on a regular basis as part of my job. Security guys, roadies, rock stars... badass, manly men didn't faze me.

*Just beautiful, batshit crazy ones, apparently.*

"I swear on my mother's grave," I told him, "you tell anyone about this, I will kill you. You won't know where or when or how, but I'll do it. I don't care if you're all ex-military and shit. You will die. Slowly. I will kill you and all your future babies, too. You don't want to fuck with me."

"Know that, Maggie," Flynn said with a little nod. A small smile tugged at his lips as he looked down at me, all tough in my sexy pink dress and four-inch heels, holding my little bouquet of tulips.

Yeah, they were tulips. My favorite flowers.

I eyed my "groom" sidelong as he offered me an elbow. I took it, feeling kinda regretful for the thing about the babies. Over the top much? Whatever. Flynn didn't even have a girlfriend as far as I knew, much less any babies on the way.

"I love it when you threaten people," Zane said, and Flynn looked away, pretending not to hear. From here on in, he was just a fly on the wall... a blind and stone-deaf fly with a gun.

"Yeah," I said, a little sheepish. "I'm pretty good at it."

# Zane

FLYNN and I strolled into the wedding chapel to find a bridal party waiting in the small lobby and a ceremony going on in the main room, beyond a set of closed doors. I could hear voices and laughter. Hopefully they were almost done.

I walked right over to the small reception desk, locking on the woman who stood behind it.

"Hi," she said when she saw me, perking up. She was about forty, nice-looking in a MILF sort of way, her blouse buttoned a little too high. She looked friendly, though. Shouldn't be too hard to get what we needed.

"Hey, sweetheart." I'd put on my cap and pulled it low; no idea if she recognized me. "Looking to get married."

"Great," she said. "We'd be happy to accommodate you. It'll just be a bit of a wait. There's a ceremony in progress and another couple ahead of you. About... forty-five minutes?"

I leaned casually on the desk and looked her in the eye. "How about instead I give you whatever you make in a month, right now, to clear this place out and marry me and my girl."

She stared at me, a little speechless, but I could see the wheels turning. She glanced guiltily at the wedding party who were chattering excitedly on the other side of the room.

"Oh, yeah," I added, tapping the small glass display case next to the desk, "and I'm gonna need a couple of rings."

Minutes later, I walked back out to the limo, reached in and took Maggie by the hand.

"Who were all those people who just left, looking pissed?"

Damn. The girl didn't miss much.

"Don't forget your flowers," I told her as she scooted toward me.

"Got 'em!" Dizzy's date, behind her, held up the bouquet triumphantly.

Maggie scowled at me as she climbed out of the limo. I held onto her hand and steered her toward the chapel door. The woman from the reception desk was holding it open for us.

"I saw a woman in a bridal dress, Zane." Maggie craned her neck to see over the limo, where the wedding party I'd just had kicked out was piling into a couple of taxis. "She did not look like a happy newlywed."

I ushered her into the chapel, shrugging. "Must've called it off."

Maggie narrowed her eyes at me, but didn't call me on my shit.

Dizzy and his date, some ditzy-looking chick in a tube dress who could barely be out of her teens, followed us inside.

When we'd knocked on the door to his hotel room, both Dizzy and Maggie had been stunned when I'd formally asked him for his daughter's hand in marriage. He'd given his consent, looking way more astonished than I'd expected him to be. Apparently Maggie was right that he didn't take her seriously, either as a member of Dirty's management team or as a woman I'd be fucking lucky to marry.

Just sealed it for me that we were doing the right thing. Maggie's old man needed to be put in his place.

Keeping my word to her, I'd made him promise not to tell a soul about the wedding until we said he could. Told him this was our night, Maggie's and mine, and we didn't need our relationship turning into a three-ring circus in the media. On that condition, we'd invited him to attend the wedding.

Pretty sure it would kill him to keep his mouth shut on this, but he'd do it for the honor of attending my wedding. And no mistake. The man was definitely more jacked about the fact that it was *my* wedding than his daughter's.

Such a prick.

He'd then produced this chick from somewhere in the shadows of his hotel room and insisted on bringing her along, and Maggie didn't seem to have it in her to refuse him. But as long as she kept her mouth shut, I didn't have a problem with it either.

We stood over to the side of the lobby as the double doors into the main room opened, and the wedding that had just finished cleared out. Maggie shook her head as she watched the staff usher out the bride and groom, a little too hastily. Then she leaned in and murmured in my ear, "You've got serious impulse management problems. You know that, right?"

"What I've got you for," I whispered back. I leaned down, nuzzling her neck and inhaling her sweet scent. "Managing all my impulses..." Then I reached around to grab a handful of her sweet ass and gave her tight cheek a slow squeeze for the first time ever.

I liked it. A lot.

She rolled her eyes but her cheeks flushed a little, and Maggie never fucking blushed.

I liked that, too.

The reception lady guided us over to the ring case and asked Maggie which wedding bands she wanted. Dizzy tried to butt in with his two cents, but Maggie wasn't interested.

"I just want to marry Zane," she announced sweetly, her arm wrapped around my waist, her other hand on my chest. "I don't care about the rings. Just pick whatever you like, sweetie." She fluttered her eyelashes up at me. I crossed my eyes and stuck my tongue out the side of my mouth. She giggled, which was totally un-Maggie. Maggie had a sexy, husky laugh.

She was really laying this shit on thick for her dad's sake.

Dizzy was either too wrapped up in his date or too clueless about his daughter to notice anyway. Probably both. But Maggie managed to steer him away, feeding his ego by asking for his input on a bunch of things I was pretty fucking sure she didn't give a shit about. Should his date be her maid of honor? Should we use the bouquet we'd brought, or use some of the flowers offered by the venue?

While they were distracted, I picked out some rings and took a look around.

It was a cheesy theme chapel, and the theme was rock 'n' roll. I'd gotten the recommendation from the hotel, but in keeping my word to take care of things myself, I hadn't let them call ahead for me. Was pretty sure I could make this happen with a little money. Didn't occur to me until the dude who was about to marry us asked me to sign a copy of a framed Dirty album on the wall that maybe the cash wasn't the only reason they'd let us take over the place.

I agreed to sign it on the condition that the staff understand this wedding was a private event, and they weren't to tell anyone about it. They agreed enthusiastically, especially when I beefed up their tip. Then I scribbled Dylan's signature on the album instead of mine, grinning to myself. My drummer's autograph was totally fucking illegible. Pretty sure they didn't know it wasn't mine. If it was, no one would believe it was mine anyway.

I was the last guy in the band anyone would ever expect to find hanging out in a wedding chapel. Which was saying a lot. My band brothers weren't exactly famous for their long-term relationships.

Then again, no one had ever seen me with Maggie.

Not like this.

Even I didn't know what it would be like. What it would feel like to actually be *with* her. But I found my eyes following her around the chapel as she and Dizzy looked around, and it felt fucking *good*.

Sure, this had started out on a whim. At least, the proposal part. A testosterone-fueled impulse, brought on by Dizzy's shitty treatment of his daughter and my own gut-deep urge to do anything in my power to protect her from him.

But it was an impulse six years in the making.

The fuse had been lit the day I met Maggie, and I'd been burning for her for a long, long time.

The closer we got to walking down that aisle? I was warming more and more to the idea of making her my wife.

Despite what my friends might think, what Maggie might think, I could totally do a wife and a marriage. If it was Maggie. Why the fuck not?

I'd had every kind of fantasy there was about the girl, and seeing her in that clingy pink dress holding those flowers? Yeah, I could be all over that.

*My wife.*

"So... what are you doing later?"

I glanced down to find Dizzy's date getting up close and personal.

"You know," she added, "after this?"

I stared at her. *The fuck?*

"I'm boning my new wife," I told her, deadpan.

She smiled a little, and that's when I noticed her eyes. She was blitzed on something. Didn't smell of booze, though.

"Oh yeah," she said, kinda dreamily. "She's so pretty." Then her thoughts seemed to wander away, and so did she.

I shook my head.

"We're in luck, sweetheart," I heard Dizzy say. "They've got my song." I turned to find Maggie's dad stuffing coins into a jukebox and looking over at Maggie.

Sweetheart?

Guess he was pretty fucking pleased with this whole event, then. Big improvement over calling her a slut.

Then the song kicked in and I cringed.

"Schoolgirl."

Christ, but the man was clueless.

My gaze slammed into Maggie's across the room. Her face was

turning pink to match her dress. I couldn't tell if it was repressed rage or laughter, or maybe some kind of allergic reaction to the song. Whatever it was, she bit it back and smiled, the epitome of the happy, blushing bride.

"Perfect!" she said cheerily.

She steered Dizzy and his date over to talk to the officiant, then came over to me while Dizzy pummeled the guy with questions, rolling her eyes. I actually felt kinda sorry for the guy, but dude was in the wedding business. Couldn't be the first time he'd had to deal with an asshole father of the bride.

"Hey," I said, taking her hand and drawing her close.

"Hey." She looked up at me and bit her lip. And yeah, I liked fighting with Maggie, but even better than fighting with Maggie was seeing that truly rare but fucking beautiful spark of mischief in her eyes, the one that said we were on the same team. "I wanted to tell you... I was never that girl who dreamed of some big traditional wedding, you know?"

"That's good, because this place is a fucking dive."

She glanced around and shrugged. "Yeah. Good thing it doesn't matter. But sometimes traditions can be nice. And since this whole thing is hella unconventional..." She grinned. "You know that 'Something old, something new, something borrowed, something blue' thing?"

"Sure."

"Well..." She glanced over her shoulder to make sure Dizzy was out of earshot and leaned into me. "Dizzy's the something old," she whispered.

I laughed. "Perfect."

"And the flowers are new," she said, twirling her bouquet. "Something borrowed... I thought maybe you could lend me that skull ring?"

"It's yours." I took it off and slid it onto her thumb again. Her thumb looked tiny and delicate engulfed in the big hunk of silver.

"And... well..." She reached down. "I know you picked the pink ones, but I needed something blue." She slid the dress up her thigh and flashed me the electric-blue lace of her panties.

Instant flood of lust, straight to my dick.

"I think, traditionally, it's supposed to be a blue garter, but I didn't have one of those on short notice." She bit her lip again, smiling. "You think this'll work?"

"Yeah," I said as she lowered her dress back down. "It works, babe."

Then I leaned in and caught her mouth with mine. Just felt like the right thing to do.

I was *marrying* the girl.

I wrapped my hand around the back of her head and kissed her slow. I held her tight, breathing with her. I didn't want to let her go. I just wanted to taste her, to smell her, to make her mine in every way.

Should that have scared me?

Maybe.

I'd never wanted anyone like this. Never wanted anyone to belong to me.

Never wanted to belong to anyone... until I met Maggie.

She pulled away, licking her lip and gazing up at me, heat and a strange unease thudding between us. Couldn't say what it was. Didn't know if it was bad or good. Just knew I wanted to kiss her again.

I leaned in and brushed my lips to hers.

"Hey, you two."

Dizzy's voice grated through the moment and I felt Maggie stiffen.

I glanced over at him. He was standing by the open doors into the main room, at the foot of the short, red-carpeted aisle, and wearing a shit-eating grin. He offered an elbow to Maggie, and I walked her over, gently handing her off to him.

"Let's do this," he said, and Maggie smiled.

"I've got something to say."

The ceremony was short and sweet, but when the dude launched into the standard wedding vows bullshit, I spoke up, cutting him off.

"Oh... I'm sorry." He looked from me to Maggie and back. "It was my understanding that you hadn't written any vows."

"We didn't," I said, holding Maggie's gaze. She looked a little panicked. Probably wanted me to just stick to the script, but fuck it. "Got something to say to my bride."

The dude cleared his throat and gestured for me to take the floor. "Of course."

"It's not much. Just something I need to say to you, here and now, in front of your dad." I didn't even glance over at Dizzy. Didn't have to, to know he was eating this up. "The first time I met you," I told her, holding her hands tight in mine and looking straight into those gray eyes, "I thought you were adorable. Also thought you wouldn't last. You had those invisible braces, remember?" She smiled a little and chewed on her lip. "And so much fucking courage. You stayed. You never gave up on me, even when you should've. Since the beginning, you've been my girl. Even though you didn't know it yet. Far as I'm concerned, this is just making official what I've always known. I love everything about you, Maggs, even the stuff that annoys the shit out of me, and I'm never letting you go."

Her gray eyes flared at that. Probably because me declaring outright in front of Dizzy that I was in this for the long haul went against her little plan that we'd soon get "divorced." Well, fuck that. She agreed to marry me.

I never agreed to give her a divorce afterward.

She stared at me, stammering out some stuff about loving me too, when the dude prompted her.

After that, I'd have to say it was kind of a blur. Maybe because my eyes were kinda wet.

# CHAPTER EIGHT

# Maggie

"YOU CATCH the look on Dizzy's face when they pronounced us husband and wife?" Zane nuzzled into me so he wouldn't be overheard; his arm went around my waist. He'd barely let go of me since we'd left the hotel.

To any observer, we probably looked exactly like newlyweds should look. Happy, a little adrenalin-buzzed, and all over each other. Random people honked their horns at us as they drove by.

We were standing on the curb outside the chapel, about to pile back into the limo, and Zane had put his cap back on, so I didn't think anyone saw his face. They were just happy for us. Total strangers, and they were probably happier for me than my own dad was.

Dizzy was happy, sure. For himself.

I sighed, because yes, I'd seen the look. Not a look I could recall ever seeing on my dad's face. Pretty sure it was pride.

Lukewarm approval was about the closest I'd ever seen before, and that was years ago, when I'd first told him I'd been hired to work for Dirty. At the time, he'd been a lot less interested in the particulars of my job than in what name I'd be using for work; he was royally pissed when I told him I'd be continuing to use my stepdad's last name, Omura, instead of his. Dizzy was adamant that having his last name would open doors for me in the industry, but I wasn't *that* naive. I knew he was more interested in what doors might open for *him* if he could associate himself in any way with Dirty.

For a moment, I allowed myself to wonder what he'd think when he found out I wasn't taking Zane's last name either. He'd probably say that was a mistake, too. Good thing I didn't care what he thought, right?

Except that I did care. Hence this whole ridiculous farce.

Yeah, I really had to do something about this fucked-up little masochistic streak of mine. Starting tomorrow.

"I saw it," I murmured distractedly, as we watched my dad making a flashy, embarrassing spectacle of tipping the chapel staff.

"Should we rescue them or what?" Zane asked, flicking his chin at the staff. They'd been pretty much trapped by Dizzy, who was waving a fistful of cash around as he told them some bullshit story about whatever great thing he figured he'd done most recently. Dizzy had a bullshit story for every occasion. Especially when he'd been using.

"No," I said, but I appreciated Zane deferring to me on this. No one could really "handle" my dad, but after the years I'd spent working with Dirty, I had a knack for knowing when to step back and let the biggest ego in the room have the floor. "Just let him have his moment."

For fuck's sake, though. You'd think *he* was the one who'd just gotten married. I just hoped he wasn't being rude.

The chapel staff had been incredibly accommodating, and my suspicion that Zane had paid them to shut down for us had been confirmed—by my dad, at his first opportunity. It was grotesquely clear to me by now that in his eyes, the fact that I'd just married a man who had the cash, the influence, and the balls to do that kind of thing meant I'd won the husband lottery. In fact, he'd warmed up extremely fast to the idea that I was marrying someone who, in his mind, was a lot like him. This, evidenced by the fact that he'd used the phrase "Zane and I..." to start about every second sentence he'd uttered since we left the hotel.

As in, *Zane and I would've preferred you in a white dress, Maggie.*

And so on.

Which just got me thinking...

I eyed my dad and tried as hard as I could to see him objectively.

The frizzy, bleached-out hair, all scraggly and black at the roots. The grossly tight jeans. The studded boots, the many necklaces and the earrings. The sleeveless Harley-Davidson shirt that showed his overly-tanned arms, now the texture of jerky; the tattoo of a voluptuous girl busting out of a bikini on his right bicep.

It all used to look so badass when he was younger. I could remember thinking he was just so cool. He'd flitted in and out of my life, and he always had some magical excuse for it. He was like a superhero to me then.

But now I was grown-up, and Dizzy was just ridiculous.

This was an extremely wealthy man who'd never treated his own daughter with much respect, forget about genuine affection or love. And now he was alone, clinging so desperately to his stoned-out youth that he was screwing chicks who were younger than his daughter and probably had daddy issues of their own.

I just hoped this one was legal.

*Shit.*

Was Zane gonna end up just like my dad in thirty years?

Didn't matter, I realized. I wasn't going to be married to him that long.

I wasn't going to be married to him at all.

Sure, I'd said my vows and signed the papers and went through the motions. I'd "married" Zane in a super tacky all-night wedding chapel in Las Vegas, in front of my dad and some girl named Maxxi. Yeah, that's with two x's. She spelled it for me.

It couldn't have been any more ridiculous, but apparently Dizzy had bought it. Big time.

Other than Zane being pretty sweet about the whole thing, it was kind of humiliating. I just couldn't decide if it was more humiliating for me or for my dad.

Zane's hand dropped to my ass and he gave my cheek a squeeze. He'd done that about ten times since we'd arrived. I didn't mind. It was pathetic to me, and incredibly hurtful, that my dad thought more of the man I was marrying than he did of me, and his comments in the hotel bar tonight still stung. If this was what it took for him to finally dredge up a modicum of respect for me, then so be it. I wanted him to see my new husband all over me, and for his part, Zane was taking every advantage of the opportunity.

"Get your sweet ass in the limo, wife," he said, his smoky voice all kinds of suggestive. Then he nipped my neck with his teeth. "It's time to celebrate."

"We are not celebrating," I said coolly, trying to stave off the shiver that pricked its way down my spine. Zane's idea of "celebrating" was bound to involve his dick in my pussy, and despite the fact that I'd been glued to his side for the last hour, I was not down with that.

I was way too sober—not to mention sane—to be down with that.

"Fucking right, we are," he murmured, and this time he nibbled on my ear, just scraping his teeth lightly over the curve of the lobe. And damn, I couldn't keep still. I squirmed a little as I shivered again, pretending to be cold as I burrowed deeper into his arms.

"No," I said into his shirt. I was putting my foot down on this. No fucking way were we "celebrating" this craziness. I just wanted this whole thing over with.

"C'mon, Maggie." Zane gripped my head and tilted my face up. "We just got married and I wanna go shake it up before you pop my cherry," he whispered, his lips hovering so close they brushed against mine. "Don't worry, we'll keep it low-key."

Right. Low-key.

And popping his cherry? Pretty sure some other woman had that honor, many, many years ago... his high school music teacher, if I remembered the story correctly.

No one was popping anything tonight, except maybe a couple of Advil before passing out.

"No, Zane," I whispered back, my voice firm. "Let's just go back to the hotel." I only heard how it sounded once the words were out.

Zane didn't miss it.

"Straight to bed, huh?" He cocked his pierced eyebrow at me, stroking my cheek with his thumb. "That's cool. We can do that instead, if you'd rather—"

"Forget it," I cut him off, untangling myself from his arms. "Let's go shake it," I announced, loudly enough for everyone to hear, as my dad and his date headed over to us.

Maxxi whooped excitedly. My dad smacked her ass and I followed them into the limo, tugging Zane along behind me as Flynn brought up the rear.

Dizzy was already opening a bottle of champagne that he'd produced from somewhere as I settled into my seat with a sigh... and pasted on my most dazzling newlywed smile.

So much for putting my foot down.

When we arrived back at the hotel almost four hours later, my head was still ringing from the music in the all-night karaoke bar that was the last stop on our whirlwind tour of late-night Vegas.

It was Zane who'd insisted on the karaoke. He'd been going on about popping cherries again while we perused the song selection, and when I realized he was planning to serenade me, I'd hissed at him, "Don't you dare sing 'White Wedding'!"

Then my dad piped up, telling Zane with a heavy slur that he should sing "Dirty Like Us," and I wasn't even sure if it was an actual mistake that he got the name of Dirty's most famous song wrong, or if he was just being an asshole getting it wrong on purpose, but neither Zane nor I bothered to correct him. I did slap my hand down over the Dirty songs on offer though, including "Dirty Like Me," since it would give him away in a dead second if Zane decided to saunter on stage and start singing that panty-wetting, now-classic rock anthem of love, hate, and soul-sucking heartbreak. "And no Dirty!" I ordered.

Instead, my wiseass "husband" chose another Billy Idol classic, "Rebel Yell." Which he sang arguably better than Mr. Idol himself, and holy fucking shit, who knew that song was so sexy? His performance, with ball cap pulled low over his eyes, raised so many eyebrows, we just barely scraped our way out of there before he lost his pants.

Flynn was sweating when we piled back into the limo.

In front of the hotel, I was wobbling a little on the curb as everyone piled back out. I gave Zane a serious once-over, and my most managerial stare down. "That was the sexiest karaoke, ever. And karaoke is never sexy. So you do the math on that."

He pulled me close and steered me into the hotel. "You're drunk," he whispered in my ear, his hot breath on my neck making me shiver.

"Am not."

I kinda was.

We said good night to Dizzy and Maxxi. They were wasted and my dad hardly noticed our departure. At least he'd stayed coherent enough to witness the wedding; that was all that really mattered.

Still... would it have killed him to offer a half-hearted "Congratulations" or a hug or something?

Apparently.

He was too busy pawing Miss Barely Legal to even say goodbye.

As Flynn dropped us at our door, I convinced myself it was all for the best. No point drawing this out. It was done, and now I could leave my dad hanging as long as I wanted to. For all he knew, I could spend the rest of my life happily married to Zane, a man he obviously admired. A lot. It's not like he'd notice we weren't actually together. My dad and I didn't live in the same city. Christ; Zane and I didn't even live in the same city. I still lived in Vancouver, where I'd grown up and where Brody also still lived. Zane lived down in L.A. most of the time.

Dizzy now lived in Vegas.

Yeah. He'd never know. Not if we didn't tell him.

He'd never been the world's most observant father.

When Zane and I walked into the penthouse suite, that fact was made abundantly clear. Not only had Dizzy bought into our little charade, he'd bought into it so hard, it had inspired him to do something totally out of character. Something thoughtful.

He'd put his staff to work for us, big time.

The big double doors leading into the master bedroom stood open. Red and white rose petals had been scattered along the floor, leading a trail up the three stairs into the room and straight to the massive bed. The bed had been covered with a fluffy white duvet, turned down to reveal white satin sheets. Giant bouquets of exotic flowers burst from vases set atop every available surface. There was a fruit tray and chocolate truffles and fresh oysters on ice. And a card, which I opened. It was signed in a hand that wasn't my dad's.

*With my deepest blessings. Dizzy.*

What a fucking tool. Like I gave two shits about his blessings.

I passed the card to Zane. He scanned it and tossed it aside.

Dizzy had never done anything like this for me before. Not when I graduated high school or college, not when Dirty hired me, not when I bought my first home. Nothing I'd ever done had warranted more than an absent "Good for you, sweetheart" when we'd spoken over the phone. Which was how I knew this had exactly zero to do with me.

This little display was for Zane.

Correction; actually, it was for Dizzy himself. To make him look like father of the year in the eyes of my new rock star husband.

*Good luck with that, Dad.*

Oh, and there was more champagne. Because that's just what I needed; more booze.

I stumbled a little as Zane let me go. He'd kept his arm around my waist all the way up to the room, and he eyed me warily as I got my footing. Whatever. My high heels were *high*. Yes, I'd had a bit to drink while we were out. Maybe a bit too much. But who could blame me? I'd just gotten pretend-married on a moment's notice to Zane in front of my dad, who thought it was real.

Obviously I understood why Zane was going dry, but I wasn't the one with the drinking problem. So why should I suffer through a night with Dizzy sober?

In the limo, it was Zane himself who'd handed me a flute of bubbly. I had no idea if my dad had a clue that Zane didn't drink. Zane just passed politely on the liquor, and no one seemed to care. Zane didn't bat an eye as I sipped the champagne, and honestly... maybe I did it to force some distance between us.

He said he didn't do chicks who'd been drinking. What better way to ensure he wouldn't try to feel me up when we got back to the hotel than getting a little buzz on?

I watched him take off his vest and kick off his boots. I still had the bouquet of tulips he'd given me, which had miraculously survived our bar-hopping. I went to put the flowers in a jug of water in the kitchen, avoiding his eyes, and told myself not to feel guilty for being a little inebriated.

This wasn't *actually* our wedding night.

Yes, it felt weird drinking in front of Zane. At least, for the first couple of drinks. But we were in and out of so many bars tonight and people were indulging all around us. What difference could it make if I had a few?

It was Zane who'd convinced me to do body shots off a waitress. That was at the strip club Dizzy decided we should hit. It was also Zane who bought me a lap dance. From a chick, which wasn't exactly my thing. She took us into one of the private rooms and I endured it for about a minute, because it made Zane laugh. But then I decided it would be a hell of a lot more fun making her sit in the chair and teach me some moves. And damn, did I ever work my tiny pink dress.

At least, it was fun until I remembered my dad was on the other side of that same room.

Luckily he was making out with Maxxi at the time, so he missed my little performance. Zane, on the other hand, didn't miss a thing. He even tipped me afterward. Also kinda fun.

But standing there in a private room in some strip club with my dad while Zane stuffed cash into my lace panties, I decided it was well past time to call it a night. This night was already fucking weird enough. Didn't think I could handle it getting any weirder.

I'd spent the ride back to the hotel quietly sipping a bottle of water and wondering why I'd let myself drink so much.

Maybe I'd been more nervous about this whole crazy thing than I'd let on... even to myself.

Still, I'd somehow managed to rationalize the booze, just like everything else, as harmless enough fun—until I stepped back out of the kitchen with my bouquet and looked up to see the weird-ass expression on Zane's face.

We stood there, awkwardly, on opposite sides of the room, staring in at the giant bed all decked out for a night of matrimonial bliss.

"If you want the big bed with the satin sheets you can take it," he said. He'd turned to look at me, and I could not for the life of me read the look in his blue eyes. "I'll take the other one. Whatever you want."

I blinked at him and set the flowers on a table, wobbling a little in my high heels. Whatever *I* wanted?

What the fuck?

"We aren't sleeping together?"

The words came spilling out of my mouth before I could think them through.

Zane's eyes twitched like he might smile, but then he didn't.

"I'm gonna go wash up. Take whichever bed you want and I'll take the other one. Cool?"

I stared at him, totally speechless.

No.

*Not* cool.

Maybe he was ready to call it a night—why??—but I'd spent the better part of the last four hours, pretty much from the second we said "I do" and he kissed me like he was devouring a bottle of particularly expensive bourbon, mentally preparing myself to spend the rest of the night, from the moment we walked back in here, fending him off.

Well, that, or fucking his brains out. If I was being honest. Hadn't quite decided which way things were gonna go yet. Blamed the champagne for that. Definitely.

But this? This was bullshit.

I watched him stroll up the stairs, through the master bedroom to the en suite bathroom, turn up the lights, and disappear inside. He closed the door behind himself. Not all the way, but still. A civilized person knew what a closed bathroom door meant.

But fuck that.

I heard the water running in the sink as I approached, and tossed the door open to find him brushing his teeth. I stalked over and turned off the faucet.

"This is my wedding night," I told him icily. "You have to at least *try* to bang me, so I can turn you down."

He pointed at the sink, which I was standing in front of. Never mind that there was another one two feet over.

I crossed my arms, staring him down.

He pulled the toothbrush out of his mouth. "May I shpit?" he asked, his mouth full of toothpaste foam.

"Fine." I shoved away from the sink to let him at it. Then I grumbled, "Like you didn't do enough of that already tonight," as he spat and rinsed.

"And like I told you," he said, eying me as he dabbed his mouth with a towel. "I don't fuck chicks who've been drinking."

"I'm not even drunk!"

He gave me a level look. "Babe."

"I'm not!" Pretty sure I was. Didn't keep me from protesting the fact. Hard. "Look, I'll brush my teeth. You won't taste a thing." With that, I seized his toothbrush and brushed my teeth.

He stood back, watching.

"See?" I spat in the sink and rinsed, then gave him a winning smile. "Minty fresh."

"You used my toothbrush," he said, eying me with mock concern. "You know that has cooties on it, right?"

I rolled my eyes. "I'm your *wife*," I shot back as sarcastically as possible. "I can't use your toothbrush?"

I strutted back out into the bedroom, still trying to prove my case. Zane followed at a distance. I wasn't sure why it was so important to me that I prove I wasn't wasted. In the bar it really hadn't seemed like a big deal, especially when he kept feeding me drinks.

Now it felt wrong.

"What do you want me to do? Walk a straight line? Touch my finger to my nose?" I did that, and thank God I actually hit the target. "What if I sing 'Schoolgirl'? Bet I can remember all the words."

Then I started singing my dad's shitty song. Not terribly, either. I could hold a tune. Couldn't hold a candle to Zane's voice, but at least I wouldn't totally embarrass myself. The booze loosened me up, so I figured I sounded even better than usual. Though my judgment was probably impaired on that.

Zane just stood there, leaning on the wall by the bathroom, silently observing as I tried to take off my strappy high heels while singing the chorus, and fell over on the bed.

"See?" I kicked the shoes off and did my best to make it look like I'd meant to sit down. "Every word."

"Uh-huh."

"So?" I stared at him expectantly. "Don't you think if I was wasted, that would be the very, very first thing to go?"

His lips quirked. "That doesn't make much sense, Maggie."

"Yes it does!" I jumped to my feet. "Come on! Sing along. It won't sound as terrible if you sing it."

"Can't do it." He shook his head slowly. "Promised you I'd never sing that song."

Shit. That was true.

"Fine. But we're not just calling it a night! I'm all amped up, and it's your fault."

"My fault?"

"Uh, yeah. You're the one who dragged me out of bed and took me out on the town, married me, poured booze down my throat, bought me lap dance lessons, and sang karaoke to me. Now I'm not sleepy. Party with me."

"Jesus," he muttered. "Never thought I'd see the day."

"What day?"

"The day you begged me to party with you."

"Whatever." I paced to the other side of the room, but something snagged at me, drawing me back. "Wait. Wait just a sec..." I walked over to him, poking him in the chest. "Did you encourage me to drink all that booze so you wouldn't touch me?" I looked down at myself and wondered how drunk I looked. "Is this like... Zane repellent, or something?"

He laughed shortly, but the look in his blue eyes was much less than funny.

Yeah. I'd hit that one on the head.

Motherfucker had gotten me drunk on purpose so he wouldn't fuck me.

"Shit. You're such a dick!"

"How am I a dick? You wanted to have some champagne, and why shouldn't you? Why should you have to deal with Dizzy sober?"

"Exactly!" I was so thrilled that he saw it the same way I did, I tossed myself against him, slapping my hands on his chest. "Come on, Zane! Get over it. I promise I won't grope you. I just can't go to bed right now. I'll just lay there eating all those chocolates and being pissed at Dizzy and that's fucking stupid."

He studied me, a bunch of shit going on behind his eyes that I couldn't fathom. "Not worried about you groping me, Maggs."

"Okay. Well, I'm not gonna let you grope me either. I'm not *that* drunk." I wasn't totally sure that I wasn't, but whatever. "Just... I don't know... get your shit together and smoke a joint or something, man. I need you."

His gaze slithered down my chest. I was still leaning on him, my breasts crushed against him. "Sure you want me to do that, babe?"

"Why not?" I asked casually, stepping back to put some space between us.

"Because I get horny as fuck when I smoke up."

He wasn't kidding. I could hear it in his voice. Could see it on his face.

But I wasn't some innocent victim here. I could keep my panties on if I wanted to.

I'd already kept them on for six years.

"You already smoked up when we were on the patio tonight, remember? And you managed to keep control of yourself."

"Right," he said. He was already pulling out his weed to roll a joint, as he studied me with one eye closed. "But I did ask you to marry me."

# CHAPTER NINE

## *Maggie*

SOMETIME LATER, Zane had smoked up, and I'd helped him. My eyeballs felt fuzzy and everything seemed really good.

Life was good, right?

I had the best job *in the world*. Every day I got up and I felt grateful for where I was. I had the respect of my coworkers, and I kicked ass at what I did. I knew I was appreciated. Needed.

So what if my dad didn't see what I was worth?

Maybe my "marriage" to Zane would change that. Fundamentally, it probably wouldn't. I'd just have to work harder at accepting it.

I wasn't going to change Dizzy Bowman. The man was an old, old dog, with no interest in picking up any new tricks.

And so what if I had no real girlfriends outside of work? I could always make new friends.

Besides... I had Zane. And right about now, that was all I really needed.

What else could I possibly need?

When he and I were together—and not pissing each other off—it just fit. It felt right. At least, when he wasn't trying to get up my skirt.

Thing was, these moments were few and far between.

Maybe that was the only real problem between us.

We sat side by side, close together on the big white bed. We'd managed to have an extremely engaging conversation about Hanna-Barbera cartoons, the kind of conversation where time just cruises on by and I, for one, didn't even notice. I was vaguely aware that the sun would be coming up soon. We'd just had a heated, nonsensical argument about who would drive the car if we lived in the time of *The Flintstones*—uh, obviously we both would; it took a lot of feet to move those stone wheels, right?—and which dinosaur would make the best pet.

How we got onto *The Flintstones*? I asked Zane if he'd ever thought about marrying a woman before he popped the question out on the patio. I really thought the answer would be no. But after what appeared to be careful consideration, he said, "Betty Rubble."

A while later, once we'd agreed to disagree about the dinosaurs, I said out of nowhere, "She already had a husband."

Zane looked confused. "Huh?"

"Betty."

"Betty who?"

I laughed, and I couldn't stop laughing. It felt so fucking good to talk about nothing at all. Forget my dad. Forget this whole fucked-up night. Forget this unbearable sexual tension that had me all tied in knots every time I was alone with Zane.

I could live with it. All of it.

As long as Zane had my back, I could put up with anything, really.

Which reminded me of something. "What did my dad say to you?" I sat up straight and turned to face him. "When we were getting out of the limo and Maxxi hugged me, he leaned in and you guys were talking for a minute. What were you saying?"

He held my gaze, his eyes a little hooded, and I couldn't tell what he was thinking. Couldn't tell if he was stoned or not. "He was asking me for a meeting."

"Seriously? Jesus Christ," I practically growled. "Fuck! I can't believe he asked you that on our wedding night."

Zane said nothing, but a gorgeous smile crept across his face.

"What?" I elbowed him sharply.

"Nothing," he said.

"What did you tell him?"

"I said we'd meet. Day after tomorrow."

"What, here? In Vegas?"

"Yup."

I blinked at him. "You're on a flight at like eight in the morning. No way Dizzy's up early enough for that."

"Yeah," he said, unconcerned.

Slowly it started to penetrate my foggy brain. "You're really meeting up with him like you said you would?"

He shrugged. "This is my wedding night. I'm all high on nuptial ecstasy. Already forgot what he and I talked about." He cocked his head like he was trying to pull up some distant memory. "Did I even talk to Dizzy?"

I smiled, big time. "You are one damn good husband, Zane Traynor."

"Always knew I would be." His eyes were locked on mine, and he was so close I could feel his breath on my face. When did we get so close? I became aware of my hand, which I'd planted on his thigh at some point, but I didn't remove it.

His gaze dropped to my lips and lingered there.

I glanced down and away, because I couldn't keep looking at his face.

"You have beautiful feet," I whispered.

I could see them now, sticking out the legs of his frayed jeans, naked, his strong, graceful toes wiggling with latent energy. Like a tiger's tail twitching just before it pounces.

When I looked back up he was cocking an eyebrow at me. Shit. I just said that out loud?

Right... now I remembered the other reason I made it a practice never to drink too much in Zane's company.

He licked his lips. "You say one more thing like that, Maggie May, and I'm gonna kiss you. Consider yourself warned."

"What? About your feet?"

"About my anything."

Turned out I didn't have to say a thing. I just kissed him first.

I really couldn't say what I was thinking when I climbed onto the bed with him; when I snuggled up to him like he was some asexual man-friend with innocent cuddling privileges, instead of a diabolical, sex-hungry man-whore with a permanent hard-on.

I couldn't say what I was thinking when I kissed him, either. If I was thinking at all.

Apparently I'd had just enough booze and pot and weirdness over the course of the night to allow myself to go there. For once, not to question his motives or worry about what this meant or warn myself I was making the world's most massive mistake.

I just leaned in and laid one on him.

His lips were soft and gentle in a way I didn't expect. It kinda took my breath away.

When we'd kissed just before the wedding ceremony, and during, those were hungry, passionate kisses. The first a slow burn, the latter a blazing fire. Maybe they were for show. I couldn't honestly tell which was the real deal; this kiss or those. Or maybe all of the above. But I fell into it, this kiss. I tilted my head a little when he pushed in deeper, opening for him. He swirled his tongue against mine, tentatively, and when I responded with a little moan I didn't even know was coming, he took my face in his hands and cranked up the heat.

After that, I had no idea what happened.

I lost track of myself in the ensuing inferno.

We were horizontal on the bed, making out like animals, and Zane's shirt was gone. Maybe it had incinerated. Somehow I was underneath him, and his hands were working their way up under my dress... and I didn't want to be anywhere else.

"Fuck... Maggie... I've wanted you... wanted this... for so long..."

He devoured me with his kisses, feasting on my mouth, my face, groaning when I kissed him back... and as I gasped for air in between

—because I'd pretty much forgotten how to breathe—an awful, horrible thought invaded my brain.

What if any of this passion was about the booze?

I broke away, panting, lightheaded and breathless.

Sure, I'd brushed my teeth. Like that could magically undrink the booze I'd drank? The truth was, I was a lot less sober than I'd let on. I was pretty sure Zane knew that.

But that meant he was breaking *his* rule for me. And his rule was a big one. As in, his life pretty much depended on it.

*Booze and women together... that's a temptation I just can't hack.*

Shit.

Just... *shit.*

All the air squeezed from my lungs and my heart kicked in a really weird way.

I could *not* be the reason Zane destroyed his life.

Wait.

My *heart?*

When the hell did my heart get in on this?

*Fuck me.* My heart was *not* allowed to do weird kicky things for Zane.

It was *Zane.*

He was looking at me, his blue eyes hazy, his face a little flushed, his skin kinda dewy as his tongue swiped the corner of his mouth. I tasted his salt as I bit my lip.

When did it get so bloody hot in here?

"What's wrong?"

"I think you were right," I whispered, my hand on his chest as I pushed him away.

He didn't let go.

"I'm right about a lot of things, babe. Be more specific."

He slid his hand around my neck and dug his fingers into my hair, pulling me closer, and I said, "Maybe we shouldn't do this."

He stopped dead and stared at me. "You serious?"

I nodded. I was dead serious.

"Fuck me."

He released me and rolled away, sitting on the edge of the bed, facing away from me. Then he got up, fast, and put his shirt back on.

Shit. Was he pissed?

Where did he get off being pissed?

I scrambled off my side of the bed. "You weren't going to before, so why should I?"

He turned and stood glaring at me. I was actually glad the bed was between us, because he was starting to look stabby again. "Because you *want* to."

"*You* want to," I shot back.

He clawed his hand through his blond hair, clearing it from his face. "For fuck's sake, woman, I've wanted to for six fucking years, and now you marry me and you still say no?"

"*You* said no."

"I'm saying *yes*," he said, with a not-so-subtle adjustment of his dick in his jeans.

"Because you *married* me."

"What the fuck does that mean?"

"It means this was all your idea!"

He shook his head. Then he rounded the bed so he could glare at me up close and I backed up until I hit wall.

"And you said yes to it," he said slowly, and really fucking quietly. "Right after I told you you weren't gonna pull this shit, remember?"

"I said yes because I hate my dad, Zane."

"You do not hate your dad."

"Yeah, I do."

He took a breath, turned away like he was looking for something to pummel, then turned back and stared me down again. "We just got married, Maggs—"

I rolled my eyes. I couldn't help it.

"We just got *married*," he repeated, leaning down close to my face. "Which means you're not gonna do that. You're not gonna lie to me. You're not gonna roll your eyes at me anymore. No more fucking wall of Maggie between us. Just *you* and *me*." He stepped in closer, until we were almost nose-to-nose. "You gonna look me in the eye right now and tell me you hate Dizzy?"

Shit. It really could be maddening as all hell the way the man saw through me.

And right now? Totally fucking inconvenient.

"No," I said softly, swallowing.

"Now do you wanna fuck or not?"

"Well... yeah."

"Good." He grabbed my face in both hands and pressed in close. "Because I'm gonna fuck you in about one minute, on those white satin sheets, and then I'm gonna do it again, and you're gonna fucking love it and I don't want you pissed off at me tomorrow."

Then he kissed me, and he was right.

I did love it.

The one thing I knew I would never forget, the moment that branded itself into my bones, was that first kiss after we were married.

As soon as the guy said the word, I'd claimed Maggie's sweet mouth with my own and thrust my tongue inside, making her mine. Officially. *Mine.*

My wife.

My Maggie.

And that stuff about never letting her go? I'd meant it.

No idea if she knew how much I meant it.

Didn't matter.

With Maggie, I'd always played the long game.

Just didn't realize until tonight that it was time for me to cash out.

Everything I'd ever wanted to do to Maggie, I was finally gonna do it. Now.

Kiss her all over. Devour her.

Totally unleash on her.

I was gonna fuck her until she rasped my name, her husky voice raw from screaming.

But first, I was just gonna kiss her. So I got her on the bed and that's what I did.

Lot of other things I wanted to do with my mouth, lot of places to explore, but I couldn't tear myself away from her lips.

Didn't even care that she'd been drinking. I should've cared. I just didn't. Didn't care about a thing but screwing her, hard. With my tongue. With my entire body. I rammed myself against her, fully dressed, just savoring the fact. Just drenching my senses in her.

I was gonna make Maggie mine in every fucking way I could think of before the sun came up.

"Zane... are you sure...?" she murmured against my lips, and I shook my head at her.

"Just shut up Maggie. For once in your life, just shut the fuck up and trust me."

Then I tore off her little pink dress and looked at her. I felt kinda breathless as I swiped my hair out of my eyes and stared at her.

She lay there breathing hard and staring back up at me. Just waiting for me.

*Zane repellent?* I almost laughed out loud. No way this woman could repel me.

Yes, I'd tried to get her drunk. Only because I thought it would keep me from taking advantage of her when she was feeling so low.

When we'd set out to the chapel, fucking right, I was planning on getting her into bed before the night was through. But then I saw how it was with her and Dizzy. She just wanted him to give a fuck, and the guy was blind to it. That, or he didn't know how to give a fuck. It hurt her. And I couldn't be a part of anything that hurt Maggie.

But now? There was nothing in her eyes but longing. Anticipation.

Desire.

I peeled her lacy bra and panties off. I just wanted to see her. All of her. She was so fucking pretty. And so strong. Her skin so smooth and soft... I started kissing her, nibbling her, licking every part of her body. I just needed to taste her, to inhale her sweet smell and get lost in her.

She could've done anything, said anything, fought me tooth and nail, and I would've wanted her.

She could've drank all the booze in Las Vegas.

Wouldn't matter.

This girl was my fucking kryptonite.

Right now, feeling her panting, getting hot beneath me, I would've done anything, given anything, risked anything to be with her.

Her breaths came faster, shorter, harder as I sucked her nipple into my mouth. As I teased her with my teeth. I had no idea if she was already regretting this. I hoped not, but I wasn't gonna let her dwell on it either.

I reached down and smoothed my fingers over her pussy. She was soft and wet. Hot. I let her nipple go and clenched my teeth as the hunger rocked through me. I was so fucking hard for her. Again.

Always.

I pressed my fingertip into her and she tensed.

"No. Wait," she gasped, reaching to stop my hand. Her gray eyes found mine, bright and clear. "I want your cock to be the first thing inside me."

She didn't have to tell me twice.

I got up and stripped off my clothes. Dug around in my pockets for a condom.

I sheathed my dick and went to her, and I gave her what she

wanted. I didn't get her ready or tease her at all. I just filled her in one fast, possessive thrust that made her cry out.

Her fingernails dug into my ass as I fucked her and everything started to rush.

I was gonna come.

Way too fucking fast.

But Maggie was clawing at me, moaning and gasping, pulling me deeper, and no way I could stop. Pretty sure I couldn't hold on like this... maybe not the first time... maybe this one would be too fucking quick, and I'd just have to apologize and make it up to her later.

*Fuck me.* What a lousy fucking lay.

Then she surprised me by pushing me off. I rolled, taking her with me. Maggie straddled me, dug her knees into the bed, and started riding me, hard.

Hottest thing I'd ever seen.

"Oh, fuck," she said, wiggling around. "These stupid satin sheets!" Her knees were slipping all over the place.

"You wanna do it on the floor, babe?" I managed to rasp out. The repositioning had interrupted the rush, so I was able to hang on. But watching Maggie's tits bounce, feeling her hot pussy bear down on my dick? No fucking way.

I was not gonna last.

"My room," she gasped. Then she was up, and dashing across the hotel suite. I lay there for a second, kind of stunned.

Then I went after her, grabbing her around the waist and throwing her over my shoulder. She squealed in surprise and I slapped her ass. Hard. I took her into her room and tossed her on the bed. We came together and fell on our sides, kissing and fucking and kind of struggling for dominance.

She wanted on top.

I wouldn't let her mount up.

Not until I'd pounded her for a while and she got a little glassy-eyed and gave in. When she softened, I rolled over and drew her on top again. I couldn't take much more of that anyway.

She put her hands on my shoulders and rode me, slowly. Teasing me.

"You're gonna come when I say," she said softly, her eyes locked on mine. Her hair was all wild and in her face and spilling over her shoulders. Her lips were swollen.

I'd never seen anything more beautiful.

"Am I?"

"Yeah," she breathed, then bit her lip. "It'll make me come."

She rode me faster, jerking her hips as she found the friction she wanted. Then she got rougher, fucking me a lot harder than I expected her to.

"Jesus... Maggie..." I said between my teeth.

"Let's just get it out of the way," she said. "I can't wait anymore."

"Uh... yeah..." I rasped out. "But you should go first."

"Nuh-uh," she said. "Trust me. Next time, we can take our time..."

I wasn't gonna argue with that. Whatever the fuck she wanted... I just wanted to be there when it happened.

Anyway, it wasn't gonna take long for her to get her wish.

The pressure was building in my balls, hot and fast. My cock hummed as she squeezed me, aching for release as she slithered up and rammed down. She pulled almost completely away and swirled her hips, teasing my cockhead. I groaned desperately, clutching at her hips, and when her eyes caught mine, she said, "Now, Zane." Then she dropped down on me, hard. "Come for me."

I did. I blew so fucking hard I lifted her off the bed. I crushed her hips down to mine, squeezing her tight. My fingers dug in... pretty sure I left bruises.

She didn't complain.

She tossed her head back and moaned, and I felt her spasm, clenching around me as she rammed down a few more times, taking what she needed.

Then I grabbed her and spun us around, pressing her down beneath me, driving her into the pillows as I buried myself in her and rode out the aftershocks. When I did that, she came again, shuddering in my arms, gasping and clawing at me and crying my name.

Afterward, she blinked up at me with that gorgeous haze in her gray eyes as she went all soft and limp.

I kissed her deep as I held her. When I came up for air, I breathed with her.

Then I kissed her again.

I just wanted to stay lost in her. To feel nothing but her, taste nothing but her... stay inside her as long as I could.

Then I wanted to start all over at the beginning... and do it all again.

And again.

And again.

## CHAPTER TEN

*Maggie*

RELIEVED.

That's how I felt when I woke and found Zane in bed with me. Naked.

For that uncomfortable moment teetering in the unreality between sleeping and wakefulness, the events of the night replayed in my head in a high-speed rush—all of them. And for a split second as I opened my eyes, I was intensely sure that none of it was real.

I'd dreamed it. All of it.

When I saw him lying next to me on his back, his head turned away, his chest rising and falling as the rhythm of his deep breaths sounded softly in the near-dark... yeah. I was glad he was here.

I was glad the whole crazy thing was real.

As I watched him, I couldn't help but feel a little happy.

Maybe sanity was overrated?

Maybe it was okay to go a little crazy, just for one night.

Then he turned his head and looked at me. He blinked his blue eyes, then locked on me.

*Oh, shit.*

I now knew that look. Intimately.

He rolled toward me. His warm hand found my stomach beneath the sheet and slid down, down... When his fingertips grazed my clit, I bit my lip to keep from gasping. I spread my legs without thinking.

Because hell, yes... I wanted more.

More of what I'd had last night.

In my defense, I was still only half-conscious, and besides, only a stupid, stupid woman would kick Zane Traynor out of bed. Only a crazy woman would let him into her bed in the first place, but still.

His eyes seemed to darken in the dim light and his hand slid further down, his fingers slicking against my already-wet flesh. Then he slipped inside, filling me. His fingers curved and undulated, doing insanely pleasurable things to my insides, and I moaned.

Okay. I was definitely awake now.

He repositioned himself above me and kissed me. His lips were hot and by this point, familiar. I liked how they felt against mine. How he sucked on my bottom lip and made soft growling noises low in his throat when he did it, like he couldn't help it. How he breathed faster and faster the more we kissed, like he was speeding toward the edge, and I was taking him there.

He slipped a second finger in to join the first, twisting both fingers around as he fucked me with them. I squirmed and moaned, unable to resist the almost-overwhelming pleasure. It just felt so good.

So. Fucking. *Good.*

I should've put a stop to it right here.

A smarter Maggie, a Maggie of twenty-four hours ago, would have. But she wouldn't have been in bed with Zane in the first place.

Which meant she would've missed out on this unbelievably pleasurable bliss.

But, yes. I should've stopped it. Last night was one thing.

A separate, one-time thing.

A crazy ending to a fucked-up night, prompted by hours of built-up, pent-up sexual tension. I'd been ditched mid-foreplay by Coop, and I was pissed off at my dad. I'd been humiliated and hurt. I was a little high. And a lot drunk.

But now? What excuse did I have for letting him do this to me?

I was no longer drunk. Not even a bit.

In the dim morning light, I was as stone-cold sober as it could get, and still I spread my legs for Zane.

I writhed and undulated beneath him, screwing his hand, wanting more. Even as I did it, I knew I was overthinking things. Zane had warned me not to do that. Actually, he'd kind of ordered me not to.

Well, fuck that. I didn't follow his orders.

I pushed him up and off, throwing one leg over him and shoving him down on his back, straddling him. His fingers were still inside me, and I rode them with all the pent-up frustration I still had left. There was a lot of it, apparently. Maybe until last night, when I'd fucked Zane—three times—I'd never realized how hard I held things in. Didn't realize it until I actually let loose and it all came rushing out.

So. Much. *Tension.*

He wrapped his hand around the back of my neck and pulled me down to him, kissing me fiercely as I kept riding his hand. The man had a wicked, talented tongue... but I gave back everything I got. I ravaged him, sucked on him, ate him alive, taking everything that was mine in this moment with my lips, my tongue and my teeth. It was hot and wet and all kinds of greedy. It was messy.

It was chaos.

It was becoming addictive.

It was only a few hours since we'd fallen asleep, but technically it was kind of a new day. The day I was supposed to get off my masochistic ass and get my shit together. Deal with the last night of the tour. Wrap things up with Brody and fly home. Say goodbye to the band, for now.

Say goodbye to Zane.

I'd see him again in a few months, when promotion for Jesse's solo album, which was coming out soon, really ramped up.

Maybe even before that.

But between now and then? Zane would do what Zane did. He

could be with a hell of a lot of other women. I had no claim on him, despite what happened last night.

I didn't want a claim on him. Or so I kept telling myself, again and again, last night in the dark, as we claimed each other... again and again.

But we were here right now, and he was willing. There was nothing standing between us anymore. No one else, no booze, no distractions... other than my busy brain. Here, in the near-dark... it was just me and Zane.

And no one ever had to know.

*What happens in Vegas...*

I was moaning, kind of panting into his mouth as I neared orgasm. He felt it. I knew he felt it as I bore down on his fingers. He groaned and rolled me over, pinning me again as his fingers dug in and his thumb pressed my clit. It almost hurt, and I wanted it to. I just kissed him harder, pulling him down to me.

He withdrew his fingers and climbed on top of me and I braced for the thrust of his cock. Just once more. Once more and then we'd go back to our lives. He'd go back to screwing everything with a pussy—except me—and I'd go back to screwing the odd random hot guy who crossed my path, up to and perhaps including the occasional rock star... so long as it wasn't the one currently on top of me, seizing my wrists and pulling my hands up above my head, claiming me, again, with his mouth, his possessive kisses.

Shit, but that was a depressing thought. Way more depressing than it should've been.

He nudged my knees apart and settled between my legs, and as I opened for him, he rammed into me with an urgency that startled me, just like that first time. I gasped in pleasure-pain as my body stretched to take him. All of him. Zane did not hold back in this, or in anything he did. This was pure Zane, and it was beautiful and it was messy and it was perfect.

His blue eyes found mine and I just nodded, breathless, for him to keep going.

He fucked me hard and slow, pinning me there against the bed, churning into me with his hips the way I'd fantasized about him doing a hundred thousand times as I wrapped my legs around him and took him.

I felt tears prick at the corners of my eyes.

It was all so overwhelming.

Suddenly he stopped and withdrew, letting my wrists go as he crawled down my body. Then his tongue found my pussy and it was all over—any over-thinking, any kind of thought at all... rational or otherwise.

He lapped the flat of his tongue over my sensitive flesh once, twice, three times, and I relaxed into the bed. Then he focused on my clit, flicking the tip of his tongue lightly over it, then swirling around, and I shuddered, gasping for breath. After the rough treatment of his hand, the warm, gentle caresses of his tongue, soft and slick, were almost too much.

"Ah... Zane..." I gasped out, my voice all raw from last night, "... I can't..."

I didn't know why I said it. I just did.

"Maggie." He fluttered his tongue against me and practically growled. "Gonna make you come so hard..." And then he did. With one long, slow lick that set me off like a rocket.

I arched and cried out, my voice raw and rasping.

"Fuck, I love your voice," he murmured against my flesh as I came down.

Then he was at it again, teasing me to climax, taking his time, taunting and exploring, experimenting as he assaulted my clit with what felt like a thousand different types of licks, nibbles, kisses and strokes from every direction. I went off again and again, until he finally rose above me on his knees, panting.

He braced his hands on either side of me and lowered his hips, stroking the long, hard shaft of his cock against my pussy... and I exploded again, coming so hard as he ground against my clit that I bit my tongue.

"Oh my God," I panted. "Shit. I bit my tongue."

"You bleeding?" His brow creased with concern as he slowed his teasing thrusts and I shuddered, still coming down off that last orgasm.

"No." I poked my tongue around my mouth. "Just... ow."

He smiled and leaned down to kiss me softly. Then he lifted my limp legs by my thighs, spreading me wide, and thrust into me. I was so sopping wet by now that even as big as he was, his cock filled me in one smooth motion. No friction this time, no pain. Just slippery wet and heat. He shoved himself in to the root, then started rocking his hips, pumping himself slowly in and out. I met his thrusts, lifting my hips off the bed as he picked up speed, making him lose his rhythm in ragged breaths.

Then I was on top of him again, riding him with abandon, and then we were tumbling onto the floor. Zane managed to shove a blanket from the bed underneath me, more or less, and then he was pounding into me, hard. Unlike the bed, the floor had no give, and his pounding thrusts felt like punishment. It was a punishment I could take. I wanted it. I wanted him. I wanted him to tear me apart.

His whole body tensed as his breathing got rougher. His dazed blue eyes met mine as he started to come. "*Zane...*" I rasped his name as his cock jerked inside me.

He growled, low and strained in his throat. "Maggie," he gasped as he erupted. "*Fuck... Maggie...*" He pounded into me a few more times, sloppily, completely losing himself.

I came then, suddenly, his messy, desperate thrusts sending me over the edge again... writhing under him as he buried his face in my neck.

"Jesus... shit," he panted when it was over.

It wasn't eloquent, but yeah, that kinda summed it up.

We were both soaking wet. My whole body throbbed with my heartbeat, every nerve humming and alive.

We lay there a long time, entangled, until the sweat on my body cooled and I started to get cold. He felt me shiver and got up, tugging me to my feet.

As I flopped back onto the bed, I made the mistake of glancing in the direction of the bedside table. My phone was lighting up.

I took Brody's call as Zane went to the bathroom to clean up. It was only then that it struck me he'd been wearing a condom. Well, shit. Thank God one of us had been thinking.

But leaving that kind of thing up to Zane? Not a smart move.

Not smart at all.

Luckily the chat with my boss kept me from examining that too closely. Especially when he wanted to know why his Twitter feed was blowing up with a bunch of cell phone videos of Zane serenading me and my dad with "Rebel Yell" at a karaoke joint last night, and also, why he wasn't invited to that little party. I sputtered through my response to that, at which he sounded amused, and mercifully turned the conversation to other business.

After I got off the call, I thumbed through my new texts, including a link from Brody to one of the aforementioned videos, which I clicked on and watched for about three seconds before Zane came back out of the bathroom.

He cocked an eyebrow at me as I stuffed the phone under my pillow.

Pretty sure he caught a snatch of the song though, and his own voice, not to mention all the lustful screaming in the background; there was a lot of it, more than I'd been aware of at the time, since when Zane Traynor took a stage, all else pretty much ceased to exist for me... and judging by that screaming, similar to the screaming that could be heard anytime he took a stage, I was not the only woman with this reaction.

I was wondering if I should just get it over with and do the naked morning-after dash to the bathroom, to avoid the awkward aftermath, when I realized I didn't need to. Instead of heading for the door with some lame excuse for needing to disappear, Zane sauntered over and sprawled on the bed next to me, face-down.

Like it was totally normal for him to sprawl out on a bed next to me, buck naked.

King of cool.

I should've gotten up and gotten dressed. Brody wanted to meet for breakfast in half an hour, and it would've been suspicious if I'd begged out. So I didn't.

It also gave me the perfect excuse to get out of here.

But Zane didn't seem to be in a hurry.

I really meant to get up. But somehow, I didn't budge.

Instead I listened to Zane's even, relaxed breathing as his beautiful feet played lazy footsie with mine.

And then, because I needed to say something to fill the air and distract myself from this growing awkwardness that was an uncomfortable mashup of embarrassment, confusion and guilt, I said, "I can't believe Elle missed our big fat fake wedding. She would shit."

"Thought you didn't wanna tell anyone," he mumbled into his pillow, the long blond strands of his hair scattered across his face.

"I don't." I reached up and smoothed the hair back with my fingertips, gently, so I could see him. I wouldn't be able to touch him like this in an hour or two, so why not? Might be my last chance.

The one eye I could see was closed, his eyelashes long and straight, nearly black at the root, lightening to golden-blond at the tips. Yeah, Zane had beautiful eyelashes. Was there anything about the man that wasn't beautiful?

Nope. I would know. Got up close and incredibly personal with every last inch of him last night, and I sure as hell couldn't find it.

He stirred a little as I let my fingers trail down his temple and around his ear where the hair, buzzed short, felt like velvet. That one blue eye opened as I brought my hand away, and froze on me.

"Fake?"

"How long should we wait to tell my dad it wasn't real?" I wondered aloud. "I mean... we can't just let him believe it forever, much as I'd love to let him dangle..." It would be cruel and pretty shitty of me to lie to my dad for any length of time, and I knew it. But after what he'd said to me yesterday... my own father called me a slut, for fuck's sake. I was prepared to let him dangle for a little while.

Hell, for all I cared we could wait until after he sent us our wedding gift. It would be something expensive, knowing Dizzy. Not out of generosity, but because he'd consider it poor form to send Zane a wedding gift that was anything less than seriously, grandiosely overpriced.

Maybe I was a terrible person, but the thought of parting Dizzy with any of his precious money made me smile. Damn right, he could send us a gift. And we weren't returning it, either.

Zane lifted up, still eying me strangely, and rolled onto his side. His legs were all tangled up with mine from the knee down. I focused on his face to avoid looking at his cock, which was now in full view.

He blinked at me, his eyes adjusting to the pale morning light, like he wasn't sure if he was seeing things right.

"It was real," he said slowly but really quietly, and the smile dropped from my face.

Zane Traynor had fucked with me plenty of times, and you better believe I knew when he was fucking with me.

He wasn't fucking with me now.

The intensity in his blue eyes said it all, as they burned into me with that look that could give you frostbite.

"No," I said, so calmly I kind of scared myself. I didn't even know where the words came from, but they were coming out of my mouth. "It. Was. *Fake.*"

"It wasn't fake."

"It wasn't *real*," I protested, my brain groping madly for an explanation that would make his words make sense.

"You thought it was fake?" he asked, his eyebrows drawing together in a dangerously pissed-off look.

What the fuck was happening?

"You thought it was *real*?"

"Why would it be fake?"

"*Why would it be real?*"

I jumped up, untangling Zane's naked body from mine and scrabbling off the bed, pulling the sheet with me as a shield.

"No. Nuh-uh. That was a pretend ceremony and you paid the chapel guy to... to..."

"To marry us?" he finished for me.

Oh. *God.*

"For fuck's sake, Zane! You *didn't.*"

"Pretty fucking sure I did." He rubbed a hand over his face, looking sleepy and irritated as fuck.

Too fucking bad! He didn't get to be pissed at me. Not when he—

"Jesus!" I jabbed my left hand in the air. "These stupid cheap rings?"

He glanced from the ring to my face, looking unimpressed as shit, and cocked that wicked pierced eyebrow at me.

"These are supposed to be stupid cheap rings, Zane," I informed him, anger rising along with the panic. "Like pretend, 'Ha ha, I just fake-married my friend in Vegas because it's hilarious' rings."

"If you say so."

He started to drag himself up off the bed, giving me an eyeful of his godlike body and his stupid gorgeous dick.

"No. No, we did not. I did not. I couldn't have. I did not just *marry* you..." I babbled on, clinging to the sheet like a lifeline.

"Actually, sweetheart," he said, "you did. Maybe you remember that part where you said 'I do' or the paperwork we signed?"

He wandered out of the room, giving me an eyeful of his sculpted ass... then he returned, holding the vest he'd worn to our wedding last night. Our *fake* wedding. "I'm gonna take a shower," he said, sounding kinda disgusted as he dug something from the inside pocket of the vest and tossed it at me. "And by the way..."

It landed on the bed just in front of me.

A small, red velvet box.

A ring box.

"... there's your legit proposal."

Against my better sense, I picked up the box and opened it... to find a gorgeous platinum ring with a big-ass diamond staring me in the face.

## WHAT A SHITTY FUCKING NIGHT.

I'd lain in bed, unable to sleep, for hours before I gave up on trying.

Zane invited me up to the penthouse to meet some girls, but I ignored his texts. Dylan wanted me to come down to the bar. I didn't go.

Instead I tried to watch a movie. I tried to write some music. I played guitar for a while, just trying to clear the argument with Elle from my head.

It had really pissed me off this time.

I wasn't fucking flirting with that chick. I was being friendly. Professional. I was pretty sure I'd know if I crossed a line, but lately, it seemed like everything I did went over some line with Elle.

I couldn't fucking take it anymore.

So I got up and went to the rooftop gym. I didn't want to be recognized. I just wanted to be alone. But I couldn't stand sitting in the hotel room any longer.

Luckily, the gym was pretty much empty.

I should've called Jude, probably. Talked it through. But I didn't call. I didn't text. I didn't want to talk; maybe I was through fucking talking. I was definitely through arguing with Elle over the same fucking things, over and again.

We just weren't working as a couple. Why couldn't she see that?

I went over and over it in my head as I worked out. But any way I looked at it, it was the same old thing. Elle and I were just too fucking different, in the ways that really counted, to make this thing work.

We could never work it out anyway, even when we tried. We couldn't even talk about shit without fighting. She got confrontational. I withdrew. She was quick-tempered. I was brooding.

To other men she was "passionate." To other women I was "mysterious."

We both drove each other crazy.

And she still loved me. I knew she did.

She always had.

That knowledge weighed like a rock in my gut. Because I knew she would do anything for me. For us.

When I was done at the gym, I paced through the hotel with my hood thrown up. It was the dead of night, and while it was Friday night in Vegas, the hotel corridors were pretty quiet.

I walked a long time, but there was nowhere for me to go to get away from this problem, and the problem was, Elle wanted more from me than I could give. She thought I was holding something back from her. Holding myself back.

Maybe I was.

I just didn't know.

But I wasn't looking to mess around with anyone else. I was just being me. That had never been enough for her, though. She just kept pushing and pulling, and it was bleeding me dry.

She wanted me to love her, unconditionally. I knew that. And it was a fair thing to want.

I just couldn't get there.

And I was tired of feeling shitty about it. Feeling guilty.

I just wanted to let it go.

I wandered toward the lobby. It was lined with a bunch of giant columns, interspersed with massive plants. I was coming through the columns lining the walkway that led into it, and that's when I saw them.

Zane, Maggie and Flynn, standing in the lobby.

They were with Maggie's dad, Dizzy. Dizzy had his arm around some girl and Zane had his arm around Maggie. Maggie looked drunk, and something made me stop short.

As they parted ways, I heard the chick with Dizzy say, "Farewell!" in a sing-song voice. She and Dizzy seemed to be heading for the bar. It was closed, but since he owned the place, probably not a problem. "Sleep tight, Mr. and Mrs. Traynor!" the girl shout-whispered across the lobby. Then Dizzy grabbed her hand and tugged her out of sight.

*Mrs. Traynor?*

I stared at Zane and Maggie, and it all came together in an instant. Las Vegas. The bouquet in Maggie's hand.

The fucking rings.

I could see them, glinting in the lights off the bank of elevators. Zane wore a lot of rings, so I couldn't be sure. But Maggie was definitely wearing a wedding band on her ring finger.

I saw it when she put her hand on his cheek.

What the *fuck*?

I watched them get in the elevator, leaning way too close together. Flynn stepped in silently behind them, and the doors closed.

They never saw me.

I wandered around a while longer. Then I went back to my room, poured myself a couple of fingers of bourbon and tried to absorb what I'd seen.

Totally impossible, and defying every law of the universe I'd ever heard of, but I was pretty fucking sure that Zane and Maggie had just gotten married.

*Damn.*

How long had this been going on? Were they fucking?

Of course they were fucking.

Were they in love?

Probably. That's usually what a wedding implied.

Weirdly, I could see it with Zane. Surprised he would ever marry anyone, and yet, I could see him falling for Maggie. He'd always had a thing for her. I just didn't know how serious it was, apparently.

Zane never seemed to take anything that serious. Wasn't really his style. But somehow... yeah, I could see him taking Maggie seriously.

Maggie, though? What the fuck was she doing marrying Zane?

Shit. I sat back on the bed and had to wonder... Should I be concerned? Should I say something to Zane? To Brody? Maggie had looked pretty drunk, weaving into the elevator in her high heels. Zane had been helping her along. I'd rarely seen her that drunk.

*Fucking hell.* I rubbed my hand through my hair and told myself it wasn't my problem. Not my business at all. So long as Zane didn't screw up what we had with Maggie. She was part of the team. Part of our family. He'd be in big fucking trouble if he fucked Maggie over.

There were a lot of people, me included, who'd have a problem with that.

I just hoped, for the band's sake, that he knew that.

*Motherfucker.*

I shook my head. But there was nothing to be done, not until they mentioned it. Maybe Zane would make an announcement at the show, on stage. Declare his love for Maggie in front of the world.

I grinned at the thought. It was actually kind of sweet.

Kinda shocking, but I was happy for them. So long as they were happy.

Anyway, I had problems of my own.

I went out on the balcony a while, looking out over the glittering city, and pondered it. Because Elle was family too, and I really didn't want to be the motherfucker who pissed everyone off.

*Zane marries Maggie and I break up with Elle?*

*Who's the asshole now?*

Shit. How would everyone react?

Would they be pissed at me?

We'd been in this band, together, for a decade. Elle, Zane, Dylan and I. And no one was gonna be happy about what I was about to do.

Least of all Elle.

But I had to do it.

I'd wait until after tomorrow's show, though. Tonight's show. It was after five in the morning; the tour would be over tonight.

The morning after the show, Elle and I were going to her place in L.A.. I was hoping to meet up with my sister when she got into town. Just planning to lay low. Write some music. Spend time with friends. Take a little break before the new album launch.

Now all I wanted to do was go home.

Have some time alone.

I was so *fucking* tired.

I collapsed into bed near dawn, feeling like I could finally sleep because the decision had been made, as difficult as it was.

As painful as this thing was gonna be.

It just had to be done.

When we got back to L.A., I'd sit Elle down. I'd ask Brody to set up a flight. Get me back to Vancouver by the end of the day. But before I left, I'd have to look her in the eye. I'd have to tell her.

We couldn't drag this out anymore.

I just couldn't do it another day.

When I woke, it was late morning and Jude had left a text. I'd missed our morning run.

There was a text from Elle, too. She wanted to talk. She said she was sorry.

As I stared at the words, a text came in from Dylan. He was hungry. As usual. He wanted to meet up for lunch.

I put the phone down. I felt groggy and over-tired. I'd slept five hours; it had been a heavy, dark, dreamless sleep, but as I gradually blinked my way to life, everything became so fucking clear.

I threw the curtains open. It was a blazing, gorgeous day. I looked down over the Strip. It was gonna be a killer fucking show tonight. I could feel it.

This band, the music, were my heart and my soul. And I loved my bandmates. I loved Elle.

But the hard truth was, I wasn't in love with her. Not like she was in love with me.

And not like she deserved.

I knew it with certainty as I showered and got dressed.

Zane had texted by then. The band was heading to a restaurant. I'd meet up with them for lunch. I'd be damned sure no one suspected anything was off. I'd be civil with Elle. She wouldn't push it.

She always knew I needed time to come back to center after a fight anyway. That was the advantage of a relationship with someone who knew you so well; they understood all your little flaws and weirdnesses.

Didn't mean they had to like them.

I texted Jude to meet me in the lobby and threw up my hood as I headed out the door. Yeah, tonight's show would be epic. I would never let what was happening with Elle and I overflow onto the band. I knew she wouldn't, either.

We would stay together, play together, always.

Just not the way Elle wanted.

There just wasn't enough chemistry between the two of us, in that way, to maintain that kind of bond, to get us past our differences through the highs and the lows of life, much less the life of a band on the road.

I needed something more.

Something else.

I didn't know what it was yet.

I just knew that when I found it... I would know it was the real thing.

# A Dirty Wedding Night

*For every reader who wanted more...*

## AUTHOR'S NOTE

In *Dirty Like Brody*, we get to attend Jesse and Katie's rock star wedding—from the point of view of Brody (Dirty's longtime manager) and Jessa (Jesse's sister and former Dirty songwriter).

*A Dirty Wedding Night* is a four-story collection about what happens between Jesse and Katie on their wedding night... and three other couples who secretly hook up that night!

The four stories in *A Dirty Wedding Night* are somewhat interwoven, and are meant to be read in order.

With love from the beautiful west coast of Canada
(the home of Dirty!),
Jaine

# A DIRTY VOW

# AUTHOR'S NOTE

Jesse and Katie's love story begins in *Dirty Like Me*, and in that book, they get their happily-ever-after ending... yet it's not really an ending. It's just the beginning of their lives together.

In *Dirty Like Brody*, we get to attend Jesse and Katie's rock star wedding at a remote luxury resort called Cathedral Cove, on the Canadian Pacific Coast.

In that book, Jesse and Katie's wedding night—*after* the wedding reception—ends with Jesse's band, Dirty, having drinks and a musical jam with a few close friends around an outdoor fire pit. We get to experience the jam, which stretches into the wee hours, from band manager Brody's point of view.

As the jam finally winds down and some of the remaining party-goers opt to take an impromptu skinny dip in the frigid waters of the cove, Jesse and Katie have vanished. Obviously, the newlyweds have headed off to their luxurious cabin for wedding night sex, right?

In this story, we get a glimpse of the relationship politics around the fire pit from Jesse's point of view. Then... we get to find out what happens when Jesse and Katie finally get to celebrate their wedding night—alone.

Or maybe not so alone...?

Though there's plenty of sex in Jesse and Katie's book, *Dirty Like Me*, there are actually no sex scenes from Jesse's point of view. In *A Dirty Vow*, we get that, and more.

So, for all of you who've asked for MORE of Jesse and Katie, even after they got their happily ever after (and thank you for that!)... this one's for you, with love.

Jaine

# CHAPTER ONE

## Jesse

THE FIRE BATHED Katie's face in lapping, golden light. She was sitting right beside me and she was so fucking beautiful, with her creamy skin and her sweet features and her dark hair... she laughed at something Zane said, and my stomach twirled.

Butterflies. The girl actually gave me butterflies.

As she raised her champagne glass to her lips, gazing into the fire, I glimpsed the platinum wedding band I'd slipped onto her finger earlier this evening; it glinted in the dark, reflecting the flames, and it gave me a total rush. That shiny band now marked Katie Bloom as married. As *mine*.

And that shit was making me hard.

Her cheeks and the tip of her nose were rosy; it was cold out, but that flush might've been from the booze. She was definitely a little drunk, but it was a cute drunk. She'd been pacing herself throughout the night. I'd made sure of that. Because sometimes when Katie got too drunk, she couldn't come, and that wouldn't fucking do.

Not on our wedding night.

Not when I was desperate to watch her come; to *feel* her come.

Several times.

She caught me perving on her and smiled. Her big blue-green

eyes widened in the firelight—and that sweetly surprised look went straight to my cock. Just like it always did.

Didn't exactly help matters that she hadn't let me fuck her in two long, aching days.

*Save it for our wedding night,* she'd said, fending off my wandering hands as we arrived here at the resort, on the morning of the wedding rehearsal. *It will be better if we wait.*

Which sounded like a nice idea at the time. Romantic. Hot.

But that was yesterday. Before she proceeded to dance with me, flirt with me, make out with me at her stagette party—in a super-thin bikini top and minuscule cut-offs—then make me sleep in a separate bed.

Today, she danced with me again, flirted with me some more, married me in a jaw-dropping-gorgeous dress, and at the reception, let me peel off her garter with my tongue. Without ever *once* giving my aching dick so much as a pity stroke.

If I'd known by "wedding night" she actually meant almost dawn the next morning, I would've screwed her senseless every step of the way.

Because fuck waiting.

I held her gaze, sipping my beer, my tongue playing idly with the neck of the bottle, thinking about all the shit I was gonna do to her the second I got her alone... until her smile melted into something else, her teeth catching on her plump bottom lip.

Then my gaze slid deliberately south... to the hint of cleavage and that alluring dip between her breasts, bared by her half-unzipped, down-filled jacket... to her sexy, curvy legs, crossed, in her tight jeans.... to her furry boots. They were new, and I hadn't fucked her in them yet.

I was gonna have to remedy that. Soon.

"Jesus Christ. Quit eye-fucking your bride and go do it already."

I glanced at Zane, my lead singer and one of my groomsmen. I had to kind of blink him into focus, I was so cross-eyed with lust.

He was sitting on Katie's other side, a dirty, cocky smirk on his face. It was the one he usually used on women he was planning to fuck. Since he was using it on *me* right now, it was meant to piss me off—since his arm was around my wife.

"You know, you're married now," he went on, his fingertips grazing Katie's shoulder. "It's not a sin anymore." The touch was so light she probably didn't even feel it through her puffy jacket. But it wasn't meant for her. It was meant for me, because this was how Zane entertained himself when my woman was around. "Unless you're waiting on some pointers...?"

"Zane, don't tease," Katie scolded him, but she was still smiling too. She liked my friends; I liked that. She even put up with Zane's flirting, which was both cool and annoying.

"Yeah, man. The fuck are you waiting for?" Dylan chimed in. My drummer was now grinning at me across the fire.

Not good.

Zane and Dylan ganging up on me was never good. Unlike Zane, Dylan rarely busted my balls when it came to Katie... which clearly meant that us newlyweds were wearing out our welcome at the fire.

Which was totally fucking fine with me.

I'd felt a little obligated to hang out with our wedding guests, even though the reception was long over, and I knew Katie did, too. After all, they'd come all the way up here, hours north of the city, by floatplane, just to attend our wedding—at a remote resort in the wilderness that didn't even have Wi-Fi—despite the fact that many of them were rock stars, or people who worked with rock stars, and therefore had other shit to do. I figured the least we could do was keep them fed, liquored, and entertained.

Still; if I didn't get to bury my dick in my new wife soon, I was gonna explode. Maybe literally. I'd been hard all fucking day.

Well, not *all* day. But every time Katie kissed me, or brushed up against me, or looked at me like she was doing right now...

Rock hard.

I adjusted a little in my jeans, thinking about the welcoming warmth of Katie's pussy, slippery wet and swollen... all hot for me and so sweet and tight—

*Jesus.*

I took a cooling swig of my beer.

*Time to fucking go.*

Only one slight problem. That being, I didn't love leaving my little sister to the wolves.

There were only a few people left by the fire, and my sister was one of them. After the reception had wound down and most of the wedding guests stumbled off to bed, my band, Dirty, and some of our closest friends had come out to the fire pit on one of the low cliffs over the cove to jam. We'd been drinking and playing songs, which had been incredible. With my sister, Jessa, here, it was like old times. The way it used to be when we were all together and she was still with the band. The *best* times.

But now the music had died and everyone was kind of paired off and chatting. Jessa and her friend Roni were huddled together, whispering in low, conspiratorial voices, glancing over at Dylan and his buddy, Ash. I didn't even wanna know what that was about, though I was pretty sure it was about Roni, not Jessa.

Dylan and Ash were drinking and goofing around, as usual.

Brody, our band manager and another of my groomsmen, was sitting back in silence next to Maggie, our assistant manager, looking tense, just like he had the entire wedding. At least, whenever my sister was around.

And there was Zane, his arm around my wife and that infamous panty-wetting grin on his face.

"Unless, of course, you aren't up to it." Jesus; was he still fucking talking? At me? "Maybe you need a little nap? It's been a long day, and you're getting old. Pushing thirty. And you've been drinking... Maybe you just need someone to fill in for you. You know, get things warmed up—"

"That kind of comment didn't fly when I was dating her," I told him, keeping my tone casual. No way I was letting Zane fuck with me tonight, and just because he was a recovered alcoholic and therefore sober did not mean he got to win some imaginary hard dick contest. I was plenty able to fuck my wife. Didn't matter how late it got or how many beers were passed around; I'd been pacing myself, too. "It's definitely not gonna fly now that I've married her."

Zane just laughed.

*Fucking guy.*

I could not wait 'til he fell in love. I'd have a fucking field day with that shit. The guy was always busting everyone else's balls; he deserved some payback.

Of course, I wouldn't hold my breath waiting on Zane to get serious about a woman. Fucking around was kind of his lifeblood.

Case in point: we'd just finished jamming on an acoustic cover of "Brown Eyed Girl"—Zane's idea. He'd sung it specifically to sere-nade my brown-eyed sister, probably in part because he was happy she was here—we all were; it'd been fucking years since she'd been home to see us all—but also in part to piss off Brody. Because nothing ramped up Zane's meddling urges like a guy who obviously had it bad for a girl—yet failed to make a play for her.

"Hate to say it, but he's right," Brody told me, low enough Zane wouldn't hear as he settled into a seat next to me; I was watching the cocky bastard whisper in Katie's ear, making her laugh. "Just go back to your cabin and I'll take care of things here. It's past three o'clock. At this rate, your wedding night'll be over before you consummate it."

That may have been so, but I didn't like being told when, how or where to fuck my own woman. It wasn't Brody's fault, though; he was just born bossy. Usually, I didn't mind.

"How about you?" I cocked an eyebrow at him. "Amanda?"

He sucked on his beer, looking gloomy. "Later."

I doubted that.

Brody had brought his latest "girlfriend" to the wedding, but that didn't mean much. It never did. They were always perfectly nice and perfectly pretty, with perfectly nice names like Amanda or Jennifer or Michelle—and he was always bored with them before they even got started. The odds of him actually sleeping with this one tonight seemed slim, what with the way he'd been acting around my sister all day... avoiding the shit out of her, then staring at her from afar like some lovelorn stalker.

My little sister was gorgeous; I got that. She turned heads everywhere she went, and not just because she was a lingerie model and looked like one. There was something about her that guys had always eaten up, even when she was a dorky little kid; I'd had to witness it all my life. It was this kind of awkward sweetness she had, some kind of dick-throttling magic that made boys follow her home from school and reduced grown men to idiots. Made them all—boys and men alike—want to get in her face, push her buttons; make her squeeze out a smile in their direction so they'd feel better about themselves.

None more than Brody.

I had no idea what shit had really gone down between the two of them, though what I'd once assumed was a more-or-less mutual infatuation had obviously turned south—and now neither one of them seemed able to either completely ignore or tolerate the other.

I looked at my sister across the fire. Jessa caught my eye and swiftly flashed her infamous bratty look—the one that earned her the nickname "bratface" among my friends, years ago, when they were all crushing on her but wouldn't admit it in front of me; it was the face she'd given me as a little girl when I pissed her off. I didn't even know she was still capable of that look, yet she'd been in Brody's vicinity for mere hours, and now there it was.

I didn't love it, but not much I could do. I wasn't exactly a relationship expert.

The fact that I'd managed to get Katie to the altar still kind of stunned me.

I looked at Brody. He pretended not to notice Jessa sulking and leveled me with a gray look. "Quit being a fucking hero and take your woman to bed," he muttered.

"Uh-huh." I stared at him, gauging his reaction to my words. "Guess someone should get laid tonight."

He didn't touch that. Just sipped his beer and pretended he hadn't heard me. But he still wouldn't look at my sister.

"Don't worry about it," he finally said, when he could feel me staring at him.

And I realized I didn't have to. Not really. Brody was one of the good ones. If I'd ever had qualms about the idea of any of my friends hooking up with my sister—and I did—Brody wasn't one of them. Still; if he didn't pull his head out of his ass and quit putting that bratty look on her face, I was gonna have to say something to him about it... sometime.

My wedding night, though, was not that time.

But at least one thing I knew for sure: Brody wasn't gonna let Zane or anyone else fuck with Jessa.

I sighed. "Babe," I said, standing up and extending a hand to Katie. "Let's go."

Katie beamed her sweet smile up at me, like she'd been waiting on those words all night. She took my hand and I yanked her to her feet. She fell against me, her tits squishing against my chest, just like I wanted them to.

I wrapped my arms around her waist and leaned down to give her a kiss. It was soft and slow, and earned us a bunch of whoops and growls from the guys.

So maybe I was showing off. A bit.

Then we did the obligatory round of goodnight hugs and kisses and backslaps. We got congratulated, yet again. Then I picked up my new wife and tossed her over my shoulder, despite her mild protests, and finally, we got the fuck out of there.

"Don't come back 'til she's popped your cherry!" Zane called after us as we disappeared into the dark of the trees.

"Go easy on him, Katie!" Dylan added. "He's new at this!"

And then my friends all laughed, which was understandable. They were, after all, jealous.

I couldn't blame them for that.

# CHAPTER TWO

# Jesse

"I'M GONNA FUCKING die if I can't get between your legs..."

We didn't even make it to our cabin.

I had Katie up against the railing on the wooden boardwalk that wound through the ancient trees. I could hear the waves of the cove crashing on the rocks somewhere below. I had her jeans down around her knees and I was kissing her chest, unzipping her jacket as I worked my way down. Quickly. Then I yanked her sweater up and kissed my way down her stomach.

She gasped and panted in response, clawing at my neck.

"Jesse... what if someone comes?"

"No one's coming."

That was probably true. We were on a section of the boardwalk between the fire pit and the largest cabin, our cabin, and no one had a reason to come this way. Other than maybe my best friend, Jude, my best man and head of Dirty's security, who was roaming around somewhere, ever vigilant. As if some crazy paparazzo was gonna parachute into this remote resort on the Pacific coast, way up Vancouver Island, in the middle of the night.

Well, possibly.

"We're alone," I told her as I got down on my knees and, yanking her white panties down with my fist, snaked my tongue between her legs.

"Oh... Jesse..." Katie whimpered in anticipation. She gripped my hair in fistfuls like reins, like she could hold me back, but fuck that. I was diving right in—

"Oh... *shit*."

*Elle*. I knew that voice, but it didn't quite compute.

My tongue froze a breath away from Katie's clit.

Elle. Dirty's bass player—and my ex-girlfriend.

"Oh—Sorry!"

That was Katie. My wife, scrabbling to cover herself, to no fucking avail, since her skinny jeans were down around her knees, tangled with her underwear.

I stood to shield her, turning around.

Elle was standing there, halfway down the stairs that led up to the wraparound deck of our cabin. It was pretty dark, but it was definitely her. Her platinum blonde hair was impossible to miss.

Maybe she didn't really see anything... but all that creamy-fair skin of Katie's under the moonlight was probably hard to miss too, even in the near-dark. And anyway, Elle wasn't an idiot.

"I was at the lookout," she said, gesturing over her shoulder.

Right... The boardwalk continued on the other side of our cabin, snaking up the cliffs to a lookout over the cove. Kinda forgot about that when I was trying to get my tongue up Katie's pussy.

"Nice up there," Elle added, awkwardly.

"Nice," I agreed. The blood wasn't exactly pumping to my brain.

"I'll... I just have to get past. To my cabin..."

"Go ahead," Katie said, clutching onto me and peeking around my shoulder. "Um... hope you had a nice night."

It was dark, but I saw Elle's gaze shift from my face to Katie's. "Yeah," she said after a moment. Then she came down the stairs and walked on by. She disappeared into the dark, without another glance in our direction.

Katie smacked my arm. "'Nice'? That's all you have to say?"

I turned back to her. "'Hope you had a nice night'?"

"Well, I do hope that."

"Katie. Any fucking way you slice it, our wedding was not nice for her."

"I know!"

"Babe." I took hold of her bare waist and softened my voice. "Don't worry about it." But I could see it already. For Katie, the moment had been ruined.

"Maybe we just... shouldn't..."

"Shouldn't? Fuck, no. Oh, fuck no." I gripped her neck and held her close, lowering my forehead to hers. "You are not putting the brakes on on our wedding night. For one thing, I'm pretty sure it's illegal."

"What?"

"We have to consummate it or the marriage isn't valid, right?"

She shrugged me off, pulling away. "I don't know. Is that even true?"

"Who cares? Let's go fuck." I caught her arm and dragged her with me toward the stairs, but she resisted.

"Jesse... don't be cold like that."

"I'm not cold, believe me. I'm burning up here."

When she dug her heels in, I turned and picked her up. I threw her over my shoulder again, pants still down.

"Jesse! Put me down."

I didn't put her down. I walked her toward the stairs, feeling my way along the handrail in the near-dark.

She slapped at my butt. "Are we seriously fighting on our wedding night?"

I set her down on the stairs and crawled over her, looking deep in her eyes. "You gonna feel guilty every time you see her because we're happy?"

"Aren't you?" Her big blue-greens blinked up at me and I softened, sighing. She sighed, too. "Okay. I'll work on it," she whispered.

"Me too." I kissed her neck.

"You'll work on feeling guilty?"

"I'll work on being more compassionate. It's hard, you know. Most of the time I'm just too damn caught up in how happy I am to give a fuck about anyone else." My hands snaked beneath her bare butt and squeezed, pulling her against me. I ground my hard dick against her for effect.

"That's not even true," she said. "I know you care about people. If you didn't, you would've hauled me off like a caveman the minute we said our vows."

"Almost did."

My lips found hers and I kissed her, softly, hungrily, the urgency building as I felt her tongue dance shyly against mine. She was holding back.

I pulled away.

"Katie, I know you have big feelings. You feel for Elle. That's part of what I love about you. But could you right now put your feelings for me and my dick ahead of those ones? We're kinda hurting over here."

I took her hand and rubbed it on my package for emphasis. Felt so fucking good... and kinda like torture. My jeans felt so tight, and they were loose fit. I couldn't remember the last time I went two days without coming.

Since before I met Katie, for sure.

"You're hurting?" she asked, giving me puppy eyes. Half-teasing, half-sympathetic.

"Fuck, yeah. I wanna make out with my wife."

She smiled. "Okay," she said softly. "Let's make out."

I had Katie laid out on her back on the stairs leading up to our cabin, moaning, my face between her legs and my tongue up her pussy, when I heard it.

"Jesus, get a room."

Katie jumped; actually, she totally fucking screamed.

I turned to find a big, dark-haired figure—my best friend—

looming on the boardwalk, grinning down at us, a fucking smug, shit-eating grin.

I rolled over and sat up, shielding Katie again. She curled into an embarrassed ball behind me.

"You know the honeymoon suite is like ten feet in that direction?" Jude drawled, pointing up the stairs.

"Yeah," I said, in my best *go-get-fucked* tone of voice. "We're aware. What brings you by?"

"Just makin' the rounds. Thought I should make myself known when I saw you there. Otherwise, maybe I don't say anything, just slip away, but Katie opens her eyes at the last moment and sees me, thinks I'm creepin' away like some perv."

"Right. Well, appreciate it." I did, actually. "Now fuck off."

Jude laughed. Then he tipped an imaginary hat at my wife. "'Night, darlin'." Then he turned and started away into the dark.

"Goodnight, Jude!" Katie called sweetly. When he was gone, she slapped my shoulder. "Oh my God. Get me out of here!"

I grinned a little. "You embarrassed, babe?"

"Yes! Take me inside before every fucking member of your posse sees you going down on me!"

"Posse? Didn't know I had a posse..."

"You know. Your rock star posse."

"I think it's called an entourage."

"Whatever. They don't need to see your face between my legs. Let's go."

She was trying to get up the stairs with her pants down and simultaneously pull them up. I rushed her instead, picking her up. I carried her over the threshold, into our huge, luxury cabin, newly-wed-style.

Then I laid her out on the dining table.

She looked like an offering to some primitive love god, sprawled there all tussled and sexy on that big slab of wood, her pants around her knees. There was a giant, three-tiered deer antler chandelier glittering above her, dappling her with light.

"What?" she asked, a little breathless.

"Just want to remember this moment," I said, admiring her.

"So remember it later as the moment you got laid." She reached to paw at me, catching a belt loop and yanking me closer. "Don't make me wait anymore."

"Me? You're the one who inflicted this bullshit waiting torture on us both."

"Whatever," she said, climbing her way up my shirt and stripping off my jacket. "So punish me."

Before she could kiss me, I grabbed her hips and flipped her over, pulling her over the edge of the table. I stood her in front of me and bent her over, shoving her chest down to the table. I yanked her jeans down as far as they would go, bunching them up against her boots. Then I knelt down and finished what I'd started, eating her upside-down. Just Katie's pussy and my face...

No more interruptions.

*Fuck.*

That sweet, slightly musky, heady taste of her... Katie's sex. I was totally fucking addicted to it. I ate her out with a passion, with a vengeance, with a fucking fury. I worked her clit with my tongue, sucked on her, until I shoved her right over the edge.

"Say it," I told her as she came, still eating her out. "Tell me you love me."

"Ah... Jesse... I totally love you..."

"Fuck, yeah," I mumbled, fucking her with my tongue as she shivered and shook.

When there was nothing left of her but a gasping puddle on the table, I stood up and turned her toward me, pulling her into my arms as she collapsed against me. Then I kissed her, good and hard.

"Come on." I scooped her up and threw her over my shoulder one last time, making her squeal.

"Aren't we gonna fuck?" she complained, sounding dazed and confused as I carried her up the stairs to the loft—the master bedroom.

"Not yet," I said.

"Oh, God... that was so unsatisfying."

I laughed as I threw her down on the king size bed.

I kicked off my boots and tore off my socks. I unbuckled my belt and unzipped my jeans, peeling them down, letting my cock free, heavy and thick with need. Letting her look at it. Her eyes darkened and she swiped her lip with her little pink tongue.

"Don't worry. I've got something to satisfy you..."

I stripped off my jeans, and Katie took off her jacket and sweater. I barely had my shirt over my head before I was on her, naked. Working myself between her legs. Her jeans and boots stayed on. She still had a tank top on, but I yanked that shit up. I shoved her bra up with it, letting her tits bounce loose.

"Ow!" she said. "Underwire..."

"Deal with it."

Then I was all over her, my face buried in her tits, my hand between her legs, my finger on her clit.

She smacked my ass, but groaned as I caressed her. Smooth and fast... just to make sure she was still with me. Her pussy was slippery-wet—from her arousal, her orgasm, from my spit. I sucked a nipple into my mouth and spread her thighs wide. Then I drove into her, my cock like a heatseeking missile, pre-programmed to hit home. I didn't have to think. I just had to fuck. Had to fuck *her*, in those furry boots that were digging into my ass.

Just smother myself in Katie.

It wasn't romantic.

It was frantic.

It was hungry and it was messy and it was fast. I bit her lip. She pinched my balls with her fingernails as we grappled and groped.

It sort of hurt.

She ended up half on top, hogtied around me by her jeans, then on the bottom again. I fucked her harder than I'd ever tried to fuck her. Once, I whispered, "This okay?" before she nodded and I kept at her. But I never really stopped.

*Yes*, she whispered, once.

Twice.

*Yesss...*

She made sounds I'd never heard her make. Sawed-off syllables supposed to be words, rasps and half-realized gasps, torn apart with need. Her voice shredded in the half-dark.

"Jesse, don't stop," she begged as I pounded her, when she knew I was close. She knew all the signs. She could hear it in my breath. Feel it in my cock, like a steel post, rigid inside her. Swollen... my balls pulled up tight. An itchy trigger just aching for release as I thrust into her. But I had control. I could hold back.

I didn't want to.

I was totally fucking sex-drunk.

I was Katie-drunk.

And I wanted to drown myself in it.

"Not gonna stop," I managed to say. "Until I blow. You gonna beat me there...?"

My question hung between us like a taunt. Like a tease.

She was already close. Her body was tightening around me, bearing down, coiling tight... sucking me in... "You're amazing," she whispered, her eyelids fluttering as I kissed her, and then she sighed. I thrust up into her. I ground my pelvis against her.

Her breath caught.

Then she came.

I rode her, hard, tumbling into it with her, both of us falling apart.

Her fingernails were pressed a half inch into my flesh.

Her furry boot was up my ass.

And I laughed a little.

Because that's what you did when you were drunk with ecstasy and the woman of your dreams had you in her arms, wrapped up in her damp thighs... lost inside her body. When she drank you in.

I collapsed there in her arms, heaving, just trying to catch my breath, and laughed.

"What's funny?" she panted after a while.

"Nothing's funny," I said with a sigh. "That's why I'm laughing."

# CHAPTER THREE

# Katie

I STARED at my husband's muscular ass as he bent over, digging around for something in the pocket of his jeans, which he'd discarded on the floor by the bed.

*Husband.*

Wow... that had an amazing ring to it.

Jesse Mayes was my husband.

My husband was Jesse Mayes... brown-eyed, badass rock star... and the most beautiful man I'd ever met, inside and out.

Just... *wow.*

He caught me staring at his ass and grinned, all cocky and sexy.

Then he yanked off my remaining clothes and flopped onto the bed next to me.

We both rolled onto our stomachs, lying naked and side-by-side, so close together his warmth radiated into me. The hairs on his thigh tickled me. Itched a little, actually, since I was all sweaty. But I was deliciously spent, my pulse still thrumming, and I couldn't be bothered to shift away.

So I sighed and relaxed, my face smushed into my pillow. It smelled of fresh northern air and cedar luxury cabin and Jesse.

He was propped up on his elbows, and I watched as he unfolded a little piece of note paper.

"What's that?"

"A little wedding night gift." His molten-dark eyes met mine. "I wrote some vows for you."

I smiled like a fool in love, unable to help myself. "We already did that part. Remember? All that 'I will always love you and honor you' stuff?"

"Yeah, but this is the really important stuff. Private vows. Too important to share in front of all those fucking voyeurs."

I giggled. "Such as?"

"Such as..." His brown eyes burned into me, all earnest passion. "I will always put you first. No matter what's going on with the band or anything else, if you need me, I'm here."

I leaned up and kissed him. "I know that, Jesse."

I did.

Jesse had been with Dirty since they were little more than kids. Ten years. And he'd known some of the band and crew even longer than that. They were his friends *and* his family.

But I was now his wife, and I knew what that meant to him.

"I needed to say it anyway," he murmured against my lips.

"I understand. And I'm okay with sharing you," I told him. "With Jessa. I mean... I know you're all she's got."

I knew that Jesse's sister, while so beautiful and successful and seemingly together on the outside, was alone. It was aching off her, that loneliness. I'd never been so sure of it as when she showed up at our wedding, looking so happy for us—and so totally unsure of where she fit in.

"If she needs you," I said, "I would never begrudge her that."

I meant it. I had an entire family to turn to if I needed support; Jessa didn't. She had Jesse, and she'd had him long before I came along. I'd promised myself when I agreed to marry him that I would never get in the way of that relationship. How could I? It was a bond that had been forged when Jessa was born and Jesse was only four; when he'd named her, after himself.

"Jesus, I love you," he said. Then he kissed me again. It was slow and hot, and I opened for him, taking him deep.

When he pulled away, his pupils were dilated. He licked his lip and groaned a little. I grinned.

Then he turned back to his little paper.

"Now quit distracting me. I have more vows to get through."

I brushed a little curl of his dark hair back from his face as he spoke, then trailed my fingertips over his shoulder and down his back, scraping him lightly with my nails, making him shiver. I had no intention of quitting; distracting Jesse was one of my favorite pastimes.

"I will always make sure you have a place to do your art. Or whatever it is you want to do."

"That's really sweet," I said. And it was. Especially when he'd already given me an amazing art studio where I could paint, and also let me set up a second, smaller studio in the sunroom of his house. *Our* house.

"I will always listen to your problems," he said, "and hold back your hair when you barf, and be patient with your moods." He glanced at me sidelong. "Even when you're on the rag and you get weepy."

"Amazing," I said, with somewhat-mock adoration. "So gallant, babe."

"Thank you. I try."

"So that means you'll eat ice cream with me and listen to me bitch about my cramps? And not judge me when I cry at cute puppy food commercials?"

I saw the gears turning in his head as he thought his way out of that one.

"I will always call someone in to do the stuff I don't wanna do, so it gets done," he said carefully.

I tried to peek at his paper, but he held it out of reach. "That's not even on there!"

"So? I mean it, babe. You've got PMS, I'll call Devi over in a heartbeat."

"Okay. That's fair." My best friend would be far more empathetic in such circumstances anyway.

"I promise to make you come almost every day—"

"Almost!?" I tickled that sensitive little notch at the base of his spine, making him buck a little. Goosebumps rippled across his flesh.

His eyes darkened as he gazed down at me. "Can't have you getting too used to that shit and taking it for granted. You'll get lazy."

"That's so flattering, sweetie," I said brightly.

"Besides..." He leaned in and kissed my temple, his lips lingering. "We both know you usually come more than once when we have sex. So in the long run, you're at a surplus."

"I like the math on that."

He kissed his way down my cheek toward my mouth. "I promise to keep you stocked with a lifetime supply of thongs... those lacy ones made of expensive dental floss..."

"Ugh." He slipped his tongue in my mouth, and for a long moment I got lost in his kiss. When he pulled away and grinned, leaving me a little breathless, I accused, "That vow's for you, though, not for me. Those things are gross. They ride up my butt."

"Yeah, but you've got a killer butt." He scanned his paper, maybe looking for something to make up for that one. "I promise to hire a personal trainer for you if you start to get fat?"

I pinched his butt cheek. Hard. "Lame! And grounds for divorce." He grinned a wicked grin, making me wonder if that one was even on the paper. "Unless it's my idea. Otherwise, I'll get as fat as I damned well want to."

He lowered his eyelids and gave me the same blatant eye-fucking he'd given me the first time we met... and countless times since. "I promise to do you, even if you get fat."

"Well, thank you. I guess."

"That one wasn't even written down. I improvised."

I squeezed his ass and gave him an overly-sweet smile. "And I promise to do *you*, even if you get fat *and* bald."

"Aww. Don't make me cry." He looked a little misty-eyed, and as usual, I couldn't even tell if he was faking or not. The man was a born performer. "I promise to clean up Max's shit even though I don't want to."

I smiled at that; a genuine smile. "Well, me and Max thank you." One thing Jesse knew: a direct route to my heart was definitely through my dog. I traced little circles, idly, on his butt. "You know," I mused, "if he didn't approve of you, I probably wouldn't have married you..."

He cocked a skeptical eyebrow. "I promise to try anything you want in bed at least once."

"Anything...?" My fingers crept toward his butt crack.

"Anything." He swatted my hand away. "Don't abuse it. Oh, this one's key. I promise if you get bored of me," he said importantly, "I'll make myself more interesting."

I laughed, hard. "That's... shit. I don't even know what to say to that. Thanks?"

"You're welcome."

My hand had found its way back to his ass, and my fingertip crept between his butt cheeks again. I just loved making him squirm...

"I promise I won't fart in bed unless I really, really have to," he said, straight-faced.

I snatched my hand back. "Ew."

"What? That's how much I respect you." He leaned in and gave me a quick, soft kiss I didn't return.

"Okay... So you'll still respect me if I have to?"

"Not allowed."

"What?"

"Deal-breaker."

I laughed, pushing him away. "What am I supposed to do? What if I'm sick or something?"

"Crawl into the bathroom and shut the door behind you."

"You are such a pig."

He kissed me again, his lips lingering suggestively on mine as his tongue teased the sensitive inner flesh of my upper lip. "You married me."

I fought the urge to open my mouth to his kiss... and suck his tongue right out of his head, the way he liked. "Are you done yet?"

"You don't like your special vows?" He nipped at my bottom lip with his teeth and tingles spread through my stomach, into my core. I was getting wet. Warming... softening to him.

Wanting him again.

"I love them." I rearranged myself on my side so I could wrap my arms around his neck and nuzzle his ear. "But there are a lot of them, sweetie. And I wanna be able to remember them all—in case you break any." I licked his earlobe and sucked it into my mouth, scraping lightly with my teeth because I knew it drove him crazy.

"Alright." He cleared his throat, rustling his little paper. "There's... uh... a bunch more sex stuff on here." His eyes locked on mine. "Or should I just skip it, and show you instead?"

I bit my lip.

He crumpled the paper and tossed it aside.

He kissed me, deep, his body melding to mine until we were pressed together, my nipples hard and tingling against his chest, his cock hard and pulsing against my stomach, my pussy throbbing with reawakening desire...

He kissed his way down my neck and I closed my eyes. Some of the urgency, the edge that had accompanied that first post-wedding fuck had been released, and now I could just bask in his touch... slow, exploratory, deliciously patient... yet hungry, as Jesse's touch always was.

He continued downward, closing his warm lips around one nipple, biting lightly, then flicking with his tongue. I gasped and arched into him, wanting more, but he released the nipple, just teasing, leaving feather-soft kisses on my skin.

"I promise not to leave you," he murmured against my other breast as he kissed the soft swell of flesh. His eyes lifted to mine beneath his dark, heavy lashes. "Unless you want me to."

"Never gonna happen," I breathed as he teased that nipple into his mouth and sucked. "Unless... you eventually get tired of me... and want to replace me with a newer model."

"Never gonna happen. And by the way, even if you wanted me to leave you," he added, kissing his way down my belly, "I'd probably stick around a while. You know, until it got really pathetic—"

"Uh-uh." I caught his face in my hands and tipped his head up. "I love you, Jesse Mayes," I whispered, holding his gaze.

His brown eyes softened as he looked up at me. "I love you, too..." he murmured against my skin, "... Mrs. Mayes."

I frowned. "I told you not to call me that. That's an old lady name."

"You are my old lady," he mumbled, kissing his way in a circle around my navel.

I stirred, growing restless and needy at his slow, teasing touch. "Jesse... don't start that crap..."

He dipped into my navel with his tongue, making me squirm. He knew that spot was hardwired to my clit; plus, it tickled. Then he fluttered his tongue down my naked belly, straight toward my—

"Oh, shit!" I sat up, shoving him off, and wriggled out from beneath him.

"The hell are you going?" He grabbed at me but I squirmed away, rolling out of bed.

"I have a wedding night gift for you, too!" I dashed into the en suite bathroom; I couldn't believe I'd almost forgotten.

"If you have to fart," he called after me, "just say so."

I rolled my eyes at him and slammed the door.

# CHAPTER FOUR

## Jesse

I LAY SPRAWLED across the bed, naked, waiting for Katie. Looking at myself in the mirrored ceiling.

What was it about looking at yourself, naked and spread out on a bed, from above, that was so... erotic? Not in a cocky way, but there was just something... Something about that view.

Yourself, submissive.

Maybe it was getting a glimpse of yourself the way your lover must see you. When she had you laid out, at her mercy...

My dick twitched at that thought, and I frowned at it, lying there half-soft.

"Babe, hurry up," I called out, as I gave my cock a few pumps. "I'm gonna fall asleep."

That wasn't true. I was too wired to sleep. I just wanted her to bring her sweet ass back out here so I could fuck her again before she got too distracted and lost the mood. One go with Katie was never enough. Especially after waiting for two fucking days.

Seconds later, the bathroom door swung open.

"Hey," she said, a smile in her slightly-husky voice, "quit touching yourself."

I rolled over to face her. "Why? You want all this hard di— *Whoa.*"

Katie stood in the doorway to the bathroom, decked out in white lingerie; some kind of slutty-bride thing.

The fucking works.

A skimpy, see-through lace corset-thing with barely any material but just enough engineering to shove her boobs up—way up; garter straps clipped to sheer stockings; skimpy-as-fuck panties. And who could miss the *fuck-me-right-now* shoes... strappy high-heeled contraptions built for sex, because they sure as shit weren't built for comfort. They stacked about five extra inches onto her petite frame.

"Holy Christ."

I knelt up on the bed to stare at her.

Katie always wore sexy shit, but nothing like this. Tiny cotton panties, sexy as all hell on her, and a smooth pushup bra or no bra at all were more her thing. I'd never seen her in this much see-through, lacy stuff. And all that white against her creamy skin, her naturally rosy cheeks, her dark hair... totally fucking stunning.

I got up and met her halfway to the bed and gripped her waist, drawing her toward me. Then I kissed her. Her mouth, so hot and silky-wet, reminding me of her slippery-wet pussy, undid me. My cock was already aching for her again, stiff. I needed to fuck her, now. I could think of nothing else but whatever was the best position to screw her in all this sexy stuff.

Throw her down on her stomach?

On her back?

Bend her over...

My hands skimmed up her sides and I felt her shudder beneath the lace. She was breathing shallow and fast as we kissed; her breasts heaved against me. The corset was fucking tight. A see-through vice.

She put her hands on my chest, her fingernails digging in as our kiss deepened. Then her hands slid down, down... and stroked my cock. One slow, teasing pump...

Then they were gone.

I felt her fumbling around below. She broke our kiss and looked down. She was struggling to unhook the straps clipped to her stockings.

"I want these stupid panties off!" she panted, frustrated. "Like right now. How are you supposed to fuck in all this stuff? It's like a chastity belt..."

I watched her struggle and swear, amused.

She managed to get one of the hooks loose from a stocking, ripping it in the process. "Oh, shit. I didn't know it would be so hard to take off..." She bit her lip a little, gazing up at me. "I wanted to do a little strippy thing for you."

I raised an eyebrow, liking that idea. "A strippy thing?"

"Yeah. Like a show. You know, peel it off, all sexy and suave." Her cheeks turned pink. "I've never done this before. I guess clothing that's actually easy to strip is kinda key."

"Uh-huh. That's why dudes wear those velcro pants." I kissed her again. "You're adorable, babe. But don't strip it off. I wanna fuck you in it."

"All of it?"

"Most of it." I slid my hand down between her legs, stroking her through the lace panties. "And for future reference... there's lingerie you wear to strip for a guy, and there's lingerie you wear to get fucked in. This is lingerie you get fucked in."

"Oh. Okay. It *was* kinda murder putting it on..."

"Katie," I told her, kissing her again and walking her toward the bed, "you don't have to wear this shit for me." Not that I didn't appreciate it... "You know that, right?"

"I just wanted it to be special," she murmured as she kissed my throat, her arms going around my neck. "I mean, we've already done everything there is to do..."

"Everything?"

She blushed as she gazed up at me. "Maybe not everything. Close."

"Okay." I stood her by the bed and got down on my knees. "I'm gonna show you what we can do..."

Then I kissed my way down her body. The parts covered in lace. The naked parts. I licked her along the edge of her panties. I nudged my nose against her clit, teasing her, then slipped a finger inside the lace and teased the crotch aside.

I swiped the tip of my tongue over her softness, making her shudder. I could eat Katie out all fucking night. Since she'd just married me, she was just gonna have to put up with my oral fixation.

Not like she didn't know about it from our very first date.

"You know I'm not gonna complain about *that*..." she said breathily, as she played with my hair. "But what's new? We have to do something new on our wedding night, Jesse."

Despite her half-hearted protests, I could feel the tension and the heat building between her legs. I groaned as I breathed her in. She was muskier now, her scent even headier, the way it always was after my cock had been between her legs.

"We did new stuff..."

She shifted, restless against me as I delved my tongue deeper. I sucked on her delicate lips and she gasped like she didn't mean to, rocking her hips into me.

"Like what?" she whispered.

"Like..." I teased her with my tongue between my words. "I ate you out on a staircase... That was new... I made you come under a deer antler chandelier... That was definitely new."

"That's just new decor," she breathed. "It doesn't count."

I looked up at her. Her face was flushed and her eyes were slightly hooded. They sparkled with lust as she gazed down at me.

I stood up, my chest brushing hers. I gripped her by the back of her neck and drew her close, brushing my lips against hers. "You're my wife. That's new. And it's more than enough to get me off."

It was true.

Katie Bloom—Katie *Mayes*—turned on... Was there any-fucking-thing sexier?

Nope.

My *wife*.

*Damn*...

I kissed her, deep, filling her mouth with my tongue like I owned it... sinking into the taste of her. I breathed her in... that familiar, sweet scent of vanilla, of cherries and cream.

That smell that always got me so fucking hard.

*Katie Fucking Mayes.*

I slid a hand down, into her panties. "Let me just help you with these." Then I thrust a finger right through the thin lace, ripping out the crotch.

"Oh," she gasped, glancing down. "*That's* how you do it without taking the rest off."

"Uh-huh..."

I lay her back on the bed, crawling right over her, and wrapped her silky, stocking-covered legs around me. Her stiletto heel bit into my ass and I growled.

"Oh! I can take off the shoes, if—"

"Fuck, no. Keep the shoes. Fucking love you in shoes..." I got busy kissing her neck, licking and sucking, lost in the smell of her. "Katie... whatever it is you do to smell so fucking good... don't ever change it."

"Jesse," she breathed, her hands roaming down my back. "Your butt looks... Wow. You have a nice ass." She squeezed my ass with both hands as she checked me out in the mirrored ceiling.

I kissed my way down, between her tits, which were still shoved up by her corset, against the forces of gravity. "Quit objectifying me..." I mumbled, my voice muffled by her cleavage. Katie had epic tits. Not huge, but full and perky on her petite, curvy frame. I once told her they were fat, as a compliment, but she didn't like that. Go figure.

She arched into my kisses. "Since when do you have a problem with being objectified?"

"Since it's distracting you from this." I swiped my tongue inside the cup of the corset and sucked her nipple out. I teased the hard pink tip with my teeth until she was gasping, squirming with need beneath me. Katie never could stay still when I touched her tits; I could *almost* make her come just by sucking on them.

I was pretty bent on getting her there one day.

"I just thought of one more vow," I told her. "And you're gonna like this one."

"Yeah?" she breathed.

"Yeah." I sucked her nipple into my mouth and teased the hell out of it with my tongue, then released it with a pop.

"*Ungghh...*" she groaned, which was Katie's incoherent way of saying, *Do that again.*

I switched to her other nipple, popping it out of the corset and teasing with flicks of my tongue, interspersed with soft, feathery kisses.

"I promise," I told her as she panted beneath me, "to keep finding new ways to fuck you. So it always feels like our wedding night."

She giggled, but it came out as a breathy sigh. "You're a true romantic, Jesse."

"You doubt my creativity, babe?"

"Well, no. I just—"

Then I spread her thighs, and sank my dick into her.

I watched her bite her lip to keep from crying out as I started stroking, in and out, but not too deep...

"I mean, really..." she said, her voice all soft and raspy. "How many different ways are there to fuck a girl?"

I tossed her a loaded look before returning my attention to her tits.

"If it's you, babe?" I let my stubbly chin rasp against her breast—she wouldn't let me go clean-shaven, even for our wedding. Said she loved me with a few days' growth. I was pretty sure she just loved the feel of it between her legs. "Fuck... endless possibilities..."

"That may be the dirtiest thing you've ever said to me, Jesse," she said sweetly.

"Just feels that way because my dick is inside you..."

"Mmm." She squirmed, raising her hips to take me deeper, urging me to it, and as I sank home, she gasped, "You're right." She rocked her hips against me. "But you say a lot of things dirtier than other people do..."

"It's a gift. Stop squirming."

Then I held her down, pinning her hips as I drove into her, making her take me the way I wanted her to—at my pace. I controlled the rhythm, the depth. And as I watched her take my cock, her tits heaved, spilling from her corset. She probably couldn't get a full breath in that thing.

"Is it wrong that you're kinda suffocating and it's turning me on?"

"No," she breathed. "It's kinky."

"Good. Then I'm gonna say... that's new. I've never seen you actually struggle to breathe while I fucked you before."

"I always struggle to breathe while you fuck me."

"Flattery," I mumbled, leaning down to run my tongue between her breasts again... and over the swollen curves, the hard tips.

"Truth," she whispered, arching her back for more. "Did you mean it, though? The 'always' part?"

"Hmm?"

"You're always gonna think of new ways to fuck me?"

"Mmm," I mumbled against her sweet skin as the blood left my head. She was covered in the lightest sheen of sweat. I could feel her pussy burning up, swelling, tightening around me, choking me as she fought to move her hips against mine. "When I'm not too tired," I said, fucking her slow... lapping her nipples with my tongue. "And, you know, if I'm not mad at you."

"What...? What... um... happens if you're mad at me?"

I paused, meeting her sex-hazed eyes, then fucked her harder for effect. Once. Then again. Hard... but slow.

"Then I'll just spank your ass and fuck the hell out of you, and you'll like what you get."

She bit her full bottom lip, twisting it in her teeth as I sped up my thrusts. "Oh, God. Shit. It's really unfair how much that just turned me on..."

I smiled and kissed her.

Then an idea occurred to me, and I stilled. Katie undulated beneath me like a snake—a snake bound in lace, breathless, sucking hungrily at my tongue.

"Baby..." she begged.

"Just a sec."

Then I tore myself from her grip and pulled my dick out, getting up. She started to sit up, awkwardly, impeded by her corset. "But—!"

"Hold that thought." I sprang out of bed and dashed into the bathroom. I didn't want to leave her hanging any more than she wanted to be left.

"Jesse?" she called after me, all breathy and confused. "Jesse Mayes...? Did you seriously just *stop* in the middle of fucking me?"

I found Katie's makeup bag on the bathroom counter and started rooting through it. Where the fuck were they? I knew she kept them in here...

I heard her sigh and flop back on the bed.

"Does trying new things involve some sort of cross-dressing thing?" she called. "Because if so, you really don't need mascara. Women pay a lot of money to get eyelashes like yours. Jesse...?"

"Uh-huh..."

"In other words, you'd make a gorgeous chick. If one could look past all the muscles and the body hair. But I can't say I want to."

"How do you know until you try?"

As I strode back into the bedroom, she propped herself up on her elbows and threw me a skeptical pout.

"We've never done *this* before," I said, holding up a packet of her birth control pills.

"You know that's birth control, right?" she said, teasing. "It's not, like, ecstasy. Or Viagra."

"Viagra? Woman, please." I popped the little pills into my hand one by one until the case was empty. Then I raised an eyebrow at Katie in silent question.

She looked at the pile of pills in the palm of my hand. Then she met my eyes.

She bit her lip a little... and nodded.

My heart thumped in my chest. Because *damn*.

I'd been planning to bring it up. Soon. Maybe not tonight.

But why the fuck not?

I slipped off one of her sexy shoes and crushed the pills to dust on the bedside table with the heel.

"Great," she said. "Now the staff will think we snorted lines off there or something."

"I'm a rock star, babe," I said. "They already think that."

"You know doing that isn't gonna make me insta-pregnant, right?"

"Don't be a smart-ass. It's symbolic."

I tossed her shoe aside and dove on top of her. My cock, still half-mast, pressed to the inside of her thigh as I kissed her, deep. She kissed me back, but I could feel her resistance. She'd tensed up. Way up.

"You're... um... really committed to this... doing-something-new thing," she said, giggling a little between kisses.

"Yup."

"You know," she mused, as I sucked my way down her throat, "a baby would be crazy new."

"Uh-huh."

"Might impede your ability to stick to your other vows, though..."

I looked at her, mildly offended. "Like what?"

"Making me come every day?"

I slipped my hand between her legs and slid my middle finger, slowly, up into her. So fucking smooth, hot and wet... I watched her eyes haze over and her mouth drop open as she relaxed a little.

"*Almost* every day," I said, my voice rough with lust. "And besides..." I told her, teasing one of her blushing nipples with my tongue, "I don't see why a baby would impede that."

She laughed softly, digging her hands into my hair as I kissed my way between her breasts. "That's because you've never had one, sweetie."

"Neither have you."

"Yet I know enough to know that orgasms may slide down the priority list for a while once I do."

"Then I'll just have to pull up that other vow... Call someone in to deal with shit for me."

Katie's hands stilled in my hair. "To give me orgasms?"

"The baby, wise-ass." I bit her nipple lightly and fucked her slowly with my finger. "I'll hire a nanny to help with the baby, so we still have time for orgasms."

"It's not just time, you know," she panted, as I worked her back up. "It's... energy. We'd be tired as shit, getting up all night with a newborn. And my boobs would be all full of milk... and sore... and you wouldn't get to oral-fetish on me all the time..."

I looked at her, lifting myself off her a bit as I withdrew my finger from her pussy. "Do I need to scrape those pills back together?"

She smiled, pulling me back on top of her. "No. Just saying. But we'll just have to deal with it like we do everything else." She wrapped her thighs around my hips. "Together," she said softly.

"Yeah," I agreed. "Together." I rubbed the length of my hard cock against her softness, all slick and warm and ready for me.

"Please, Jesse..." she purred as she kissed me.

"God, I love it when you beg..."

"Just give it to me, for fuck's sake," she said. "I didn't marry you so you could fuck off into the bathroom halfway to my next orgasm..."

I grinned. "You've always had a way with dirty words yourself, you know that?"

"Only with you," she murmured, shifting beneath me. She was

trying like hell to line up the head of my cock with her wet pussy. Too bad for her, I outweighed her by a hundred bucks.

I grabbed her hands and pressed them into the bed, above her head. Then I used my full weight to pin her down, my cock lined up —but just out of reach.

Then I looked her in the eye and asked her, "Yeah?"

She smiled, even as she panted with anticipation. "It's not magic, and it's not instant, you know. I'm not gonna get pregnant tonight. It's not even the right time in my cycle—"

"Don't be a party pooper, Katie. I told you, it's symbolic."

At that, her eyes softened. She reached up to kiss me with her sweet, full lips... and that light touch, Katie's warm breath against my face, feeling her need building as she panted in her corset, so hungry I could almost taste it... it sent lighting bolts of lust ripping down my spine.

"Then, yeah," she whispered.

I rammed into her then, deep. She cried out as she took me, biting my lip. Then I thrust my tongue in her mouth, filling her at both ends as I drove into her, again and again.

She murmured against my lips when I eased up to let her breathe, begging me for more.

"Harder, Jesse... I wanna be yours..."

"You are mine."

Her tits swelled against me as my weight and the corset smothered her, and when she came, it was with a desperate, ragged, feral cry like nothing I'd ever pulled from her before.

*God... Jesse...*

*Yes...*

It pushed me right over the edge.

I shoved into her, coming like a rocket, just blanking out and giving in as I collapsed against her... Riding the waves of ecstasy as our bodies melded, shuddering together.

My fingers laced through hers, I squeezed her hands.

And afterward, when I could move again, just enough to see her face... to shift myself to the side so I didn't crush her... I looked into her big blue-green eyes. And she looked back at me.

"I promise," I told her in a rough whisper, "I'll be a good dad, Katie. Actually, I'm pretty sure... I'll be an exceptional dad."

She smiled, and happy tears sparked in her eyes. "I know you will, Jesse."

And in that moment, I saw it, so clear: a little girl or a boy with those eyes, and Katie's sweet smile...

And I fell in love with her all over again.

# A DIRTY SECRET

## AUTHOR'S NOTE

If you've read *Dirty Like Us*—and you really, really should before reading this story, *A Dirty Secret*—then you know the big secret about Dirty's lead singer, Zane Traynor, and Maggie Omura, the band's assistant manager. There are a couple of scenes in *Dirty Like Brody* that address it as well. So if you want every last detail of Zane and Maggie's story so far, you'll need to read the other books first.

*Dirty Like Brody* takes place many months after Zane and Maggie's crazy night in Las Vegas in *Dirty Like Us*, and for all that time, they've both kept their secret.

But what's been going on behind the scenes? Are they fucking or what? More importantly, are they in love? Whatever's going on, why is it all still a secret? And what the hell are they going to do about it?

Well, as the pragmatic Maggie puts it in *Dirty Like Brody*, it's complicated. And to quote her: "If I knew the answers to such questions... I wouldn't be drinking wine straight from the bottle."

The night of Jesse and Katie's wedding in *Dirty Like Brody*, we see

Maggie, in her wet undies, being hauled off into the woods, caveman style, by a naked Zane after their midnight swim.

So what the heck happens next?

I'll give you one guess...

Jaine

# CHAPTER 1

# *Maggie*

I SAT BACK and watched as my good friend, Jessa, did something I never thought she'd do: she walked straight out the dock, stripped down to her underwear, and hopped into the just-slightly-above-freezing waters of Cathedral Cove.

I laughed and applauded wildly.

Seconds later, her head popped above water. "Jesus!" she screamed. "Fuck, that's cold!" And I kept laughing—from my cozy, dry seat by the fire.

It was January and this was Canada; we were way up on the Pacific Coast of Vancouver Island, but with the fire—and several layers of clothing—it was fine. The naked crazies in the water could suit themselves. I was more than happy where I was.

It was the middle of the night and we'd been drinking and singing songs, jamming around the fire pit—just the members of Dirty, the mega-successful rock band I'd co-managed for almost seven years, and a few close friends. It was the night of our lead guitarist's wedding; Jesse Mayes—Jessa's brother—had just married his fiancee, Katie Bloom. The wedding was incredible and the party had gone late, but only a few of us had lasted this long.

Jesse and Katie had disappeared up to their lux newlyweds' cabin a while ago, and while I was privately jealous that they were most definitely fucking like bunnies right now... as a girl who hadn't gotten any in a lot longer than I liked to think about—well, I was trying not to think about it.

Likely, some of us were still up because we were still hoping to hook up, while the rest of us just weren't ready for the party to end, for reasons of our own.

I was looking right at my reason.

Zane Traynor, lead singer of Dirty; the living definition of a rock god. The man with the biggest ego of any man I'd ever met, but the killer voice, gorgeous face and otherworldly body—big, swinging dick and all—to back it up. No surprise, he was one of the crazies in the water. Actually, he'd kinda led the naked charge.

I watched as he threw his arms around Jessa, his slicked-back blond hair gleaming in the moonlight. I couldn't see them clearly in the near-dark, just their heads bobbing on the water, but somehow, I knew Zane was watching me.

"Maggie!" he hollered as he held Jessa close. "Get your ass in the water!" For a split second I let myself wonder if he'd ever fucked her; I wondered that about most women who got near Zane.

At least, the hot ones.

But no, I concluded as I sipped my beer. Zane and Jessa had never fucked, even though she was super-hot. Mainly because she would never do that to me.

Thank Christ, for both her sake and mine.

"Don't let the old man cramp your style, Maggs," Ash put in. The lead singer for the alt rock band Penny Pushers, Ash was also in the water, along with our drummer, Dylan, and Roni, a girlfriend of Jessa's; the lot of them were all amped up on liquid courage. All except Zane, who didn't drink.

Unlike regular mortals, Zane didn't need booze to fuel his crazy.

I glanced over at my boss, Brody, Dirty's longtime manager and close friend, who was sitting beside me, and rolled my eyes. Old man, was it?

When even Dylan started mouthing off at us next, I knew it was dawning on all of them what total morons they were, freezing their asses off while Brody and I lounged by the fire pit.

"Maggie May!" Zane thundered at me, using the full force of his lead singer's pipes and drowning everyone else out. "Get your ass in the water before my dick falls off!"

"Jesus Christ," I grumbled, but finally, I stood up. Because apparently there was a little moron inside me, too. "Doesn't he ever shut up?" I sucked back my beer and set it aside.

Brody didn't bother answering, just smirked and drank his beer.

I walked straight out the dock and did the only thing I knew for sure would shut Zane up. I stripped down to my underwear— quickly—to a bunch of appreciative catcalls, and jumped in the water.

And *fuck me*, it hurt.

Kinda like my body was crashing through ice.

I fought back to the surface as the pressure, at once numbing and so incredibly *burning*, squeezed in. I gasped brokenly for air. Then I screamed—the most bloodcurdling, jagged scream I'd ever heard, and until now, I didn't even know I could make.

My friends howled in the water around me.

I heard Jessa's teeth chattering as she said, "M-maggie, we're g-gonna d-d-die!"

Yep. Totally fucking felt that way.

Ash was already climbing out, the big man-baby, and streaking buck-naked up the dock toward the trees; with all the tattoos and piercings, you'd think the guy could handle a little pain. Roni was next, then Dylan, also bare-assed. They dashed up the boardwalk and into the old-growth forest, leaving their clothes behind.

I was already doing a frantic doggy-paddle back to the dock myself—I'd never been the world's strongest swimmer—when Jessa, all long-limbed and lithe, glided past me and hauled herself up the ladder, water sheeting off her swimsuit model's body.

I was close behind, shaking so hard I thought my clawed hands might slip off the metal rail, but I made it up to the dock, wheezing.

I'd never felt anything so shockingly fucking cold. And now the pain was *really* sinking in.

Yeah; fuck clothes.

I ran up the dock as fast as I dared, afraid of slipping in the near-dark, hugging myself so hard I thought my ribs might crack. Brody was on the dock with Jessa, wrapping her in a blanket, but I didn't see another blanket anywhere and I didn't stop.

I heard Zane behind me, roaring as he barreled up the dock. "Holy mother of fuck! My balls are up behind my eyeballs..." He grabbed me by the waist, swung me around, and threw me over his shoulder—like a fucking Neanderthal.

A scream tore from my lungs, partly out of relief. I should've told him to put me the fuck down, like now, but Jesus *fucking* Christ.

Never so cold in my life.

Instead, as he hauled me up the boardwalk, I slapped his bare ass as hard as I could. My hand on his wet cheek made a satisfying smacking sound; I would've hoped it hurt, but he was probably in too much pain to notice. "Do not drop me," I said. "I'm freezing!" Then the deeper dark of the woods swallowed us... and I got hit with a sickening rush of vertigo. "Oh my God, stop!"

Zane slowed down, but he didn't stop. "S'okay, Maggs," he said, teeth chattering. Was that a sign of hypothermia? "I'll take you to your cabin."

"Just s-slow down," I ordered, my own teeth starting to chatter, and he slowed a little more. "It's so dark... I can't see shit except your ass and your f-feet flickering out of the dark. It's gross."

"Just shut up and tell me where your cabin is."

"I have a r-room," I said, "in one of the b-big ones, east of the lodge."

"Where the fuck is east?"

I tried to lift my head, looking around, but I couldn't see. Everything was passing in disorienting flashes. Snatches of trees and the boardwalk handrail catching the moonlight; pools of light pouring from the windows of cabins or the little yellow lights above the doors. Darkness; moonlight; yellow light; darkness.

And music. It had to be almost four in the morning, but we weren't the only ones still up.

"Jude," Zane remarked as we passed the cabin where the Stone Temple Pilots' "Sex Type Thing" was throbbing into the night. "Guy never sleeps. Probably got all the single chicks herded up in there..."

I didn't touch that. But clearly "all the single chicks" didn't include me.

It really should have.

Except that I wasn't single, not technically—and Zane was the only one who knew it.

He was right about Jude, though. Of all the guys in and around the band these days, it was Jude, our head of security, who was most likely to trash a hotel room—or in this case, a luxury resort cabin. It didn't bother me, much, as long as he forked over a generous sum to cover the damages in the morning, along with a hefty tip.

"Whatever," I said. "Just g-get me to my cabin so I can p-put some pants on before anyone else s-sees me."

Because despite what I'd just done, I really didn't need a bunch of my coworkers seeing me in my wet underwear.

Somehow, I managed to guide Zane to my door, though we got lost in the labyrinth of the trees several times and had to backtrack.

He carried me inside, and I stumbled a bit as he put me down, kinda dizzy from the ride as I found my feet.

I wasn't drunk; I'd made that mistake with Zane once, and ended up with a hangover in the form of his naked body in my bed, a round of electrifying morning sex, and an engagement ring with a rock the size of Gibraltar. But this had been a long day—especially for me, since I'd helped organize the wedding—and I was wobbly with exhaustion and the painful ache of the cold in my bones.

Zane caught me, steadying me with his hands on my hips.

On reflex, my hands clamped onto his arms. We were both shivering as we stood there, frozen, locked together.

And then, predictably, he moved in.

We were alone, he was naked, I was near-naked; it really didn't take much. And he was definitely gonna kiss me.

Couldn't fault a guy for trying, right?

*Wrong.*

I dodged and dashed, extracting myself from his grip, and put space between us.

"You can go now," I said, hugging myself and hopping up and down. I held his gaze, carefully avoiding his cock. Because yes, he was *completely* naked. And I really didn't need to see *that.*

Even if I kinda really wanted to...

"Christ, Maggs, just let me warm up." He rubbed his hands up and down his arms and barreled past me, shivering.

"I'm too cold to fight with you, Zane," I snapped, still hopping around.

"Then don't."

"Don't you *dare* get into that bed all wet!"

I hurried into the bathroom as he headed toward my bed, emerging with a towel and throwing it at him. He got to work drying off, quickly, trying to warm himself as he rubbed the towel on his body. Not that I was watching...

Jesus, though. There were women who'd *pay* for this private show.

Shrinkage or no, the man was stunning. Lean, tall and blond, his sculpted body all tense and shivering from the cold, muscles twitching and flexing as he ran the towel over his long, hard thighs...

*Video: Zane Traynor towels off after midnight skinny dip.*

Instant viral sensation.

"You need to go, before I die," I gritted out between my teeth, still hopping as I turned away.

He ignored me, heading over to the fireplace. I tried not to peek as he bent down, his bare ass in the air as he rooted through the logs on offer, obviously intending to start a fire. Well, shit. I was hardly gonna stop him from that endeavor.

"Bloody *fuck*," I swore instead, giving up.

Then I dashed into the bathroom, slamming the door behind me, and blasted the shower on hot. Shaking, I dove right in, then gradually peeled off my wet panties and bra. I was so cold, it took several minutes before the warmth actually soaked in and my body started to register it. But when it did...

*Pure ecstasy.*

"You better quit making those sexy moaning noises..." Zane opened the glass shower door and stepped right into the spray, crowding into me. "If you expect me to keep my hands to myself."

I turned my back on him, fast. "Zane! Get the fuck out!"

"What? I'm warming up. You want *me* to die?"

I rolled my eyes and tried to ignore him. Which was totally fucking impossible. I edged forward as far as I could go and still get some of the spray, but he was right behind me. The bulk of his body —his pecs, his thighs, his fucking dick—brushing against me.

At least he wasn't hard. Yet.

"Quit hogging the water, Maggs," he said, pushing in closer behind me, and I stiffened as more of his body came into contact with mine... just lightly, nudging against me. He shivered violently— setting off a wave of goosebumps on my newly-warmed skin. Then he groaned, long and low, as the heat soaked into him. "*Jesus... fuck*, that's good..."

Fucking *hell.*

It was like listening to a live porno, custom-calibrated to my exact fantasies, only inches behind me.

Worse, his words reminded me of the things he'd said to me, and the *way* he'd said them to me, that first night we'd spent together.

Our wedding night.

"Get warm and get out, Zane," I said, my tone cool and detached. It was a well-practiced tone, used over many years in Zane Traynor's presence. The one that said, *I'm not buying your shit,* when I totally was.

Because this was the only defense I knew: denial.

My body was anything *but* cool as the hot water and Zane's increasing body heat began to smother me. My brain was no help either. My thoughts raced ahead, full-steam, imagining all the things my body could be doing with his, right now. I berated myself, half-heartedly, for failing to lock the bathroom door. But the truth was, I left it unlocked on purpose. Because apparently that little moron inside me just loved tempting fate.

So maybe there was no point in even trying to deny it anymore. It was beyond official: I was a masochist, plain and simple.

When it came to Zane, maybe I'd always been one.

Maybe I'd always *be* one.

He sighed raggedly, a sound of deep contentment. And I couldn't even pretend that I didn't like hearing him happy.

Because again, masochist.

"Babe," he said, his voice relaxed and husky in my ear, his breath and his devilish blond beard tickling my neck, "you think turning your back on me is making you any less of a temptation, you're stupider than I thought."

"What!?" I turned my head to skewer him with my eyes.

He gave me the world's most charming—yet evil—grin. Because he was messing with me. And I was falling for it.

And Zane just *loved* that shit.

"Whatever," I grumbled.

*Damn*, though. What the fuck was wrong with me?

I went to one wedding with Zane—well, besides our own—and I turned to useless, horny goo inside?

I'd promised myself, like pinkie-swear promised, after the last time I let him stick his giant dick inside me and fuck me into the stratosphere that it was the *last* fucking time. That from that day on, he would be nothing to me but a work associate. A sexless, boring-as-fuck colleague, afflicted with some nasty, putrescent venereal disease.

Yes, I'd totally made up the VD part—to trick myself into believing that Zane Traynor was *way* less appealing than he actually was. I'd even convinced myself—as I came down, sweating and shuddering, from that last Earth-shattering, mind-blowing orgasm—that tricking myself might just work.

Because I was desperate enough to believe it.

I would've believed anything, if I thought it might save me from getting naked with him again.

And now, here I was.

Naked.

With him.

*Again.*

"Take your 'temptation' and go, Zane," I said. "I just wanna be alone."

"No, you don't," he said, his tongue just happening to lick my neck as he spoke, slowly and lazily, almost like it was an accident. Which maybe it was. Hard be it for Zane to keep his dick in his pants or his tongue in his mouth when wet, naked pussy was to be had.

"Yes," I said firmly, "I do."

"Okay, how about this..." He edged in closer. His cock, which was now definitely hard, pressed against my butt. "We get warm *together*, then I go. *If* you still want me to." He said it like he didn't believe for a fucking second that if I let him get me warm, I'd want him to leave.

He was probably right about that.

And I fucking hated it that he was right.

"Just keep that thing away from me," I grumbled, as the familiar tension built, hot in my core, desire for him surging with an urgency that always threw me off-center.

Overwhelming.

Irresistible...

"What thing?" he prompted, not even feigning innocence.

I tossed him a dark glare over my shoulder and his wicked pierced eyebrow arched. Water droplets shimmered on his chiseled, godlike face and his dark eyelashes, spiky and wet, made his already-gorgeous ice-blue eyes even more striking. Totally reminded me of how he looked onstage toward the end of a show—his clothes soaked through, his golden skin dripping with sweat...

So completely unfair that he looked even hotter soaking wet.

I probably looked like a drowned rat. Or a drowned raccoon; I hadn't even taken off my makeup.

"Your dick, asshole. Put it back in your pants."

"Why?" he asked, his dick still pressed against me as he smoothed his hands lazily through his wet hair.

"Because it's fucking dangerous."

"Dangerous?" I turned away but I could still hear the smile in his smug voice. "Just think of it as a loaded gun, babe. Only dangerous if you pull the trigger. And, sweetheart... your hands are on your tits."

I dropped my hands. *Damn*... He made it sound dirty, like I was groping myself, when all I was doing was trying to shield myself from him.

I couldn't exactly help it if my nipples had started throbbing as his dick pressed against me, my body going totally fucking haywire in response to his proximity... like it always did when Zane got me alone.

And I couldn't fucking take it.

Three months. That's how long it'd been since I got off with a man.

Three. Long. Months.

Since the last time I let Zane Traynor, my husband but not really my husband, fuck me to hell and back.

My latest lapse in sanity. Though probably not my last.

Because I had some sort of sickness. An inability to resist him for more than ninety days. A debilitating weakness for his smoking-hot voice, his cocky swagger, his blue eyes and his big dick.

Just to name a few.

Yeah; I glanced back at those blue eyes of his, and I knew it.

If I didn't get out of this shower, right now... I was fucked.

# CHAPTER 2

# *Maggie*

I SIGHED IN FRUSTRATION, and pressed my hands to the shower wall so I wouldn't touch anything else—Zane's or mine. And the worst part? He wasn't even touching me anymore.

He'd edged back a couple of inches so his dick was no longer feeling me up. It was fully erect, though, pointing at me like an accusation when I glanced back. Heavy, swollen, long, and totally unapologetic. There was nothing at all polite about that dick.

He knew it, and he didn't bother covering it up.

*Fuck*, but I wanted him inside me.

"Look..." I said, with some struggle. "You know exactly what you can do with that thing. What you do to women. I'm not gonna sit here on some high horse and pretend I'm immune, but—"

"Women?" he said, feigning confusion. "Like Jessa?"

I frowned. "No, not like Jessa, but—"

"Elle?"

Right. As Dirty's bass player and Zane's longtime bandmate, Elle probably wouldn't fuck Zane in a last-man-on-Earth scenario. They'd been friends too long, business partners too long, irritated the shit out of each other too long. "Well, no. Not Elle. Just—"

"Katie?"

I scowled. Jesse's new wife was so off limits to Zane it wasn't funny. And he knew it, too. Jesse would murder him in his sleep if he ever made any kind of serious play for her. "Not Katie. Don't even fucking say that."

"Hey, I'm just trying to follow, Maggs. You said I do something to women. I'm dangerous. Or my dick is. But I just named three women in like a split second who don't give a shit about my dick."

*Jesus*, the guy was irritating. "Okay, so maybe not *all* women—"

"So just you, then."

"Right. Just me," I said in my most sarcastic tone. "Go ahead and play innocent. Put this all on me. I don't care. Just get your big dick and your six pack and your blue eyes and your devil's smile the hell out of my shower, and go find someone else to harass."

"Harass?" He laughed his cocky laugh. "I'm just showering, babe. Getting warm. You're the one fixating on my dick."

"It's *hard*, Zane."

"It's a biological function," he said, eyelids lowering. He was so totally enjoying the fuck out of this. "I can't always control it."

"*I know*," I said, slowly and with all the ice I could summon in all this steaming heat. "That's kind of the fucking problem."

His smile faded, eyes narrowing. "What is?"

I turned to face him, covering my goods as well as I could with my hands. Not well enough. His gaze fell, molesting every inch of exposed skin.

"You and your dick," I said flatly, doing my best to ignore the throbbing between my legs, the way my breasts felt heavy, my nipples fucking ached, and my breathing was getting all rough and uneven. Because I *did* know exactly what he could do to me, in seconds, if I let him, and I was already wavering on that precipice between control and total abandon—between caring and totally not caring if fucking the shit out of Zane, right here and now, was a good idea. "The both of you are catnip for horny pussy, and you fucking know it."

His eyes lifted to mine. He blinked, once. Then he laughed, his infamous Viking laugh, big, bold and all-conquering, right in my face.

And for just that split second, control won out.

"Yeah, I'm going."

I darted into the narrow space between his large frame and the glass shower door.

I didn't get far.

He grabbed me by my waist and spun me around, pressing my back up against the tile wall. It was easy. He was big, I was small.

Plus, I didn't actually want to go. My control was so quickly abandoned, it was surreal; my head spun as he pinned me there. But I didn't fight.

So maybe I just wanted to protest a little before I gave in?

Shit. Did that make me sick? Kinda *felt* sick.

But maybe not in a bad way...

His fingers dug into my hips and held me tight as he pressed in, and a shudder of nervous anticipation ran through me.

"Horny pussy...?"

He wasn't laughing anymore. His gaze moved slowly down my face, from my eyes to my parted lips, like he was reading me. And I felt totally exposed. He could probably *smell* my arousal. The man was a total bloodhound when it came to sex *and* my discomfort.

And when Zane and I had sex, discomfort was always a part of it —for me.

Worse, I'd come to learn that my discomfort turned him on. As did my increasingly feeble protests.

Maybe to him, this was all just a long, slow, sometimes painful game that he was gradually winning.

But I really couldn't help any of it. The protests. The struggle. The giving in.

I wanted him, like I'd never wanted anyone in my life.

And... I wanted not to want him.

I was breathing too hard, hanging on by a thin thread. I pressed my hands to the wall behind me, spreading my fingers and trying to dig in, like I could somehow leech onto the tile. But my hips stirred in his hands, restless, and I bit my lip, twisting it in my teeth, hard.

"You telling me you're horny, Maggs?" he asked slowly, his

smoky voice dropping dangerous-low. His tongue snaked out to lick his lip.

I swallowed.

"Telling me you're horny's a bad, bad move, Maggie May," he pressed, his mouth so close to mine I could feel his breath on my face. I could almost *taste* him. "If you want me out of this shower..."

"Get over yourself," I managed. But my voice was all breathy and pathetic.

"Why don't you just let me take care of that for you..." he said, casually, like he was offering to scratch an itch. "You know I can take care of it..." His thumbs stroked the indents between my hip bones and my groin, slowly.

And I knew I was getting wet down below, in a way that had nothing to do with the shower. My whole body was thudding, aching, hungry for him.

So fucking ready.

So fucking tired of waiting.

So fucking scared of giving in.

"But I really... I don't..." *Shit.* I was breathing faster, heavier, as the words failed me. And words rarely failed me.

His gaze dropped to my chest, which was heaving.

"Sure, you do," he murmured.

And I did. I so *fucking* did.

He knew it, and the shitty truth was, I'd wanted him to know it.

Every single thing I'd said to him tonight—actually, for the duration of this entire event—had told him *Nuh-uh...* Yet the hunger behind every word, every stolen glance, had told him *Yes.*

Actually, it had told him *Please.*

*Fucking please.*

*Give it to me.*

*I want it.*

*Hard. Fast. Just give it...*

And he knew he could give it, that I'd take it, that I wouldn't actually stop him if he tried. But he hadn't tried; at least, not hard and fast.

Instead, he was taking his time, drawing this out; savoring it.

My discomfort. My resistance. My inner struggle...

*Touch me.*

*Don't touch me.*

*Please fucking touch me.*

"You looked pretty tonight, Maggie," he whispered. Then he smiled a little, the corner of his mouth curling up in that impish, boyish way it did when he was being cute. Not coy cute and not fake cute, not kiss-her-ass-because-I-want-to-do-her cute. Just cute.

And it made me go all stupid and squishy inside.

"Don't," I said. "Don't do that."

Lethal. Zane being sweet to me; it was as dangerous as his hard dick waving at me in a hot shower.

Actually, it was worse.

"Do what?"

"Don't be nice," I said.

"Okay. Have it your way." He moved in, shoving up against me. "I've got more practice being an asshole anyway."

He grabbed my hands and pushed them up above my head, pinning me against the wall. I felt every inch of his long, hard cock pressed against my stomach... so slippery and wet. I felt him throb against me as his desire surged, as he leaned into me with his weight. His balls, full and heavy and firm, pressed against my clit. His nipple piercing dug into my chest.

And it was kind of a relief.

I exhaled, like I'd been holding my breath all fucking night.

Then he said, "But you did look pretty," his blue eyes on mine. "In that little black dress, with your hair all twirled up..."

"Just shut up, Zane."

"Kept imagining what you were wearing underneath it," he went on, his hands digging into my wrists as he moved his hips, grinding his slippery dick against me. "And how you'd look with it all bunched up around your waist... while I bent you over and fucked you 'til you screamed." Then he tipped his face down as if to kiss me.

But he didn't.

Instead, he took his sweet fucking time.

"Fucking love it when you scream..." he murmured.

Then he fit his mouth to mine.

And it fit so fucking good, like he was born to kiss me. Like I was born to be kissed by him.

He did it slowly, too, just to rub it in. To give me all the chance in the world to pull away, to shove him off, to say no, to slap his face.

I did none of those things.

I opened to the slide of his wet lips, all slippery and warm, and I moaned desperately as he slid his tongue inside my mouth, hot and aggressive but slow... lapping against mine in a torturous dance that made my entire body curl up into him.

Then he slid his mouth away just as slowly, making me groan.

"More?" he asked with a half-smile. But this time it was a happy smile, not a cocky smile, his blue eyes dancing.

Joy, not victory.

*Worse.*

"Yes, more," I said, half-desperate, half-angry as I struggled to lean into him. But he held me pinned to the wall as he kissed me again; as I kissed him back.

And I closed my eyes, so I didn't have to see that terrible joy on his face.

He shifted my wrists into just one hand and, keeping them pinned, ran his other hand down, between my legs. I gasped as he touched me, my body responding in that way only he could make it respond, stroking all my sweet spots with just the right pressure... teasing at first, letting me warm up to his touch, and gradually delving deeper... making me want just that little bit more.

"More..." I whispered when he kissed his way down my neck, his finger slipping inside me. I bit his shoulder and groaned as a second finger joined the first.

"*Fuck*... We need a condom," he muttered. "I need to be inside you..."

I sighed, shuddering as his fingers moved inside me. "I have some."

"You have some?"

I opened my eyes to find him looking at me. A grin played at his lips, but I could tell he was trying to keep a damper on it. And it made me hella surly; the grin and the damper.

"Yeah," I said, twisting away from his hand. "So?"

He released my wrists and I crossed my arms over my chest, but he slid his hand back between my legs, unfazed. "Maggie May," he said, stroking me slowly, "were you planning on getting laid at Jesse and Katie's wedding?"

I bristled, trying not to let what he was doing down below affect me, but *shit*. I was not that good an actress. "No. Not planning. Just... being prepared."

"Prepared." He seemed to roll the word around in his mouth, as he rolled his fingertips over my clit. "Because... you knew... once you saw me walk up the aisle in my suit, you'd just have to have me?"

I pushed his hand away and looked away, over his shoulder, when I said, "Because I know I can't trust you."

And that was true.

Simply put, I didn't know if I'd *ever* be able to trust a man who was so like my dad. That absent, self-involved and reckless man who had, unfortunately, shaped me, who'd cast a shadow of neglect over my whole life, yet had never actually been *real* to me. Had never really been there when I needed him.

Zane, on the other hand, had always been there for me.

And yet he was so, *so* like my dad.

Rock star.

Egomaniac.

Womanizer.

My dad was even badass and blond. At least, he was when he was young.

As soon as I became conscious of the resemblance—at our wedding—it had snaked its way into my bones and taken root, ensnarling me with irritating tendrils of resentment. It was a terrible itch I couldn't scratch, couldn't rid myself of, because—unlike my dad—Zane was always here. In my face. In my life. In everything I did. My employer. My friend.

My worst fear.

No, I most definitely could not trust a cocky manwhore who treated bedding women like a convenient pastime. Get up in the morning, scratch your ass, have a coffee, go screw someone.

My dad had lived that way, had never put me before the needs of his own libido and his own inflated self-worth, and I did not want another man like that in my heart.

*Ever.*

But I did, unfortunately, want the rest. The rest of Zane.

A man who was caring, passionate and there for me. A man who would probably *kill* for me.

Sexy. Talented. And yes, a little dangerous.

Just the coolest guy I'd ever met.

That Zane, I knew I wanted.

But you couldn't take one without the rest.

He touched my chin lightly, turning my face back to his. His blue eyes held mine, and there was a challenge in them. "You mean, you can't trust yourself with me."

That was true, too.

And I felt myself shutting down because of it.

"They're in my purse," I told him. "In the zipper on the side. You can go get them and I'll be right there."

"Or I could bring them back in here..."

"Out there," I said. "I wanna dry my hair or I'll get cold."

"I'll keep you warm," he said, sliding his hands down around my ass and squeezing, his fingers biting in deep, sending shivers of lust through every part of me. Then he kissed me again, hot and deep.

I kissed him back, my movements feeling forced, even to me. I could feel myself reeling back in, tucking my emotions back behind my neat and tidy wall—the one Zane had always accused me of putting up between us.

He pulled away, his hooded eyes on mine. Surely, he could feel that wall going up.

He always did.

From his point of view, my wall was probably the root of all our problems.

"I'll meet you out there," he said, giving my ass a final, lingering squeeze. He held my gaze until I nodded.

Then he left, and I took a deep breath.

I turned and pressed my forehead to the tile wall.

I just needed to get some air that wasn't his, some space that he wasn't all pressed up in. A moment to let my body cool down. So I could think straight...

And figure out how to get out of this.

# CHAPTER 3

## Zane

THERE WERE EXACTLY six of them, in a strip. Ribbed, and the size was XL. Which gave me a wicked surge of satisfaction.

Because clearly, the condoms she'd brought were for me.

Unless Maggie was hoping to have some other dude with an XL dick drill her this weekend...

But fuck that.

If she was, I'd just have to fuck that idea right out of her.

When she came out of the bathroom a few minutes later, I was lying on the bed with the fire burning and the lights out. She stood there in the doorway, looking at me. Her dark hair was half-dried, the ends still damp, and it was smoothed down neatly around her face.

Her body from neck to knee was covered in a hideous army-green thermal that fit her like a tent.

I laughed.

Maggie scowled.

"Wearing another man's shirt again, Maggs?"

She crossed her arms at her waist and I could almost make out her curves. "Jealous?"

"Kinda takes me back. You know, to our wedding night, when you almost fucked Coop before you married me..."

"It's Dylan's," she gritted out. "Because *some* men are thoughtful enough to lend me an extra shirt when I'm helping the staff set up, in the cold. You know, while other men sleep in half the day."

Well, that would explain the fit. Dylan was six-and-a-half feet, a maniac drummer built of solid muscle, and Maggie was about five-foot-nothing and weighed as much as a small bird soaking wet. "That was thoughtful. If he was trying to keep you from getting laid."

"I'm not getting laid."

"Let me guess," I said, sliding my arm behind my head like a pillow. "You've changed your mind."

"It's a woman's prerogative."

"Well, it's a man's prerogative to try again."

She didn't budge from the doorway. "You know, your cabin is way nicer than mine. I know, because I did the rooming assignments. Which is also why it's way the hell on the other side of the resort."

"Geography can't keep us apart, babe."

"Actually, it can. Your dick isn't that long."

I laughed again. "You should've just put us in the same room and saved yourself the trouble."

"Why would I do that?"

"Because you know I'm just gonna end up in here."

"And how do you figure that?"

"Because we're married."

She rolled her eyes. "It's the middle of the night. I wanna go to sleep, Zane."

"So go to sleep. There's room." I glanced down at the bed. It was a double, not huge, but big enough... if I wasn't sprawled across three-quarters of it. "If you can't fit, we can snuggle."

She sighed heavily, walked over, and stood by the bed. She hesitated there, looking at me. Totally fucking unsure.

"Zane. I really don't think we should do this."

"Okay." I moved over to let her in and pulled the sheet over myself. "Hands to myself." I was serious, too. If she really didn't want me to touch her, I wasn't gonna be that guy.

But she'd come around.

She stalled, fussing with the blanket on her side and fluffing up her pillow.

Then she got in the bed. She tucked herself in under the covers, lying stiff as a board on her back, and closed her eyes.

"I mean it," she said. "I'm going to sleep."

"Wouldn't dream of disturbing you," I told her. "I won't even touch you. Promise." Then I took hold of the covers and slowly dragged them off of her.

All of them.

She opened her eyes and looked over at me as I tossed the bedding behind me, on the floor.

I held up my hands. "Not touching you."

"For Christ's sake, Zane. Grow up."

"I'm working on it."

My hand snaked over to her and drew the tent of her shirt up her thigh. Not touching her, just the shirt. Underneath, she'd put on what she probably thought were conservative panties. Plain black ones, like little shorts.

Sexy.

I ran a fingertip along the edge of the panties, over the curve of her hip, the fabric a thin barrier between my skin and hers. "I wonder how hot I can get you without even touching you..."

"Touching my panties counts as touching me, Zane."

"C'mon, Maggie. Where's the fun in that?" I shifted closer to her, and my bare dick poked her in the thigh. By accident. "Does touching you with my dick count?"

She gave me a nasty look. "Zane. I told you. This isn't a good idea, okay?"

I ran my finger back over her panties, and down between her legs, stroking her pussy through the soft fabric. She squirmed, but in a lazy, tired way, like she didn't really have the will to fight—at least, not physically.

As usual, Maggie's body was totally at odds with her stubborn mind.

I slid my hand up and peeled the panties down, carefully, hooking my fingers inside... slipping them slowly down over her hips... my skin never once touching hers.

"Zane..."

"Trust me, Maggie."

She frowned. "Right."

"Okay... so don't trust me. But give me a chance. Two minutes." I slid the panties down her legs and off her feet. "I don't manage to change your mind in two minutes, without touching you, you put your panties and your tent-shirt back on, and I leave you alone."

Then I slipped the shirt up and pulled it off, over her head, with Maggie's semi-cooperation. She flopped naked and half-resistant beneath me, tense and soft, firelit and beautiful.

I put my hands on the bed, on either side of her waist, and leaned down, closer... shifting over her... so close she could feel my breath on her skin. I hovered over one nipple, then the other, as if I might kiss her there, but I didn't.

She arched a little and squirmed beneath me, her breathing getting faster.

Then I moved down... until I was in position to lick her pussy. I didn't. I breathed on her instead, slow and hot, and just let her want it.

When I looked up at her face, she was biting her lip.

"This is ridiculous..." she said. Her tone was bored and tight with contempt, but her words were breathless with need.

And it *was* ridiculous. My speeding heart was ridiculous.

The incessant throbbing of my cock was worse.

I got up and went to the bouquet on the table by the door. I'd already read the card while she dried her hair. It was from Jesse and Katie, thanking her for helping out with the wedding. It was huge, several dozen flowers. I had no idea what they were, but I plucked out one of the big fluffy pink ones with all the fluttery, silky petals. Then I took it back to the bed.

Maggie watched me every step of the way, her eyes wide. She looked so young and sweet and perfect lying there in the firelight, I paused by the bed to look at her. All the hard, accusing lines of her face were softened, her eyes and mouth, usually tight when she looked at me, more relaxed than usual.

I knelt over her on the bed, not touching her at all, and lowered the head of the flower between her legs.

She twisted her full bottom lip in her teeth.

Just before the petals whispered over her clit, I pulled it away. She groaned a little, fisting the sheet beneath her, and my cock jerked.

I just hoped my two minutes were gonna do it.

I drifted the flower over her left breast, spinning it slowly so the petals fluttered over her tight nipple. Then I did the same to the other nipple. Maggie's mouth fell open and her body arched into the light touch—just before I took it away.

Then I fluttered the flower down, down... toward her pussy. I paused, meeting her eyes. She was watching me, and she was losing it. I could see it... her wall was slipping, the way it always did before she gave in to me, before she threw herself right over.

I lowered the flower and fluttered the silky petals over her clit.

Maggie gasped and spread her legs. Her thigh bumped against mine.

"That didn't fucking count," I taunted her, spinning the flower and fluttering it down between her legs. "You touched *me*."

"Zane," she whispered, breathless, "your two minutes are up, okay?" She bucked beneath me as I lifted the flower away.

"You want me to stop?"

"No," she said, pretty much panting. "I don't want you to stop."

A smile spread across my face. I couldn't help it.

I fluttered the flower down again, teasing her... drifting it over her pussy, her inner thighs, as she writhed.

"*Zane...*"

Then I got serious. I got down between her legs and swiped my tongue gently over her sweet flesh, lapping at her clit. Then I drifted the flower over her again. Her hands delved into my hair, trying to hold me down, to make me give her more. She bucked and moaned. But I took my time, holding back... even as it drove me insane. My tongue, the flower... Maggie's cries.

Then my tongue deep inside her... Then the flower whispering over her clit.

Then my mouth on her clit and her cries growing louder.

Her clit tightened under my tongue, her pussy swelling, juicy and wet as my fingertip caressed her opening.

"Do you want me to stop?" I whispered, kissing her pussy, then caressing her with the flower.

"*Do not* fucking stop..."

I got up, and as quickly as I could I slipped a condom on. Then I went back at her... my mouth, the flower... my fingers... Maggie's cries.

When I couldn't take anymore, I moved up her body.

"I know you want me, Maggie," I said, as I kissed her neck. My hand delved between her legs and she bucked against me; her arms flew around my neck and she held me tight. "Why do you fight it so much?" I licked my way up her throat. "You know we're good together..."

"We aren't together," she protested.

"No?" I pushed her thighs farther apart and lowered my hips. I shoved my cock inside her, sliding in deep. She was so wet... she took me, hot and fast. "Sure feels like it to me..."

She moaned, but said nothing.

"I'm gonna fuck you all night if that's what it takes... to get through to you..."

"The night's almost over," she said, breathless, gasping as I rammed into her.

"Then I'll fuck you all morning. You're gonna stay in this room, with me, and you're gonna take my cock, every which way I wanna give it to you... until you see the fucking light..."

Her breathing got rougher as I fucked her, harder, my thrusts gradually picking up speed until she was crying out. I almost lost myself in those ragged, breathy screams of hers...

Music was coming through a wall. Loud. Arctic Monkeys... I wondered vaguely if someone had put it on to drown out Maggie's cries.

At the moment, she didn't seem to give one fuck.

Neither did I.

She was getting close and all I cared about, right now, was getting her there. So I slowed down. Because I knew, with Maggie, that would only get her there faster...

I put my hand on her face, gripping her chin, and made her look at me. "You sure you can handle this?" I challenged her as I looked into her gray eyes... as I pressed her thighs apart with my hips and gave it to her slow. I was almost out of breath as I held myself back, so fucking wrapped up in her I was forgetting to breathe.

"Can you?" she said, peering up at me, her voice just a whisper in the dark.

And the answer was no. I could not handle this.

There wasn't a thing about this I could handle.

The thing about me was... I'd do it anyway.

# CHAPTER 4

# Zane

I FUCKED Maggie right to the edge, and when I felt her tensing up, her nails digging into my ass, her breathing getting all jagged and desperate, I whispered, "What if I can't handle it?"

"What?" Maggie blinked at me, dazed and panting. "What? *Why?*"

"Maggie." I ran the tip of my nose along hers, brushed my mouth against her full lips. "Because I love—"

"NO! No, no." She twisted her head away and tried to push me off. "We need to stop."

So I stopped. I stopped thrusting and just tried to catch my breath.

"I mean *stop*," she said, shoving at me. "*Pull out.*"

I stared at her. "Are you fucking serious?"

She glared at me.

"Maggie."

"*Zane.*"

"*Christ*, Maggs." I pulled out. "Please tell me you're fucking kidding me," I said, panting, "and you're about to shove me on my back and hop on for a ride. 'Cause I know you love going for a ride."

She scowled at me, also panting, but it was true. Maggie loved being on top. Taking it on her back was not her usual style.

Neither was telling me to pull out seconds before she had a screaming, scorching orgasm.

"If not," I added, "that was about the shittiest thing a chick has ever done to me. And I once had a girl stab me."

"With a hair brush," she said, totally unsympathetic.

"It was sharp."

"I know. Who drove you to the hospital?" She shoved at me again and I sighed, shifting off her as she scrabbled to detach herself from me in every way.

"What's the deal, Maggie?" I fell back on the bed beside her. "You want me. You don't want me. Now you decide you don't want me right in the middle of wanting me? What the fuck."

"What I *want*," she said, still panting, "is to fuck. And you just messed up a totally decent fuck by opening your mouth."

"Yeah? Well, I'm so totally fucking sorry for sharing my feelings with you. I won't do it again."

"Yes, you will. You're *dying* to share your feelings. But news flash, Zane: I am not gonna magically start trusting you just because you tell me you love me."

"Why the hell not?"

"Because you *don't* love me."

We locked eyes like a couple of bulls locking horns, and I wondered if I should take the condom off. My cock was still throbbing, and she just lay there glaring at me, gleaming with sweat in the firelight, her breathing gradually calming, her dark hair fanned out on the pillow.

I propped myself up on an elbow and looked down at her. "And how the hell would you know that?"

"Because," she said, stone-faced, "you don't know the meaning of the word." But her gray eyes looked soft and vulnerable. She was pissed at me, but she was afraid. That much was obvious.

Maggie and her motherfucking wall.

My gaze trailed down her throat, where her heartbeat thrummed in a frantic rhythm. My hand drifted over, my fingertip tracing a line along her delicate collarbone.

"Is this, by any chance, about Dallas?"

She bristled, her body twitching in protest and her face screwing up like there was a rotten taste in her mouth. But she didn't push me away. "No. It's not about..." She stopped, unable to say the name, apparently, and swallowed. She wouldn't look me in the eye, either. "Women named after cities have enough problems. Who am I to criticize?"

"Uh-huh." My fingertip continued down toward her breast and around the slight swell.

"Or flowers," she went on. "You know, like your little friend Daisy. And what was that other one, in Toronto? Rosie? Or was it Petunia? Who can keep track?" Her tone was cold, but her gray eyes sparked as she finally looked at me.

*Fuck me.* Maggie, jealous?

Total fucking turn on.

Shouldn't be. I knew that. But my dick never lied to me.

Maggie was hot *as fuck* when she was jealous.

Slowly, I encircled her rosy nipple with my fingertip, and it tightened, rock-hard and begging to be licked. "I never cheated on you, Maggie."

She scoffed.

I held her gray eyes. "You said so yourself. You're not my wife."

"I'm not."

"Well, you can't have it both ways, babe. You're not my wife, then I'm not your husband." My finger slowly circled her nipple again. "And if that's so, doesn't that make my dick a free agent?"

"Your dick can do whatever the fuck it wants," she grumbled.

"Good. Because my dick wants you." I leaned in to flick my tongue over her nipple. As I licked her, she stirred and kind of growled in her throat.

So I took her hand and put it on my dick. I stroked myself with it, slowly, up and down. Then she squeezed her hand around me, vicious-tight. Probably meant to hurt me.

Didn't work.

I looked up at her. "Do you want this or not?" I asked her, my voice low and raspy.

She licked her lip, slowly. "I want your dick." Her gray eyes held mine, cool and controlled. Those eyes that said, *I don't want you.*

But I didn't believe them.

I never did.

So I grabbed her by her hips and flipped her over. She gave up a surprised squeal but she didn't fight.

She didn't tell me to stop.

I straddled her, my knees on either side of her hips, and lifted her ass toward me.

"You want this?" I ran my dick down between her legs, slick against her pussy.

"Yeah," she breathed.

So I rammed myself in. Her hands clawed at the sheet, squeezing it in fistfuls as I sank into her. I leaned down against her, the curve of her back to my front, and ground my hips against her ass. She gasped as she took me, as I forced my way deeper.

I grabbed her neck and held her tight.

"This is all you want?" I asked as she moaned with each thrust.

"*Yes...*"

I fucked her, harder, reaching around to rub her clit with my fingers. Maggie pressed her face into the pillow, shuddering and moaning.

"Then beg for it," I told her.

"*Ung...* Zane," she groaned.

I slammed into her again, and again, until I knew her eyes had to be rolling back in her head.

"Beg me for it."

"No..."

"Fuck, Maggie."

I pulled out. I flipped her over and got between her thighs. Her legs went around me, her arms around my back as I lowered myself on top of her. Then I fucked her the way I wanted to fuck her most; the way that was always hardest to fuck her—face-to-face.

Because, as usual, she evaded that shit.

She buried her face in my neck. She refused to look at me, no matter how I gave it to her. Hard or fast or slow, didn't matter.

She wouldn't look me in the eye.

So I pulled out most of the way, until just the head of my cock was in her, teasing her. Her body protested, her thighs clamping around me, her nails digging into my back.

"Beg me, Maggie," I said.

"*Please*," she spat out.

I gave it to her, hard but not fast, and lifted up a bit so I could see her. So she couldn't hide.

Her eyes were closed. But she was tensing up, her breaths cutting off, shallow and fast.

I leaned down and kissed her neck, licked my way up to her ear. She shivered beneath me.

"If this is all you want..." I whispered as I thrust into her, "then you don't want me to stop... not when you're right on the edge. I can feel it, babe. Know how you feel right before you go off."

She opened her eyes then, just a little, looking at me under her lashes. Those gray eyes... *Christ*, those eyes.

She wasn't the only one riding the edge.

"Say my name, Maggie," I ordered, my voice harsh and ragged.

"Don't—" she said, her breath catching.

"Say it. I wanna hear it when you come."

I pounded into her, slow and deep, snapping my hips up, dragging my pelvis against hers, so she couldn't resist it if she tried. Even if she just lay there and went limp, she'd go off. Because I knew just where to hit her, and how hard, and at what angle, and how many fucking times.

Maybe we hadn't fucked more than a handful of times, but I paid attention.

As she started to come, she said, "Zane... *please*..." and a flare of victory went off in my gut, spreading heat through my insides, even as I shuddered with the force of holding myself back... just waiting for her to go first.

"Yeah, babe..." I held her down as she cried out. As her pussy clenched, choking my cock. As the pleasure rolled through her body... rolled through mine. "I'm gonna fucking blow. Tell me you want it."

Her hazy gray eyes looked up at me. "I want it."

"Fuck... *yeah*... Maggie... I'm gonna give it to you..."

Then I totally fucking lost myself as I blew into her. All I could see was her face. Those gray eyes... just Maggie, gazing up at me, as I gave her everything I had.

Three fucking months of it...

All for her.

"Let's tell everyone."

"Tell everyone what?" Maggie looked at me as I collapsed on the bed beside her.

I'd gone to get rid of the condom and discovered my legs were pretty wobbly. Not only had fucking Maggie left me weak in the knees, as usual, but the time of night was really setting in. I was fucking tired.

"You know what," I said, closing my eyes. The idea had hit me in the bathroom, and it was fucking brilliant if you asked me. "We can do it today, at brunch. Our closest friends are here, and there's no media, no internet. Perfect place to tell everyone and ask them to keep it private while we figure our shit out."

"You're kidding me, right?"

I opened my eyes and looked over at her. The firelight flickered on her pretty face, her full lips puckered in an angry pout. She had the sheet all wrapped around her like a cocoon, her head and arms the only bare skin in sight.

"I've never been kidding about this," I told her.

She shook her head, slowly, making an aggravated noise in her throat. The kind that usually got me rock-hard, but all the fighting and fucking at four a.m. had really worn me out.

"Or not," I mumbled, closing my eyes again. So much for that brilliant fucking idea. "It was just a suggestion, Maggs."

"Uh-huh. And let me guess. You came up with it about two seconds ago."

"So?"

"So, you think announcing to everyone, at Jesse and Katie's wedding, that we secretly got married in Vegas almost a year ago, is appropriate?"

"Fuck if I know."

"Zane." She shoved at my shoulder and my eyes cracked open. "We are not doing that to them. This is *their* event, not ours."

"Okay. Whatever."

But Maggie was just ramping up. "Do you have any fucking *clue* how much work went into this wedding? How much they *spent* on it? How many people with other shit to do flew up here, just for them? Because I do. I can tell you what it cost and how much work went into it. *A lot*. Because when people *really* want to get married, that's what they do."

I sighed and closed my eyes. *Here we go again*. "Nice dig, Maggs."

"I can also tell you what it *means* to Jesse and Katie," she went on. "*A lot*." She poked me in the ribs with her tiny finger. "And since, unlike you, I don't think the entire universe revolves around me and my impulses, I can assure you that despite what you might think, pissing all over their parade with our fucked-up gossip is *not* an appropriate wedding gift. So I really fucking hope you got them something else."

Finally finished, she flopped onto her pillow.

"Of course I did. A pool table." I opened one eye. "You know, so I have something to do at their place when they disappear for a quickie, which they always fucking do."

"So it's a gift for yourself."

I opened the other eye and rolled toward her. "They get to use it when I'm not there."

"That's so thoughtful, Zane."

"I know."

"And anyway, we're not telling anyone about Vegas," she said, not looking at me, "because we are not married."

I sat up, rubbing my eyes. The music next door had suddenly shut off, and the silence was too fucking loud. Didn't realize how loud the music was, actually, until the silence set in.

"Jesus Christ," I muttered. "Enough of this shit." First the wedding, for which I'd endured wearing a fucking suit *and* tie, then the almost two-hour show I'd played after the wedding, many more hours of partying and jamming, a frigid skinny dip, and sex with Maggie—which meant feeling like I'd just gone twelve rounds in a cage match with a feral cat—and I was fucking done. "*Yes,*" I told her, "we fucking are."

"Not if we get a divorce."

I leaned down and looked her straight in the eye and told her, just like I already had, several times, "I'm not getting a divorce."

"*Because...?*" she said. "It goes against your principles or something?" Then she scoffed, like I didn't have any.

"Yes. We got married. Let's fucking deal with it already."

She rolled her eyes. And I fucking hated it when she rolled her eyes at me. "You call this a marriage?"

"It could be."

"Just because we had a wedding doesn't mean we have a marriage, Zane."

I rubbed a hand over my face. "So maybe I don't know what the fuck a marriage is. Maybe I don't know *how* to have one."

"Maybe you don't."

"Maybe I wanna try." Was that really so fucking hard for her to believe?

"Well, excuse me if I'm not interested in playing house with you," she said, sitting up abruptly and peeling off the sheet.

"The fuck does that mean?"

I watched her yank on Dylan's giant shirt. Then she tossed me an accusing look. "It means, you wanna run a social experiment in monogamy and commitment, you can do it with someone else."

I stared right back. "So I guess snuggling and pillow talk are out?"

There was a knock at the door and Maggie stiffened. She whispered, "Shut up!"

I didn't even say anything.

"Do not say a word," she hissed, grabbing a pillow and hugging it, like that could make her disappear. "Do not make a sound." Then she reached over and her hand closed on my wrist.

She looked at me, her gray eyes wide—like the thought of whoever was outside that door seeing me here, with her, was the most appalling thing that could ever happen.

Which rubbed me *way* the fuck wrong. Especially since she'd just come all over my dick.

The knock came again.

*Fuck it.*

I got up. Because right now, I did not give one shit who was on the other side of that door.

"ZANE," she cried, "DON'T!"

But I did. I went straight to Maggie's door, and I opened it.

Naked.

# A DIRTY LIE

## AUTHOR'S NOTE

The night of Jesse and Katie's wedding in *Dirty Like Brody*, we see
Jessa Mayes' friend and wedding date, Roni, hauling (naked) ass into
the woods after a midnight skinny dip in the frigid waters of Cathedral Cove, accompanied by (naked) Dylan and Ash.

Lucky girl.

Shortly thereafter, Brody thinks he hears Roni "entertaining" both
men (loudly) through the wall of Jessa's cabin room.

So, what *actually* happens when sexy "wild card" Roni disappears
into the dark with two hot, naked rock stars?

Not what you think...

Jaine

# CHAPTER 1

# Roni

"CO—CONDOMS," I wheezed.

My lungs hurt, bad. Well, everything hurt. Because about five minutes ago, a midnight skinny dip seemed like a great idea.

Now? Not so much.

I'd just reached the door to my cabin, but turned around to face Ash and Dylan, who were right behind me, shivering. Both of them watched my naked boobs jiggle as I jumped up and down, trying to get warm. "You've got... condoms?" *Shit*. My teeth were chattering.

"Uh..." Ash glanced at Dylan, then down at his naked self. "Not *on* me." They were both naked, so where they'd carry a condom, I had no idea. But that really wasn't my problem.

All three of us were completely naked, and fucking freezing. The guys were cupping their balls against the cold and dancing from foot-to-foot like some badly-choreographed strip routine. Dylan, big and burly and auburn-haired, and Ash, sleek and edgy and black-haired, muscles and tattoos gleaming in the moonlight. Hot drummer. Hot lead singer.

The stuff girlhood fantasies were made of, right in my face.

Didn't matter. They weren't stepping foot in my room without condoms.

Just because they were crazy-hot rock stars and I'd been flirting with them mercilessly—and them with me—ever since I'd arrived here at the resort, yesterday, for the wedding of Dylan's Dirty band-mate Jesse Mayes, didn't mean I owed them shit. Besides, I learned years ago never to provide the condoms. If a man couldn't make the effort to rustle one up himself, he wasn't worth my fucking time, much less a place in my bed.

If two of them couldn't do it...

"Kinda fucking cold here, Roni," Dylan offered jovially. "Maybe we come in and warm up, then we figure out the condom situation?"

"No dice," I said. "No cover, no lover."

"Hey—*ho*. Sorry."

We all glanced over in unison as Dirty's bass player, Elle, materialized out of the dark, her platinum-blonde hair flashing in the shadows between the trees. She walked right past us, up the board-walk that connected the various cabins, a tote bag slung over one shoulder, holding up a hand to block her view of the naked guys.

She nodded briefly at me, wearing a small smirk. "Didn't see a thing." She continued on, waving at us over her head, her back to us. "Have a good one, boys and girl."

"*Damn*," Dylan muttered, totally unfazed by the interruption, but slowly absorbing that I was serious. "I'll get the condoms." He gave me a super-quick kiss on the cheek, then dashed off, presumably in the direction of his cabin.

I looked at Ash. Our eyes met, and even in the near-dark, I could see the conflicted expression flicker across his features. A kind of distracted look I'd glimpsed on his face throughout the night. He swiped a hand through his jet-black hair as he bounced on the balls of his feet. I couldn't tell what he was thinking about but, oddly, it didn't seem to be me. Odd since I was standing right in front of him, naked, and presumably, he was about to fuck me.

I opened my mouth to speak but didn't get the chance.

"Me too." He took my hand and kissed it. Then he backed away and took off up the boardwalk.

*Okay...?*

I hurried into my cabin and straight into the shower, got it scalding hot, and thawed myself out. While I did that, I got a strange feeling. The kind of feeling you had no reason to feel, about things you had no reason to know, and yet you did know.

Ash wasn't coming back.

Pity.

*Guess I'll just have to do Dylan twice.*

As I got dressed in a flimsy, filmy nightie—with knit leg warmers and a sweater, at least until Dylan got back—I blow-dried my hair on the hottest setting. I'd washed off my wedding makeup in the shower, so I reapplied just a little. Natural yet polished. Fuck-ready.

Then I waited.

As I did, that look on Ash's face came back to me; like he was looking through me, rather than at me. And it started to bother me.

Like *really* bother me.

Five minutes into waiting, I decided *Fuck waiting.*

When had I ever waited around for a man? Even a hot one?

Even *two* hot ones?

Well, there was a time... But that was years ago. And totally didn't count. Everyone was allowed to be a little stupid when they were eighteen.

I was no longer eighteen or stupid when it came to men.

I was more than aware that these ones, in particular, didn't exactly take me seriously; to the boys of Dirty, I was just the wild card. The party girl. That's what they'd called me, ever since I was sixteen, when I met Jesse's sister, Jessa, in high school and we became friends. Roni "Wild Card" Webber. Translation: easy lay. So it hardly surprised me if Dylan, Dirty's drummer, and his best friend, Ash, lead singer of the Penny Pushers, were blowing me off.

Hot as they both were, it was fine by me.

I could blow them off, too.

Dylan was beautiful but really not my thing. Too clean. Too whole. Too... undamaged.

And Ash? I'd met him for the first time at the wedding. I knew who he was, but I'd never really taken notice, per se, until I met him. Smoldering blue eyes, tattoos and piercings and an angsty restlessness just under the skin. Hard to peg. Probably more my style, but I had no idea what his deal was. The guy was hot and cold. Last night at Katie's stagette he was all over me, but then he'd up and disappeared, and Jessa had been so rough—in other words, hard up for Brody, Dirty's manager, but too stubborn to admit it—that she and I had ended up staying up together, drinking until dawn.

And tonight, at the wedding reception... Ash and his general air of distraction had barely even seemed to notice me in my sexy red dress.

Well, fuck it. Waste of time.

And we only got so much time, right? Personally, I had none to waste.

So I got up and I got dressed. I slipped on a g-string and a pair of my skinny, sexy cargo pants, fawn color, with woolly socks and my little hiking boots; totally outdoorsy-chic. I hoisted up the girls in one of my most gravity-defying push-up bras, because I never did anything halfway. Even if no other man laid eyes on me tonight, *I* had to see me, and that totally counted.

People who took one look at me and assumed I dressed the way I did for men assumed *wrong*. I did not need a man—or a hard dick—to make me feel good about myself.

So why did I feel so crappy?

I decided, immediately, not to dwell on that. Evasive action was what was needed here. The frigid cold of that skinny dip had shocked away the totally decent buzz I had going on, and it was time to remedy that. And I just so happened to know where I could find myself a drink.

I layered on a super-low-cut T-shirt, a super-low-cut cashmere sweater, my cute down-filled satin bomber jacket, and walked out the door—and straight into Dylan. All six-and-a-half feet of him. Actually, I plowed face-first into his hard chest.

"Hey," I said, bouncing back.

His wavy auburn hair had mostly dried and he'd gotten dressed. Jeans, cozy sweater, green plaid lumber jacket. Outdoorsy-chic-fucking-delicious.

"Sorry that took so fucking long," he said. "Had no booze left at my cabin. Thought I'd find some in the lodge, struck out. Bar's locked. Ended up raiding a party up at Jude's cabin." He held up two fists, one with a bottle of vodka and the other with a jug of orange juice. "Screwdriver?" He cocked an eyebrow at me and his green-eyed gaze drifted to my mouth as I put on a smile. "Also brought condoms. Studded... for your pleasure."

"I do like a man who's resourceful," I said.

But... *Jude's cabin*...?

I noticed the throb of music in the distance now, muffled through the dense trees, echoing the strange throb of my heart. Unmistakably, it was Nine Inch Nails. "Closer." Heavy, aggressive, fucking sexy song. Yeah; that sounded about right.

Dylan's eyes flicked past me, into my cabin, through the door I was about to close. "Where's Ash?" Then his gaze scanned slowly down my body, the unspoken question in them: *And why the fuck are you dressed?*

"No idea. But... hey, sorry it didn't work out." I shut the door behind me, firmly.

Dylan lowered the bottles.

"I mean, look, you're sweet..."

His lips quirked in a half-smile. "Ah, shit. Not the 'you're sweet' talk..."

I laughed a little. "Okay. How about this. I like you. Let's be friends?"

"Right. 'Cause I'm sure neither of us have enough of those."

I smiled back, genuinely this time. Dylan Cope had an easy, relaxed charm that was impossible not to smile at. Add to that a killer body he tended to show off in a kilt; I'd even heard he was about to add "underwear model" to his incredibly long list of talents.

So what the fuck was I doing?

Why did it bother me so much that Ash had bailed? Because yeah, it really did.

And not because of Ash.

Because I was on a mission to prove something to myself at this wedding. Well, to myself... and to someone else. Because when Jessa invited me to come as her date, I saw a golden opportunity to indulge my baser self.

Revenge: a dish best served cold...

But apparently, my feelings hadn't run as cold as I'd thought. And now, thanks to Ash bailing on our little threesome, I'd failed to prove shit to anyone, including myself.

Either way, not Dylan's fault.

"No need for sarcasm," I said, cocking my head and flirting just a little. "It's the lowest form of humor, you know."

"Guess I'm just not that funny." With a hooked smile, he hit me with his gorgeous green eyes again. "Anything I can do to change your mind?"

"Unfortunately, no."

"Got it."

He was still standing there, blocking my way. If he was any other guy, I might've just told him to get over it and left him there in the dark. But he really was sweet. And gorgeous.

I wasn't about to tell him that, though. Give him the wrong idea. I'd said the f-word, and if we were gonna be friendly, I couldn't play it both ways.

Nobody liked a tease.

His eyes darkened, like maybe he was reading my mind. Then he leaned in, slowly enough that I could dodge if I wanted to, and kissed me. Slow, and a bit heady-hot, but no tongue. I kissed back, but I held back, too. Way the hell back.

When it ended, he growled a little in his throat, his lips hovering close to mine. "You're a dangerous woman, Roni."

"So I've been told," I whispered.

Then he leaned back, and the moment passed.

"Thanks for not breaking my heart," he added, in what I'd noticed was his lighthearted, easygoing way of handling pretty much everything. Even getting turned down by a potential lover.

"Please." I smoothed out his sweater like a proud mom about to send him off to school. I felt his solid muscles under my hands, his pecs flexing... responsive, willing... eager to please. He watched me do it with hooded eyes.

So maybe the moment hadn't totally passed...

*Fuck*... he'd be a good lay. Dirty's drummer just had that certain vibe. Pure. Full-steam. All stops pulled.

Like a thoroughbred.

"Think I'm gonna head up to Jude's," he murmured. "You wanna come with?"

"No. Thank you." No fucking way was I going to *that* party. I patted him on the cheek. "Go get laid."

"Yes, ma'am." His eyes sparked with amusement. Then his expression grew serious.

He stepped back and nodded at me, once. It was a nod I'd seen before. The one a guy gave you just before he walked away, to make sure you knew what you'd missed out on. And I did, more or less.

Then he turned and walked away. Just as the darkness was about to swallow him, he paused and held up the vodka. "You wanna keep the drink? Kinda look like you could use it."

"No, thanks. You save it for the girl who's about to blow your mind."

He shook his head. "'Night, Roni," he said, and disappeared.

Well, *fuck*.

That kinda sucked. And yet...

I just wasn't in the mood for a convenience fuck.

And that's all Dylan Cope would've been to me. And me to him.

A wild threesome with two hot rock stars was one thing. Memorable—even to those who weren't involved in it. The kind of thing that got around, even at an event like this. Sure, people were probably hooking up all over this place tonight; what else did you get when you stranded a bunch of hot rock stars and a bunch of women at a remote wedding with an open bar?

But who cared about that?

You wanted people to talk in the morning—you wanted that certain someone from your past to hear about your sexploits—you didn't bang a hot rock star. You banged a hot rock star *and* his best

friend, another hot rock star, at the same time. Then at least you got
an honorable mention over morning brunch.

*Shit.* Was that really what this was all about?

And if so... when had I become so lame?

I could see now, since the buzz had worn off and the hot, naked
distractions had evaporated into the night, that that was a really
stupid reason to fuck someone. Or two someones.

But truth be told, I'd fucked a man for stupider reasons. Like, for
instance, thinking I was in love with him. Or worse...

Thinking he was in love with me.

I took a breath of the amazingly fresh night air and told myself to
let it go. Just forget about it.

*Nobody cares.*

*Neither should you.*

I started around the deck, heading away from the music that
surely led to Jude's cabin. Away from the direction both Ash and
Dylan had disappeared. Just trying to get present in the moment
and absorb my surroundings, because this place deserved nothing
less.

Rainforest on the Pacific coast, with ancient, towering trees and
water crashing on the rocks below. It was crisp-cold tonight, the
resort notched into a cove off the dark ocean, secluded. No snow.
Just riding that edge of frozen, everything chilled and green and
ready to unfurl in spring.

Winter paradise.

The sun would be up in a few hours; I could probably just
wander around all night, fall asleep under the stars. Maybe curl up
on one of the couches on the wraparound deck of the lodge with a
couple of blankets.

And a nightcap. A toast to me and my lack of any need for a
man. Just enjoy my own company for a while.

Because it really didn't matter what anyone else thought or said
about me, good or bad, in the morning.

Since when the hell did I care what anyone had to say about my
sex life anyway?

## CHAPTER 2

# Roni

AS I WALKED past Jessa's room, I noticed her light was on and I stopped. I thought about knocking on her door, maybe staying up all night chatting like we did last night, but decided against it. Tonight, I really didn't mind being alone.

But just then, the door opened.

And Brody stormed out.

Tall, dark and broody Brody Mason, Dirty's manager and the guy Jessa, apparently, had it super fucking bad for. Not that she'd said as much to me. She didn't have to.

"Roni," he growled as he shut the door behind himself. He looked frazzled as he clawed a hand through his hair; wound up.

Recently fucked?

No. Definitely not. Way too much tension rolling off him for that.

"Hey," I said, wondering if I should check on Jessa after he left.

"I was just gonna knock on your door," he said abruptly. "Jessa's in the bath. Can you look in on her? She's drunk."

"Oh. Sure."

"Good." Then he stormed off, just like that.

*Hmmm...*

I went in and knocked on the bathroom door. I could hear what sounded like weeping. *Great.* I'd never been good with weepers. And Jessa Mayes had always been one. Lucky for me, she didn't often get weepy with me. "Babe. You okay?"

"Roni?" Sniffles and a little splash. She was still in the tub.

"Yup. Should I come in?" *Please say no.*

"No. I'm okay. I'll be out in a bit. Can you stay?"

"Yeah." I sighed. "I can stay."

I grabbed a tiny bottle of Baileys from her mini fridge, opened it and sipped. Then I flopped onto her couch, zoning out to the tunes she had playing. Arctic Monkeys. Some depressing thing about crawling back to someone when you've had too much to drink...

Just a little too fucking fitting for my liking.

I turned it off.

A few minutes later Brody stormed back in, tossed some black fabric thing at the couch, and left again. It hit my boot and plopped on the floor.

What the hell was that about?

I picked it up. Some old Led Zeppelin T-shirt.

When Jessa finally emerged from the bathroom, she looked a wreck. Her eyes were puffy and bloodshot from boozing and crying.

"Wow," I remarked. "Good thing you don't have a photo shoot tomorrow. You'd be incredibly fired."

Despite her current appearance, Jessa was a model, but she'd never been stuck up about it. She giggled all bubbly, like baby Dumbo after he'd gotten smashed in a bucket of booze in that old Disney cartoon. "Thanks." Then she blinked at the Zeppelin shirt I'd draped on the back of the couch, seeming to sober a bit, and glanced forlornly at the door. "Is he gone?"

"Does it look like he's here?"

She hugged herself and didn't answer.

I steered her over to a chair and sat her ass down, and blow-dried her hair. Then I tucked her into bed.

"You're amazing, Roni," she gushed as she cuddled into her pillow.

So, yeah. Pretty drunk.

"You okay?" I smoothed her hair back from her face. "You want me to find him, ask him to come back?"

She blinked up at me with her big brown eyes. "Why?"

"You tell me."

"Yeah..." she said. Then, "No." And about three seconds later, she was asleep.

I waited a few minutes to be sure Jessa was out. Then I got the hell out of there and knocked on the door to Maggie's room, next door.

There was only so much nurturing I could handle, and I'd just maxed out my annual quota when I brushed another woman's hair. But as Dirty's assistant manager, Maggie was probably used to handling other women's hair—like holding it out of toilet bowls while they puked and stuff. Much more suited to this gig.

There was a fire burning in her room; I could see it through the window curtain. But no movement, no noise.

I knocked again. Maybe she was asleep. Or—?

"ZANE, DON'T!"

I heard some footsteps, then the door opened and I glimpsed Maggie, sitting on the bed across the room. She was hugging a pillow. And there was Zane Traynor, lead singer of Dirty, the gorgeous golden god of rock, in my face.

Naked.

He smirked when he saw me and leaned casually on the door frame, as if his legendary cock wasn't hanging out. "Wild card," he said. "How's it hangin'?"

I glanced down because I couldn't really help it, given that question. Impressive, sure, but I wasn't impressed. I was aware that Jessa had assumed Zane was the reason I'd wanted to come to this wedding with her. But she was wrong about that.

Way wrong.

"Not bad," I said, unfazed.

When I looked at Maggie again, she was covering her face. I heard muffled swearing into the pillow.

Zane's gaze crept down to my cleavage, his smirk widening into a grin. "Yeah? Dylan and Ash treating you well?"

Maggie exploded out of bed. "Don't answer that. It's none of his *business*." She grabbed the door from Zane's grasp, elbowing him aside. "How are you?" she asked me, with way too much enthusiasm for this time of night. Up close, she looked a wreck. She was wearing the ugliest tent of a puke-green shirt, with no pants, and her hair was all messed up. I'd never seen the girl with a hair out of place.

Actually, she looked fucked.

I knew what a well-fucked woman looked like.

"Uh... okay," I said. "I was wondering if you could pop in and check on Jessa? You know, make sure she's still breathing? She's been sucking back booze like a sorority girl and she's passed out now, but I wanted to go for a walk. I mean, if you're not busy..." I glanced at Zane, who was still grinning.

"Yeah. For sure," Maggie said. Again, too much enthusiasm. "We're up. I'm up. We were just talking. Zane was helping me with something. We can check on her. I can check on her. I can go stay with her. Because I'm not staying here. I mean, this is my room. He's not staying..."

Her awkward babbling trailed off. I didn't know Maggie well enough to know if this kind of babbling was normal for her or not, but it definitely didn't seem healthy to spew out so many words without breathing.

"Okay," I said when she seemed finished. "Thanks."

Then I walked away.

I heard Zane laugh and Maggie swear as she shut the door.

No idea what that was about, but at least everyone except me was getting laid tonight. And I happened to know for a fact that Zane Traynor was an amazing lay.

So kudos, Maggie.

At least, he *was* an amazing lay five years ago... back when I was twenty-one and screwing rock stars seemed like the world's best idea.

Especially if they were friends with Jude Grayson.

The lodge was faintly aglow in the night, its wraparound deck rimmed with golden lanterns, the chandeliers inside the windows dimmed, a fire burning low in the hearth. Everything else was dark, still and silent as I approached. I didn't see a single other person around. Even the staff had cleared out.

Perfect.

I found one of the glass doors along the deck unlocked and slipped it open, stepping inside.

Dylan said the bar was locked, but I'd made a point of flirting with the bartender at the wedding reception and found out where he kept the key. Not that he'd told me; I'd watched him stash it in a drawer. You just never knew when information like that might come in handy, right?

I headed straight for the bar, across the grand room.

And that's when I saw him.

A man, sitting alone in front of the fireplace, on a small love seat facing the fire. I saw his dark head of hair tipped back, resting against the back. Sleeping, maybe. Hopefully.

I'd just have to slip out before he saw me...

But as I neared the bar, the side of his face came into view... that unmistakable face.

It was *Jude*.

Of all fucking people.

Jesse's best man. Dirty's head of security.

The worst mistake of my life.

His big body came into view. And *big* was definitely the word. He was lounged back on the love seat, thighs spread wide, and I saw it.

I saw it *all*.

I stopped short... and it took me a delayed moment to process what I was seeing.

I was seeing Jude's dick.

He had his dark T-shirt shoved up, showing his thick, washboard abs, his sweats shoved down to expose himself, and his long, swollen dick was in his hand.

He was *jerking off*.

I glanced around, but there was no one else here. I half-expected some hot young bimbo to come crawling out from behind the couch at any moment.

But no. There was no one but him.

And now, me.

I couldn't tell if his eyes were closed, but his dark eyelashes were lowered. His heavily-tattooed arm flexed as he pumped. His mouth was open a bit and I could hear him breathing, low and strained, as he worked himself...

And heat crashed through me in a wave.

I swallowed.

*Well...* There was something I never thought I'd see again.

I just stood there, staring. Wanting to laugh, wanting to run, wanting to strut right over and lend him a hand... all in equal measure. Instead, I did something else.

I started singing, loudly.

*"HEEEYYYYY JUDE—"*

"Fuck!" He sat up like a shot. "Jesus! Don't sing the fuckin' song."

I laughed. I fucking *howled* with laughter. "You should see your fucking face!"

"Shit. She sings me the fuckin' Beatles while I've got my cock in my hand." In no particular hurry, he wrestled his hard dick into his sweats, which tented rudely. "You think I haven't heard that song enough in my goddamn life?"

"So blame your parents."

"I do. Fuckin' hippies." He swiped a hand through his thick, almost-black hair and fell back on the couch, heaving out a sigh. "And now she's talkin' to me about my parents. Christ."

I was still laughing, doubled-over. Actually, I was crying. Tears leaked out the corners of my eyes, shimmering in the firelight. He was getting blurry, but I could still see him scowling at me.

"Wow. Oh, shit. I haven't laughed like that... Well, since the stagette last night." I wiped the tears away.

"So fuckin' glad I could provide your nightly amusement."

"Oh, don't pout." I stood up tall and crossed my arms under my chest. "It's so pathetic when men pout. And please, don't let me stop you." Against my better judgment, I sauntered over and perched on the arm of the love seat, totally fucking in love with the fact that I'd caught him in a vulnerable moment, even if it barely fazed him. Because clearly, it didn't.

Despite the fact that he'd put his dick away—more or less—his sweats were still riding so low I could see the shadow of his closely-shaven treasure trail, his shirt still halfway up his abs as he lounged back. The man was dead fucking sexy. Sexist man I'd ever...

But I didn't plan on letting that faze me, either.

"Please, carry on. I wouldn't dream of leaving a man hanging."

*Well, tell that to Dylan...*

"I'm good," he said, but his cock didn't look any less put out. I could see the thick head clearly outlined as it pressed against the fabric of his dark sweats.

*Damn...*

Jude had a monster dick when he was twenty-one. Guess that hadn't changed. In my fantasies of him over the years, it definitely had; like maybe he'd started doing 'roids to pump up his hot bod, and his dick had shrunk to the size of a raisin, and his life had fallen apart.

Yeah; those kinds of fantasies.

I met his eyes. Dark and smoldering and totally fucking dangerous.

So those hadn't changed, either.

Jude had been hot back then, but now he had a monster body to go with his dick, and he'd really grown into his rugged-gorgeous looks. Had a lot more tattoos, too. He pretty much lived the life of a rock star, managing security for one of the biggest bands in the world, working alongside his best friends, and if that wasn't enough, he was a patched member of a powerful outlaw motorcycle club, alongside his brother. All of which meant that he had big, fat bank and pretty much his pick of any pussy that drifted his way.

So no, Jude's life hadn't fallen apart. More likely every boyhood fantasy he'd ever had had come true.

Because life was fair like that.

"May I ask why you're jerking off?" I inquired, busting his balls a bit. "You know there are women here, right?"

He shrugged a shoulder but the look in his eyes, which were still fixed on me, was not casual. It was sex-hazed, rough and ready. "Just felt like it." He shifted over a bit, his gaze dropping to linger on my breasts, so purposefully I couldn't even pretend not to notice. He patted the seat cushion next to him. "Have a seat."

Right.

There were about five inches between him and the end of the tiny love seat, and my ass was not that small. And I definitely wasn't sitting on that monster in his lap. Even though, clearly, he was offering it up... as he spread his thighs a little wider, his arm tossed up on the back of the love seat. Casual, not casual. Just putting it out there to see if I'd bite.

And I had to wonder... If another woman had happened to walk in on him while he had his cock out, and she had her cleavage out, would he have asked her to sit down, too?

*Yes.*

*Well, maybe.*

"I'm good," I said.

I started to get up, but then paused. I looked at him just sitting there, staring at me.

I sat back down.

"You wanna smoke a joint?" I pulled one from the pocket of my jacket. "I was just going to."

Stupid.

Actually... really, *really* stupid.

When the hell had I become so stupid?

When he didn't answer right away, I got up to leave for real. Like I really didn't give one fuck. I was just being polite, right?

"I'm on duty," he said. His tone was serious, but it was hard to take him seriously when his dick was still up.

I started backing away as I spoke. "So... you'll jack off on duty, but you won't smoke up?"

The barest hint of a smirk curved his full lips. "Man's gotta have his ethics."

"Suit yourself." I turned away before his dimples could make an appearance and I got even more stupid. But as I walked away, I could *feel* his eyes all over my ass.

"Roni."

I stopped, my heart thudding in my chest at the sound of my name in that low, soft growl.

"I'm just messin' with you, darlin'."

*Jesus.* Darlin' was it, now?

I turned back.

"You know," I mused, "being 'on duty' never would've stopped you before. I remember you, twenty years old, working with the band..." *Shit.* What was I doing now? Flirting? "Just a lowly roadie back then, bouncing parties and hauling gear, but partying as hard as anyone else." Yeah. I was totally flirting. "Harder, I bet."

He stared at me with that look in his eyes.

*Hellfire.*

Jude's eyes had always reminded me of hellfire. A deep, molten brown that burned right into you. It wasn't a stare that looked through you, to all the other women you could've been but weren't... like Ash's did.

Jude looked at me like he really saw me.

He'd always looked at me like that.

"I remember you, too," he said.

And with that, I should've turned and walked away. Just left things on that high note.

Instead, I kept flirting.

Because old habits die hard.

"So now it's all work and no play for poor Jude?"

He cracked a rare smile, the deep dimples flashing in his cheeks. And I felt the tiniest surge of victory—even as that smile hit me, right between the legs. "I play when I want to."

"And?" I challenged. "Can't some of your boys take over? I don't see any imminent security threats around here."

"My boys are off for the night. Having a party in my cabin. That's the thing about boys..." His eyes roamed down my body as he spoke. "Gotta let 'em blow off steam sometime."

I planted my hand on my cocked hip and perused the scene. "So... you escaped to blow off some steam of your own, in front of a crackling fire?"

He raised a dark eyebrow, his dimples still on display. "You laughin' at me, V?"

I stared at him, my heart beating a little too hard in my chest.

*He called me V.*

Which gave me a very unexpected—and yes, stupid—surge of hope that he still had a soft spot for me?

Well, not that he ever really did. Not exactly.

More like a hard spot...

"No," I said. "It's very romantic, Jude." I made sure to look deep in his hellfire eyes and hold his gaze when I said, "I just never thought of you that way. You know, as a romantic."

Then I turned and walked away, in no particular hurry, giving him ample time to appreciate my ass in my tight cargos... and ponder what he'd been missing.

"V," he said.

And I couldn't resist. I stopped and turned back to him, again.

He gestured at his crotch, at the stiff bulge of his cock in his sweats. "Just gotta give me a minute here, darlin'."

"Uh-huh." I turned on my heel. "There's a key for the bar cabinets in the drawer by the sink," I told him over my shoulder as I walked away. "I like tequila."

"I know you do," he said, and I could hear the smile in his voice as I walked out the door.

# CHAPTER 3

## Jude

RONI. Fucking Veronica Webber.

Blast from the fucking past.

I tried not to think about that. Thought, instead, about how bad Dylan's shoes stank after playing drums all night, all the times I'd walked into some shared bathroom on the road that reeked of puke... the time me and Brody had to pick broken glass out of a nasty gash on Zane's ass...

Yeah, that worked.

Once my cock was down, I threw on my hoodie and got that key. I swiped a couple of shot glasses and a bottle of tequila. Then I went to the door and looked outside. Watched her standing there against the deck railing, her profile to me as she looked out over the dark water below.

Glad I didn't say anything ridiculous while all my blood was in my dick.

Yeah, so I'd pretty much offered up my cock, when I was hard as fuck and she was sitting right there, still laughing at me. But that was all horny bullshit and bravado.

Truth was, a woman with Roni's talents deserved better than a quick fuck. And quick was what it would've been. Was about ten seconds from blowing my load when she interrupted me.

And glad she did.

Been a lot of girls in and out of my life. My bed. Was like that for a lot of guys I knew in the rock 'n' roll life. In the MC life. But for some guys, lucky or unlucky, there was that one girl you remembered, different from all the rest. The one you sometimes thought about out of the blue, no matter how long it'd been since you last had her. And you wondered, *Would she be that fine if I had her again?* Because she was that epic.

Sexy, obviously.

Pretty.

Had some other qualities like a big, infectious laugh and a lack of self-consciousness, a freeness you could admire and didn't see a lot in other women.

And something else. Something you couldn't put your finger on, and maybe that was the attraction. That unknown quality that worked its way under your skin and stayed with you.

That something different.

More than just the taste of her or the wild noises she made. The feel of her, naked and soft, against your skin... How hot and wet her pussy was. How tight her ass was. How good she sucked you off.

It wasn't just fucking her.

It wasn't just her fucking you.

*More.*

Some crazy head-spinning shit, some kind of magic you made as your bodies slammed together.

As I watched her standing there, the curve of her slightly arched back as she leaned on the rail, the way her pants hugged her round ass, the way her thick, black hair hung down her back and framed the side of her face, I remembered it. Like a tug in my stomach. Lower... like a pull.

Like a tiny blade twisting when she looked over. Just one of her bright green eyes glittering at me.

*Come the fuck over here*, that eye said.

I opened the door. Went to her and poured her a shot. She sparked up her joint and passed it to me.

"You roll this fatty?" I asked, impressed.

"It's a talent."

I offered it back. "Ladies first."

She shook her head. "I insist."

So I took a drag and passed it back. I poured myself a shot. Then we clinked glasses and she said, "To good times."

"To epic times," I said, and we shot back the liquid gold.

She smiled, but it was a guarded smile, like she hadn't decided if she was happy or not. "How was it?" she asked.

"How was what?" I leaned against the railing next to her.

"You know." She flicked an eyebrow toward the lodge. "In there. You see stars? Or was it more of a utilitarian wank?"

I chuckled. "Come again?"

"Your tug fest," she said, and took a drag on the joint. "What kind of orgasm was it?"

"The nonexistent kind."

Now she raised her eyebrow at me. "I thought you finished."

I laughed again. "While you're out here waitin' on me?" I took the joint as she passed it back and took a drag.

"You took long enough."

I let my gaze drift down her open jacket, her low-cut shirt. I could see the full curves of her juicy tits, mocking me. "What can I say? You look good in cargos." I watched as she poured us both another shot. "Took a while to cool off."

"That's very sweet," she said, like it wasn't sweet at all. "But it wasn't my cargos that got you there. So you don't need to loop me into it. I'm not that fragile."

"Never thought you were." A lock of her black hair had fallen across her cheek. I reached up and smoothed it back from her face so I could see those green eyes. "Was definitely your cargos that would've finished it off, though."

She smiled a little, again, but in that flippant way that meant she didn't believe me. She raised her shot in toast. "To... even better times? Whatever's better than epic." She cocked her head at me. "Is there such a thing?" And as usual, I couldn't tell if she was flirting with me or mocking me. Teasing me, just because she could.

"To the best times," I said.

We clinked and shot the booze back.

I handed her the joint. She looked down over the water and leaned over the rail as she smoked. I watched her dark hair dance in the slight breeze. Let my gaze wander down the curve of her back, to that round, tight ass. To the hit of memory: Roni bent over in front of me, my hands digging into her hips, that sleek arch of her naked back, gleaming with sweat.

I looked away, out over the water.

"This place is insane," she said with a small sigh.

"Yup."

I leaned farther over the rail, just like her, to see her face. There was a sweet, dreamy look on it as she took another drag on the joint, then handed it to me.

"You gonna invite me when you get married here someday?" I asked her.

Roni stared at me. Then she looked out over the water again, her gaze unfocused like she wasn't really seeing it. "A young man told me, years ago, that I'm not the marrying kind."

I took a slow drag off the joint, thinking about that. "Must've been a real douche. And you listened to that shit?"

"No. I never really listened to any of the shit you said. You said a lot of shit back then."

True enough.

"Did piss me off for a while," she admitted.

"You still pissed, darlin'?"

She poured us another shot. "I'm here, aren't I?" Those unreadable green eyes held mine. "Besides, I don't really do pissed anymore. Pissed implies attachment to outcomes, and I don't have those. Cheers."

This time, we drank without toasting anything.

"No?" I licked tequila from my lips. Despite the cold, my insides were growing warm.

"Nope."

"Never?"

"Not usually."

"How 'bout tonight?" I asked, handing the joint back to her. Because I saw her at the wedding reception in that sexy-as-fuck red dress, looking like a five-alarm fire, waiting on Ash to notice. "You got outcomes for tonight?"

"Nope," she said.

"Ashley Player not an outcome, then?"

She looked out over the water again as she smoked. "Nope."

I shifted closer to her and nudged her shoulder, lightly. "Thought you were lookin' to hook up with him tonight."

She looked at me, not quite turning her head, just glancing around the curve of her hair. Then she smiled, just a little, her green eyes sparkling. Girl could play a tough game.

Hardest chick to read I'd ever met.

"Dylan, too," I added.

She passed me the joint. "Is that what it looks like?"

"Looked like. Actually, you ask me, looked like pussy purring up the wrong tree."

She laughed. "Excuse me? Pussy what now?"

"Ash," I said. "Kid's mind is somewhere else."

"I noticed." She poured us another shot and handed one to me. "You wanna tell me where?"

"Nope. Not my place."

We clinked and drank.

"And now?" she asked, looking out over the water again as she licked tequila from her lip. "Where's my pussy purring?"

My gaze lingered on her plump lips, flushed and moist from tequila. I stared so long she finally turned to look at me, and her eyes met mine.

I raised the joint to her lips and held it for her, while she gave it a little suck.

"Up to you, V."

She just looked at me as she exhaled smoke.

"The way I see it," I added, "you could be with Dylan or Ash right now. But you aren't. And in my experience, darlin', when you're choosing between two options, even two good ones, there's always a third."

"Hmm," she said, like that was mildly interesting.

But she didn't ask what that third option was.

I took a long, deep pull off the joint, filling my mouth with smoke but not breathing it in. Then I let my gaze trail down her face again, to those swollen, cocksucking lips.

"C'mere," I murmured.

She didn't come, but she didn't pull away when I leaned in. Her lips parted, and I fit my mouth to hers, almost... never quite touching her lips as I breathed the smoke into her mouth.

She breathed it in.

Then my lips brushed hers, lightly, hovering.

She drew away an inch.

"You still call me V," she said softly. Her eyes were soft, too. Maybe the pot going to her head.

"Your name, isn't it?" I licked my lip without meaning to. "Fucking Veronica."

"Yeah," she said. "No one else seems to remember it." Then she moved to pour us another shot.

I stopped her. "No more booze."

She glanced at me, then looked away, letting the bottle go. I set it aside. I watched her watch the water rush over the rocks below.

"You don't like Roni?"

"Roni's good," she said.

I took a drag from what was left of the joint, considering. "You don't like it when the boys call you wild card."

"Fuck, no. They might as well call me slutbag and get it over with. For a bunch of rock stars, they're a bunch of fucking prudes."

I chuckled. "Slutbag would be a compliment. Trust me. They mean wild card as one."

"No, they don't."

"You'd be surprised."

She raised an eyebrow and I leaned in closer to her.

"Brats on a playground. They're all jealous of what they don't have. Shiny toys... All the boys want 'em, even if they're not supposed to."

She smiled a little. "Did you just call me a toy?"

"Not if you didn't like it."

She smiled again. A genuine smile, for once. It lit up her face, her cheeks kinda glowing in the cold. But those green eyes were still wary.

"How 'bout me?" I asked casually. "Am I a prude?"

"You were never a prude. Just... selective."

"That right?" I looked down, watching the waves lick the rocks below. Dropped the roach into them, watched the ember sparkle down and snuff out. "Did I mention you look good in those cargos?" I turned my body to face her, letting my gaze move slowly down her curves. "Looked good in that red dress, too."

"Didn't know you noticed."

"Notice a lot of things, darlin'."

She turned to me, her gaze drifting down my body. "So do I."

I was hard in my sweats, again, and I knew she could tell. No way I could hide a hard-on this size, even in the near-dark.

She looked up at me and I saw the options there, flickering behind her eyes.

Go back to her cabin, alone.

Wander the woods the rest of the night, alone.

But there was always that third option...

"So..." I asked her, "you gonna play nice, V? Or make me work for it?"

Her eyes narrowed a little as she considered that.

"I never play nice." She glanced at my cock again before meeting my eyes. "But why don't you take it out, and *I'll* do the work."

# CHAPTER 4

# Roni

IT WAS JUST TOO FUCKING sweet to resist.

The ultimate revenge.

As Jude pushed the front of his sweats down, baring his big dick... hard... so totally fucking hard and swollen, for me... I'd never felt anything like the rush of it. I watched him jerk, tightening in anticipation, swelling even more as he waited for it. As he thought about what I was about to do.

*Yeah*... hard, swollen, straining revenge, just aching for my attention. What could possibly be better than the man who'd once rejected you wanting you again?

I could've walked away from him right then, just to rub it in.

But where was the fun in that?

There was no higher high, nothing I'd ever felt that was better, more delicious, more intensely arousing and at the same time totally fucking *gratifying* than the sensation of getting on my knees in front of that big, hard dick... and taking a taste of him.

Slowly.

While he groaned.

While he shifted and stirred and put his hands in my hair. Just lightly.

*Shit*. He was being sweet with me. And that, I didn't expect.

I couldn't blame him for taking my mouth when I offered it. But he didn't have to be sweet about it. He didn't have to be gentle with his hands, as he held my head and let me take control.

He could've been a total fucking cocky asshole about it.

But then again, Jude had never been an asshole.

And as I teased his fat cockhead with a slow, torturous lick, and flickered the tip of my tongue over his slit, tasting that delicious taste, that first drop of his salty fluid... it hit me, hard. Made my head spin with the question...

*Who was really in control here?*

I took him then, fast, not bothering with the slow buildup, the tease. I just stroked my tongue along his shaft, once, to get him wet, then took him deep, making him groan again. I sucked him off, hard and fast, wrapping one hand around the base of his cock and squeezing hard, strangling him, the way I knew he liked it back then, cupping his balls and tugging with the other hand.

"*Jesus Christ, V...*" he growled.

Then he pulled away, ripping his dick from my mouth.

I looked up at him. We were both panting.

He cupped my face and held my eyes. "You gonna make my night or what?" he asked, stroking a thumb lightly down my cheek.

"Was just about to," I said, swiping my tongue over my lip, still tasting him.

"Not what I meant."

He pulled me to my feet. Then he cupped my face again. He leaned in, and as his mouth met mine, it was foreign and so familiar... like being kissed by a stranger and someone you knew like the palm of your own hand—someone you'd kissed a thousand times in your dreams, or on the edge of sleep, half-conscious as your hands roamed over your own body... as you got yourself off to the half-remembered smell of him, the slippery fullness of his lips, the slight roughness of his stubble, the soft scrape of his teeth against your skin.

I broke away, drawing back for air.

He stared at me.

Then he caught my hand. He drew me with him, moving toward the lodge.

And I went with him, letting him take me there.

Inside, he walked me over to the little love seat and stood me right in front of it, close to the fire, and said, "Take off your clothes."

Then he sat down in the middle of the seat, watching me.

"Don't you wanna do it for me?" I asked, still catching my breath.

"I want to watch," he said.

So be it.

I got undressed, and I did it slowly. I started with my jacket. My boots, then my socks. My sweater went next, peeled slowly over my head and tossed aside. My T-shirt, then my jeans. Every zipper pulled slowly, every button popped with a slight pause. Watching his eyes grow darker as he drank in the curves of my body, all rimmed in firelight.

I unhooked my bra and let it slide loose down my arms, holding it in front of me, teasing him a little before I dropped it.

My panties went next in a slow, slow peel.

As soon as I was naked, he got up and prowled the two paces it took to get right in my face. He raised one hand to my breast and cupped lightly, skimming his thumb over my nipple as it hardened in response.

A delicious, tingling shiver ran through me.

And... *no*. This was not just about revenge.

I knew it as he leaned so close to me that I could feel his heat, could smell his clean, manly smell, could feel the hairs on his arm dusting my skin... and my whole body wound up tight with anticipation—even as I held back.

This was about me—getting what I wanted. What I'd *always* wanted, if I was at all honest with myself about it.

Namely, the dark-haired beauty, the beast right in front of me.

He leaned down to touch his lips to my neck, breathing in my ear. "Get on your back," he murmured. I shivered again as his lips skimmed along my jaw and briefly hovered over my mouth.

I kissed him then, softly, my lips just catching his, making him pause. The feel of him, the heat of him, went straight between my legs. I felt giddy-hot and restless with need. I sucked a bit on his bottom lip, before he drew back.

His hellfire eyes flashed at me.

"On your back," he said.

"I wanna get you off," I whispered.

"You will." He leaned in and skimmed his lips across my cheek, to my ear again. "I want you on your back," he said, his teeth catching on my earlobe. My pussy throbbed... ached as he bit down, lightly. "Wanna hold you down and give it to you, while you beg me for more."

*Not gonna happen.*

That's what I would've said to any other man.

To him, I just said, "Where?"

"Wherever you want."

I looked around. The love seat was too small for both of us, if he wanted me on my back. Otherwise, there were no full-sized couches, just chairs.

Of course, there was always the floor...

But I went over to the love seat and climbed up onto the velvety upholstered back. I reclined back on it, keeping myself propped up on my elbows, for now, so I could watch him as he lost his hoodie, kicked off his shoes and pulled his shirt over his head, then stripped off his socks and sweats. He wasn't wearing underwear.

When my gaze landed on his naked cock, it hit me.

"Oh, *shit.* Condom," I said, sitting up.

"I have some." He reached for his hoodie and dug around in the pockets, and I snickered a bit.

"You always carry condoms when you jerk off?"

He smirked. "Always come prepared."

"What is that, some Boy Scouts thing?" I teased.

"It's a smart thing," he said, his gaze roaming down my naked body, "obviously."

I put my feet up on the back of the love seat, my knees bent, pointed my toes and arched my back, like a pinup. "Well, come and get it then," I said, as he rolled a condom over his hard length.

"Intend to."

Naked and totally fucking gorgeous, he stalked over to me. I lay back as he lifted my legs. Without hesitation, he straddled the back of the love seat, one foot on the seat and the other on the floor, and wrapped my legs around his waist. Then he notched the swollen head of his cock into my pussy. I was already wet and ready to take him; I braced for his thrust as my heart hammered in my chest.

But he hesitated. "You want foreplay, darlin'?" he asked me. "'Cause that look on your face says you don't."

"Fuck foreplay," I said.

He smirked a little. He ran his hands up my body and cupped my breasts, squeezing hard... then he shifted his hips forward, sliding into me.

And *God*... that feeling.

Cock.

*Big* cock.

*Jude's* cock...

It fucking *shattered* me.

*This*. God, I wanted this...

I writhed, arching my back as I took him, as he stretched me to my limits with that long, slow push...

He didn't let up until he'd filled me. Then he paused, closing his eyes as he took a breath, savoring the feeling.

And my stomach twirled. My chest tightened. A whole lot of unfamiliar, fucking disturbing feelings ripped through me as I stared at his face.

He opened his eyes, locking on mine, and pulled back... then shoved into me again, still squeezing my breasts. Harder this time. Faster.

And I just tried to hold still.

To keep calm.

He shoved into me again and again as I lay there on my back, my thighs wrapped around his hips, gripping the love seat beneath me with both hands. Not because I was afraid of falling off. Jude would never let me fall.

Because I didn't want to touch him with my hands.

I didn't want to feel his warm, silky skin and the bulge of his muscles beneath, flexing as he drove into me. I didn't want to pinch and tease his rigid nipples and hear him growl.

Most of all, I didn't want to grab him and pull him down to me so I could kiss him again.

If I did that, I was gonna lose it. Start whimpering and panting and making a total fucking fuss that I couldn't take back. Jude's face in my face, his mouth on me again... I just couldn't fucking stand it while his cock was inside me. I *knew* I couldn't.

He fucked me harder, but slowing right down, gripping my breasts to hold me where he wanted me while his hips did the rest. He swiveled them as he dug in, working the head of his cock against my front wall—studying me the entire time, even as I lay still.

Then he slammed his pelvic bone against my clit.

I cried out. I couldn't help it.

And a slow, wicked smile transformed the dark, controlled look on his face. His dimples flashed.

I closed my eyes.

Because I'd just flashed forward. To the moment when this ended. When he pulled out... and walked away.

And I got a serious lump in my throat.

I covered it all by throwing my head back and letting myself go a little, moaning as he gave it to me, letting the heat and friction and longing build inside me, even as my throat got tight and my heartbeats sped up.

Would he walk away? Right after this?

*Yes.*

But how fast would he do it?

And how much would it hurt?

*Shit.* Just... *shit.*

Since when was I afraid of casual sex?

There were always more trees to purr up, right?

But Jude... Jude was different.

Shouldn't be, but he totally was.

There was nothing about this that was casual. At least, not for me.

"You with me, darlin'?" he asked, and I opened my eyes to find him watching me with those hellfire eyes, the hint of a smile still on his lips. "'Cause I'm about to lose it and I wanna take you with me when I go. Would love to make this last for you, V, but it's been a long fuckin' night." He was panting as he drove into me, and I could see the slight shake of his muscles as he held himself back.

"Yeah," I choked out. "I'm with you. Almost."

Couldn't make it too easy for him, could I?

"Then you better start askin' for it. Tell me what you want. What you need..."

I met his eyes again and said, "You know what I need."

At least, he used to.

His smile faded and with that, he fucked me, harder... harder, until I was sliding back along the love seat and my head was hanging off.

"Yeah... You feel so fuckin' tight, babe. So hot... Your tits are so... *fuck*," he said, squeezing my breasts until it almost hurt. So, yeah: he definitely remembered two things I needed... dirty talk and rough handling. "Can't believe I almost forgot how fuckin' fine these tits are."

Then he leaned down over me and shoved one breast up to meet his mouth, flicking and lapping his tongue over my nipple... until I groaned through my clenched teeth.

Oh, no. No, no, no.

None of this gentle tongue stuff.

"Harder," I told him, gasping for air.

He obliged, but it wasn't enough. Not enough to rid me of that feeling, his tongue flickering over my nipple, tasting me...

Then he did it again... licking, then sucking gently on me.

"*Harder*," I rasped. "You know I like it hard..."

"Yeah," he growled, slamming into me. "I remember."

"And don't fucking suck on my nipple like that."

"Like this?" He sucked my other nipple into his mouth and teased it with his tongue, lapping slowly, deliberately.

"Fuck... *Fuck off*, Jude... seriously."

He chuckled, but he didn't stop teasing my nipples, suckling, licking, kissing...

Then one of his hands slid up around my throat and grabbed me, squeezing just a little, holding me pinned as he pounded into me. I couldn't move, he had me pinned down so tight.

"*Harder*," I gasped as I fought for breath.

He let my nipple go with a pop.

"*Fuck*, V..."

He caught me up then, pulling me toward him, yanking me into his lap as he gave it to me. He held my hips down against him and fucked up into me, hard and deep. I wrapped myself around him, shuddering as he pummeled my clit, meaning to bury my face in his neck as I came, but he wouldn't let me. He nudged my face back with his and found my lips, kissing me, his strong tongue plundering my mouth.

I lost control, then.

Totally lost it...

I came, hard, as his tongue stroked mine, slippery wet and warm, as his mouth slid against mine, sucking... as he held my hips and fucked me in short, harsh strokes. I would've screamed bloody murder if his tongue wasn't filling my mouth, but as it was, I just moaned and rode him, frantically, and bit his tongue. Hard.

He growled into my mouth and a shudder tore through his body, seconds before his hips snapped up and he exploded into me.

Then he broke his mouth away, groaning.

I rode him slowly, drawing out the waves of his pleasure, kissing his face with my eyes closed and holding him tight... just savoring his ecstasy... riding it right along with him...

Until his body gradually relaxed and he hugged me, heaving a deep, satisfied sigh.

I opened my eyes.

His hooded gaze moved down my face and he smirked a little as he said, "That hard enough for you?"

"I could take it harder."

His eyes darkened and he kissed me, softly.

Then he lifted me and got up, setting me gently on the love seat. I watched him move toward his clothes—but I wasn't just gonna sit here while he got dressed and left. As rubbery as my legs were, as hard as my head was still spinning, even though most of my blood was nowhere near my brain... I got up, and started getting dressed first.

When I was fully dressed, I glanced over at him.

He was dressed too, watching me as he zipped up his hoodie. "You want me to walk you to your cabin?"

I looked away. "Nope. I'm good."

I felt him move toward me. He hooked a finger under my chin and lifted my face to meet his gaze. He searched my face, slowly, his dark eyes dead serious.

"You feelin' me, V?"

I scoffed. Then I lied to him.

I totally fucking lied.

"No," I said.

But *come on...*

Maybe Jude *was* an asshole. Fucking me like that—worse, *kissing* me like that—and then asking me if I was "feeling" him moments later?

I turned away, zipping up my jacket.

He caught my chin again and turned my face back to his.

"That's good." His dark eyes held mine in challenge, but his tone was gentle. "'Cause I told you long ago, you and me, darlin', we're not goin' down that road."

"And I told you," I said cooly, "that all roads lead to fucking. Which means this road is now closed."

He chuckled, his gaze dropping to my lips. "And what was that other thing you used to say..." His thumb brushed my cheek. "You never go back for seconds?"

I shrugged and pulled away, but I managed a small, coy smile. "First time for everything."

"Second time," he said, "the way I remember it."

"Yeah, well. I've never been great with math."

He laughed. Then he swatted my ass—like I was some fucking puppy he was sending on its way.

"Don't let the wild card thing bother you, V," he said. "You *are* wild. Nothing wrong with that."

Then he did the worst thing of all.

He grabbed my jacket so I couldn't leave, and leaned in and kissed me. I long, deep, passionate kiss that made my clit throb and my toes curl and my guts turn inside-out. It was the way a guy kissed you when he really, *really* liked you.

Except that Jude's affection for me only went so far.

Far enough to fuck me, apparently. But no further than that.

Well, *fuck him.*

I pulled away and walked away, without looking back. Letting him believe that was all I ever really wanted to be to him—the wild card; the party girl—and pretending I was okay with it.

But I wasn't okay.

I knew it as I pushed through the door and out into the crisp night air, and the cold reality of what just happened hit me, full force. Because it *wasn't* just a fuck.

And in the end, it had zero to do with revenge.

I *was* feeling Jude. A lot.

Just like I did back then.

# A DIRTY DEAL

## AUTHOR'S NOTE

In *A Dirty Vow*, when Jesse and Katie head off to their luxury cabin to finally enjoy their wedding night alone, they don't go straight there. Instead, Jesse decides he needs to enjoy his new wife, *now*... And when they stop to go at it along the boardwalk in the woods, Jesse's ex-girlfriend, Elle, unfortunately—for her—sees them.

Later, in *A Dirty Lie*, we briefly glimpse Elle again, as she walks past a naked Roni, Dylan and Ash, outside Roni's cabin—just before Ash disappears into the night.

So, where is Elle headed in the dark all alone? And how is she doing? *Is* she having a nice night? Well... no. As Jesse so aptly puts it in *A Dirty Vow*, any fucking way you slice it, this wedding is not nice for Elle.

But fortunately for Elle, her night is about to take an unexpected turn...

Jaine

# CHAPTER 1

## *Ash*

ELLE.

Long, platinum-blonde hair.

Unmistakable.

Wearing a puffy silver winter jacket and ripped jeans. Five-foot-seven, slim and tanned, with a tight ass, slender hands, steel-gray eyes, and a mouth I'd very possibly kill to kiss.

Dirty's bass player. My friend.

And the groom's ex-girlfriend.

Walking right past me, up the boardwalk.

I was standing there, naked and fucking frozen, cupping my goods in my hands, right next to Dylan. In front of Roni. The three of us were standing outside Roni's cabin, and she'd just informed us that we—Dylan and I—weren't stepping inside until we coughed up some condoms.

And now I was glad she did.

Because then Elle walked by.

And I forgot why I'd wanted into Roni's cabin in the first place.

What was Elle doing all alone? With a tote bag over one shoulder, wandering around in the dark, in the dead of night...

"Didn't see a thing," she said, a note of amusement in her voice, averting her eyes as she walked on by, waving us off. "Have a good one, boys and girl."

"*Damn*," Dylan muttered, his head already somewhere in Roni's bed, the rest of him shivering next to me. "I'll get the condoms." He kissed Roni on the cheek. Then my best friend and eternal wingman took off into the night.

I looked at Roni, and she looked at me.

We were alone. She was gorgeous. Sexy, curvy and willing. The guys didn't call her "wild card" for nothing. I'd heard the stories. Zane. Piper. Even Jude. They all had a story about Wild Card Roni.

And I could see why.

I'd kissed her last night at Katie's stagette party, danced with her, made out with her a bit.

But Elle wasn't at that party.

This was the first time Roni and I had ever been alone, and I really couldn't say what it would've felt like if we'd gotten to this moment without Elle walking by. Because the thing was, Elle *had* walked by.

And now *this* felt all wrong.

I raked my hand through my hair, bouncing on the balls of my feet, just fucking choking on it. Roni opened her mouth to say something, but I cut in first. "Me too." I took her hand and kissed it. I'd probably never kissed a woman's hand before. At least, not a woman who wasn't naked in my bed. Just seemed like the right thing to do now.

Because I couldn't remember ever getting this close to screwing a woman and blowing her off, either.

Then I took right off.

And fuck if I knew what I was doing.

All I knew was I had to get out of there.

I hightailed it up to my cabin and got dried off and dressed. Then I dug out some condoms and stuffed them into my leather jacket. Wasn't even sure why I did that.

All I was thinking about was Elle.

When she disappeared from the fire pit a while ago, I'd just assumed she went to bed. I'd tried to walk her to her cabin, but she wouldn't let me. Said she wanted to be alone.

But clearly she wasn't sleeping, and I didn't even know what to think about that. Except that it bothered me.

Bothered me enough that I couldn't fuck around with Roni, or even go to bed myself, while she was out there, alone.

On Jesse's wedding night.

Because that shit wasn't right.

When I headed back out into the night, the choice was easy: get laid, or go after Elle and make sure she's okay... as I approached Roni's cabin along the boardwalk, I just kept going. I went the way Elle had gone, down toward the fire pit, where the wedding after party had gone all night, with music and booze and skinny dipping.

But she wasn't there.

No one was there anymore, but at least some responsible soul—one of Dirty's management team, Brody or Maggie, no doubt—had put the fire out.

So I continued on... to the only other place the path delivered me: the hot springs down below, on the rim of the cove. As I wound my way down the rocky path, I saw her there.

Elle.

She was sitting in one of the little rock-lined pools, alone.

Her bag—and her clothes—were discarded on the rocks. Her back was to me; I could make out the curves of her slim shoulders in the moonlight.

Just as I opened my mouth to say something clever, hoping I wouldn't scare the living shit out of her, she said, "Fuck off, Jude. I'm fine."

"Not Jude," I said, pausing on a rock above her.

She glanced up at me over her shoulder. "Oh. Hey, Ash."

Not exactly the warmest welcome a guy could hope for, but it would have to do. I knew this wasn't exactly a great night for her.

Who wanted to attend the wedding of an ex—an ex they were still in love with?

"Mind if I hop in?"

Even in the near-dark, I saw her eyebrows pinch together and her arms float protectively around herself.

"It's dark, Elle. I can't see shit."

It was true. Mostly because she was buried in water from the armpits down.

She sighed deeply and said, "Whatever." Then she sank back, resting her head against a rock she'd covered with a towel.

Good enough for me.

I ditched my jacket and boots, then stripped all the way down to my briefs—quickly. It was fucking frigid out, and I still hadn't warmed up after that skinny dip. I didn't see any panties on her pile of discarded clothes, but that was hardly conclusive evidence that she was naked in the water. Either way, I kept my underwear on, out of respect.

Naked or not, didn't seem like she was in the mood to deal with anyone's dick in her face. Even one as awesome as mine.

I got into the water and sank down next to her.

"*Shiiit...*" I sighed raggedly as the warmth hit me. Found a smooth spot to get comfortable against a rock and closed my eyes, letting the heat soak in and the cold melt away until I stopped shivering. Took a while.

Once I'd thawed out, I ventured, "Jude been up your ass tonight?"

"Yeah. He's prowling around here somewhere," she grumbled. "Checking up on me. The usual."

Yeah. I could understand how that might get annoying, given that Jude, while Dirty's head of security, was also Jesse's best friend.

I looked over at her. She was tense as fuck, her pretty face screwed up tight and shoulders up around her ears.

"I'm not even gonna ask how your night's going," I told her, "so you can relax."

Her shoulders dropped a little as she unclenched.

"How about you?" She eyed me sidelong. "Roni?"

"Not happening."

She cocked her head, assessing me. Maybe she was considering busting my balls a bit. Probably. I'd seen that unimpressed look on her face before. Many times, actually. Usually backstage or at some party while I was surrounded by willing groupies and she was on her way to somewhere else. "Dylan win the coin toss?" Her tone was all sarcasm, but the mood rolling off her was frigid with contempt.

"We don't coin toss for girls anymore," I informed her, unfazed. This girl could be a stone-cold bitch to me tonight and it wouldn't faze me. I knew her well enough to know what she was so pissed off about, and it had shit all to do with me.

Anyone who knew Elle would know why she was miserable today.

"Only did that when we were young and immature," I added.

"Uh-huh. So how do you decide who gets the first go?"

I smirked a little, considering how to word it. "We've learned to share."

"Hmm." Her tone was dismissive. Clearly she didn't want any more details on that. Usually she didn't want any details at all, so I wasn't sure why she was curious about this.

"I guess Roni's just not my flavor," I elaborated.

"Right. And what is your flavor these days?" Again, the contempt. Like it was my fault that Jesse Mayes, Dirty's lead guitarist and the man of her dreams, broke up with her like a year ago.

So maybe she was deep in a long-ass man-hating phase.

Still didn't faze me.

I just stared at her, admiring the way the moonlight kinda glowed off her long platinum hair, watching the strands float around her shoulders in the water. The way her face looked smooth and kinda silvery under the stars... and way too fucking young for such a bitter expression.

I wondered how long it'd been since she smiled, a giant, unstoppable smile. How long it'd been since she actually good and laughed.

Or got good and fucked... So good it made her toes curl, and she forgot about Jesse Mayes for a couple of fucking seconds.

"If you tell me yours," I said, deciding to go ahead and straight-up flirt with her, "I'll tell you mine."

What harm could flirting do?

We were undressed, in a hot pool under the stars, it was the middle of the night, and we were alone.

But Elle looked away, staring out over the waters of the cove, where the force of the ocean broke the waves against the rocks just below us.

*Damn.* I lost her there.

Of course, Elle and I rarely discussed sex or relationships. Not my choice. But she was incredibly careful about that. With me, even with her Dirty bandmates Dylan and Zane; basically all her male friends. Ever since the breakup with Jesse.

Actually, since things fell to shit between the two of them, she didn't talk to me about much at all. Not like she used to.

When she was crushing on Jesse, I couldn't shut her up about him. When it became more than a crush, I heard about that, too. When she fell head-over-heels in love... I heard more than I could ever want to know about it.

Now? Not a fucking word about her feelings.

It was as if when she got dumped, she decided not to feel anything at all—other than to freeze up like an ice queen and loathe men.

"Alright," I offered, trying to keep things light, "I'll go first. I like shy, virginal girls who turn into nymphos once I get them in bed."

She scoffed under her breath. "That's a load of shit, Ash."

"Is it?" I challenged, deadpan. "I also like shy, virginal guys who turn into nymphos once I get them in bed."

"That's an even bigger load of shit."

"Why?"

She looked up to the sky and gave a small sigh. "Because I've seen the girls, and the guys, you hook up with." She was really starting to sound irritated. Though why my hook-up preferences would irritate her, I had no clue.

Other than occasionally checking me out when she thought I

wasn't looking, Elle had never expressed an interest in hooking up with *me*.

But she was in a rough mood. She needed a punching bag, she could go ahead and take her frustrations out on me. I didn't mind.

"True fact..." I lounged back against the rocks, sinking deeper into the water. "I like churchgoers I can corrupt. The more virtuous, the better."

"Bullshit."

"I'm partial to nuns, actually."

She shook her head. "So full of it."

"Monks..."

She threw me one of her steely-eyed gazes. The kind that might send a lesser man running for the hills, tail between his legs.

"I'm serious."

"Don't try to play me, Ashley Player," she said. "You like bad girls and bad boys. The *badder* the better."

I shrugged. "Just because I hook up with them doesn't mean I like them."

For some reason, that seemed to rub her the wrong way. I could practically feel the night frosting over between us. Surprised the water didn't turn to ice. "You like the pretty party people, Ash. Admit it."

"Had a thing with a priest once," I mused, even as she made an annoyed huffing sound. "Actually, he was a priest-in-training, or something."

"You like Dylan."

Her words crackled in the night, like an assault weapon fired out of nowhere.

I did *not* see that coming.

She stared at me, and I stared at her.

Silence fell.

Actually, it slapped me in the face.

For a long, sharply painful moment, I couldn't breathe.

Not that *what* she'd said surprised me, exactly. I was just surprised she *would* say it. Because it really wasn't any of her business how I felt about Dylan. He was her drummer and her friend. But he was my *best* friend.

And it wasn't like I had a choice in how I felt about him.

When I found my voice again, I said, as cool as I could, "When are you gonna stop liking Jesse? That gonna happen anytime this goddamn century?"

She stood up with an abrupt splash. Water streamed off her body. And she must've been really pissed, because she was naked.

Like, completely naked.

No panties to be found.

Elle was famous. She was famous enough when I first met her, as Dirty's bassist, but these days she was a veritable one-woman empire, with a solo music career on the side, a rising star in Hollywood, a charitable foundation, and a hot-as-shit makeup line—to list the highlights. Which meant she was incredibly fucking famous; way more famous than me.

She was also private as all hell about her personal shit.

Which meant you'd never find her flashing her goods on a "private" beach for the paparazzi or doing nude photos for Rolling Stone or "accidentally" leaking a sex tape to the media. She didn't skinny dip when the rest of us dropped our drawers and dove right in. She didn't go streaking through parties or humping randoms on the tour bus for everyone to see.

Which meant in the five years I'd known her, and our bands had toured together, I'd never seen her naked before.

I was seeing her now.

All lean and toned and sun-kissed and wet.

I saw her tits. Kinda medium-sized and that perfect tear-drop shape. Her nipples tight and flushed against the cold. The slim curves of her waist. The jewel in her navel ring glinting in the moonlight.

I saw her pussy. Neatly ladyscaped with just a delicate strip of blondish hair... right in my face.

I would've taken a closer look if I'd had the chance, but she was about to climb the fuck out of the pool, so I grabbed her arm and stopped her and looked her in the eye.

"I apologize," I said, sincerely. "Forget I said that. Now retract your claws and stay. It's not me you're really pissed at."

She stood there stubbornly for a long, tense minute as I stared into her eyes, willing myself not to gawk at the rest of her.

Then she softened and sank into the water, shrugging my hand off.

I let her go.

But my heart was beating, thudding, fast.

Elle settled back against a rock, an arm's length from me, and fell silent.

I could've reached out and touched her.

I didn't.

After a while, she said, "It's none of your fucking business, Ashley."

"I realize that."

"You're not in my band."

"Painfully aware of that."

Her eyes flashed to me and she softened some more, finally giving up on being pissed at me.

"You want a smoke?" I offered. I stood up to get one, because I couldn't sit still. A restless, frustrated energy was roiling inside me, making my guts twist.

And making my dick hard.

Lust. I was totally in lust with Elle. No matter how irritated she was with me, my dick didn't seem to care.

But this wasn't exactly a new discovery.

"No thanks," she said, not looking at me. "Just a beer, if you're getting out."

I hopped up out of the pool and grabbed a beer from her bag, popped it open and handed it to her, then fished a joint out of a cigarette case in my jacket, along with a lighter. I lit up and stood there a moment, just looking up at the moon, breathing in the pot smoke and the fucking freezing air, letting my lungs shudder and burn as my muscles jittered with cold.

Letting the discomfort of that other shit roll through me.

*You like Dylan.*

I took another drag, and as the weed gradually did its thing, I mellowed out.

I tucked the joint between my lips and got back in the water, setting the cigarette case, stocked with extra weed, on a nearby rock.

Elle glanced at me as I sank back beside her. "For the record," she said quietly, "and just so we're clear, and you never have to ask me again, I will always like Jesse."

"Fair enough."

"But," she added, "I don't love him anymore."

*Right.*

"Well, I'll always like Dylan." It came out before I was sure I should commit to saying it out loud, but here with Elle, what the fuck did it matter? I'd probably tell her anything she wanted to know, if she asked. And not like this was new information, either. "You say anything to him, though, and I'll have to kill you. You know that, right?"

"You think he doesn't know?" she said simply.

I didn't answer that.

"He's not stupid, Ash."

"Don't wanna talk about it, Elle."

I didn't. Admitting it to her was one thing. Didn't mean I wanted to have an open forum discussion. I didn't really give a shit what Elle or anyone else thought about it.

She went silent. And I could tell she was feeling a little sorry for bringing it up. She never had before, though obviously she'd figured it out.

Maybe the whole fucking world had figured it out by now.

I really didn't give one fuck.

As long as it didn't weird Dylan out and mess things up with the best friend I'd ever had.

"You know I'd never say anything," Elle said with a small sigh.

"You've always been cool about my bullshit with Jesse." She looked at me. "Everyone else gets all tense and tiptoes around it. Even Dylan. Zane. 'How you doing, hon?' They talk to me like I'm some car crash victim recovering, too slowly, in the hospital. Like they can only approach me during scheduled visiting hours and speak in hushed tones. Like they're just waiting for someone to magically appear and give them an update on my prognosis."

"Things are looking up," I said, turning on my best charlatan doctor voice. "She really came through that last bout of screaming diarrhea. She's a real trooper."

Her lips quirked in a slight smile. The first one I'd seen all night. "See? That's what I mean. It doesn't scare you."

"What doesn't?"

She got quiet, for a long moment. Then she said, "My broken heart."

I stared at her, just trying to come to terms with that. With how totally fucking wrong she was.

"It scares the shit out of me, Elle," I told her. "That's why I make jokes."

And for some reason, that made her smile.

"When did you become such a good friend to me?" she mused, sipping her beer. It sounded like an accusation.

"Who knows." I took a drag off my joint. "You're tight with Dylan. I'm tight with Dylan. Guess it was just part of the deal."

"Uh-huh." She narrowed her eyes at me. "You're very sneaky about it, you know? One minute, I'm walking into my dressing room backstage to find you screwing a bunch of groupies on my makeup table... Disgusting, by the way."

I just shrugged, as if to say *All in a day's work.*

"And the next... you're baking a five-layer cake for my birthday."

"Guilty as charged."

She was skewering me with her cool grey eyes, but she didn't have me fooled. Elle could act like an ice queen all she wanted, but I knew she was all warm, soft pussycat inside.

You just had to figure out how to rub her the right way.

"You are one confusing specimen, Ashley Player."

"Ah, but I'm never boring."

"I'll give you that. You're about the farthest thing from boring I can imagine."

I took that as a compliment.

"Just following my mom's advice," I said, using that same humor I used to deflect everything that had ever come close to hurting me. "'Whatever you do, never bore the ladies.'"

Elle half-smiled, but seemed to catch herself before she committed to anything like laughing. "I call bullshit. Your mom never said that."

"She did. Right before she left." I took a drag off my joint and looked her in the eye. "As it turns out, the bored ladies leave."

# CHAPTER 2

# Elle

WELL, shit.

Ash had never told me that before: that his mom had left him. I didn't exactly know that. Just knew she wasn't in his life.

He'd never really been the kind of friend who talked about that kind of thing. Like a lot of men I'd known, he tended to shy away from emotional stuff. Or made jokes about it.

At least, his own emotional stuff.

My stuff... a different story. Ash minced no words when it came to my shit. And as it turned out, that was just the kind of friend I'd needed this past year.

Someone who could look me in the eye and treat me like a normal, whole person instead of some broken disaster victim.

Someone fun, who made me smile when I couldn't even remember how.

Somehow who kept the party rolling. Who kept life rolling.

Who took it upon himself to bake me a five-layer chocolate birthday cake with custard in the middle and cherries on top. Not because I was a huge fan of chocolate cake, but because he knew I'd appreciate the surprise party he threw me along with it, with just a few of the most important people in my life in attendance, and that they—my friends and family—*would* like the cake. That it would make them happy, which meant making me happy, at a time when I'd almost forgotten *how* to be happy. When I was so caught up in other things that I'd almost forgotten it even was my birthday.

That kind of friend.

But it was somewhere around that party that I started to get the feeling Ash liked me as something more than a friend. Which was to say that it became apparent he wanted to fuck me.

Very soon after I met him, Ashley, the legendary Player, went and got himself a girlfriend. My friend Summer, actually. She wasn't my friend then. I didn't know her. But when my band met his at a festival, over five years ago, and Dylan and Ash became fast friends, Ash's band, the Penny Pushers, quickly became a staple on our tours. I met Summer through Ash, and she and I had become great friends over the years.

Somewhere along the way, Ash and Summer broke up. He went on playing. I drifted in and out of a few relationships.

Then I was with Jesse.

Then Jesse broke up with me.

And Ash threw me an amazing birthday party.

And I started to get that feeling when he looked at me. Especially when we were alone.

The feeling I was getting right now.

"When did your mom leave?" I asked, carefully, half-expecting him to blow it off with a joke.

But he just gazed off into the night as he smoked his joint and seemed to be thinking about it. "I was thirteen. She was never mother of the year, even when she was around," he added lightly. "So don't feel too bad about it. I have an aunt who kicks ass, so it all balances out."

"Aunt Ginny," I said. "I remember her. The one in Montana?"

"Colorado."

"Right."

A silence fell, not uncomfortable, though I could still feel that look he was giving me, even when I wasn't looking back at him. *Especially* when I wasn't looking.

No way I could ignore that smoldering interest, burning into me.

Ash was all smoldering heat and angsty intensity, and even though I knew his lighter side—his ridiculous side, the one Dylan brought out in him more than anyone—I could imagine the kind of flaming beast he'd be in bed. All lean and cut and tattooed...

Not that I'd ever really allowed myself to dwell on those thoughts.

It was too... strange. He was a friend. So many of our friends were friends that he felt, weirdly, like family.

Though Jesse felt like family too, and I'd still fallen for him.

Ash, though... he just wasn't my type.

Except that he kind of was.

I stole a glance at him. Inky black hair, gorgeous face. High cheekbones, straight nose, all chiseled, fascinating angles, the kind a girl could get lost in. Dark eyebrows drawn together over blue, blue eyes. Tattoos visible on his shoulders, and a surfer's bod—though most of that was hidden beneath the water right now.

Not like I hadn't taken a good, long look—or a hundred—before. It was pretty epic, as far as male bodies went.

Ashley Player was a thing of beauty.

So maybe I just wasn't exactly sure why I hadn't jumped his bones yet? Or let him jump mine...

Other than the fact that it had never felt quite right to me.

Or maybe it was because he didn't exactly get his last name, his stage name—*Player*—solely because he played guitar.

Or maybe, just maybe, it was because some small part of me was measuring him against Jesse Mayes... and no living human male had yet risen to that bar in my mind.

*Right.* That bullshit.

"You remember that time in Colorado?" he asked, kind of dreamily, which meant the pot was probably going to his head. "In the hot tub." His slightly-hooded eyes roamed over my face as he spoke. "You were all steamed up, like you are now, in that hot silver bikini of yours..." He roamed off there, and I got a little uncomfortable imagining where his mind was at. "You were so fucking drunk," he went on, "and happy, and that preppy douche tried to pick you up? Had no idea who you were. He was all fascinated with your platinum hair and your belly button piercing. Like you were some kind of exotic creature out of his wet dreams he couldn't actually believe was real."

"If I recall," I said dryly, "you got me drunk." I remembered that night alright, too clearly. Ash and his bright ideas. The man could bartend with the best of them, and decided to make homemade Bailey's Irish Cream. It tasted so good I made the mistake of drinking about a blender full of it myself. I was epically sick the next day. "I can't remember ever feeling that gross."

"You were a hot mess," he agreed. "You got lost looking for ice, and ended up in my hotel room in the middle of the night."

"I remember."

"I would've kept you there, tucked you in and kept you, if Jesse hadn't come to collect you." He stared at me with that smoldering, one-hundred-degree Fahrenheit look of his. "You know that, right?"

Yeah, I kinda knew.

I also knew he was flirting with me, and it wasn't the harmless kind of flirting friends sometimes did, that didn't really mean a thing.

There was heat behind it.

And a not-so-subtle challenge.

Actually, he was being downright cocky. Which meant he was being his usual Ashley Player self, but for some reason, it was more flattering than usual. More welcome.

Usually I just let Ash's attempts to flirt with me roll off. He threw it out there, I ignored it.

This time, I smiled. Admittedly, Ash seemed to care a lot about making me smile.

Too much, maybe.

But right now, I'd take it. Because when had it become okay for me to go through life without smiling?

Smiling was something I used to do easily, and regularly. Why wouldn't I? I had an amazing life. I had the band, my career. I had the music. Unlike a lot of other rock stars I knew, I had a solid family, too. Two loving parents, and I grew up with money. I never really wanted for anything, including love.

But then there was Jesse.

And everyone on Earth knew how that turned out.

I took a swig of my beer and just tried to feel grateful, for everything I had. I tried to feel, really *feel*, deep down, happy for Jesse and the love he'd found.

But just like every other time I'd tried to do that since we broke up, and he met Katie... I just couldn't.

I felt the tears sparking in my eyes before I could stop them.

And Ash said, "It's okay to still be pissed. And hurt. And totally fucking sad. Or whatever the fuck you feel, Elle. Maybe no one's told you that. But it's okay."

"Summer's told me," I said. "And Jessa, and Maggie. And now you. But I think everyone else is just waiting to exhale when I stop feeling what I'm feeling, so we can all go back to life as usual."

"Well, fuck them," he said. "There is no 'life as usual.' Life is whatever the fuck it is, right now. And if it's you with a broken heart sitting here with me drinking beer on Jesse's wedding night while he fucks his bride in their cabin, so fucking be it."

Yeah. Never one to mince words.

But I kinda loved that about Ash. The truth was, I was surrounded by yes men, and yes women, all fucking day. I preferred it when people gave it to me straight. Never more so than after Jesse broke up with me—and told me he hadn't really been happy with me all along.

Because who needed that?

I never wanted to be in that situation again. Thinking things were something that they totally weren't.

"Alright," I said, and I raised my beer, sniffing back the half-formed tears. "Here's to me and my broken heart. And to Jesse and his bride."

Ash raised what was left of his joint and tapped it to the neck of my beer bottle. I took a swig and he took a drag.

"Her name's Katie," he said, in the silence that followed.

"Uh-huh."

How could I forget? Her name was as cute as the rest of her. And now her name was Katie *Mayes*. So there was really no getting away from it.

"If you use her name, it humanizes her, and makes it harder to hate her."

"Thanks for the tip."

"You need any others," he offered, "I've got a few."

"I'll keep it in mind."

He was still watching me. Actually, I didn't think he'd taken his eyes off me more than once or twice since he joined me in the pool.

And right now, it was more than flattering.

But it still wasn't enough.

"Do you think I'll ever have that?" I asked him quietly, as if anyone could hear us. "You know, what they have. The way they looked up there at the altar..."

Ash seemed to consider that. "Do you think I will?" he countered.

"I don't know. Do you want that?"

He shrugged and kind of smiled at me. That killer, *I'm a crazy-hot-lead-singer-without-a-care-in-the-world* smile. "I don't know."

I nodded, like I understood that. But really, I didn't. Then I confessed, "I do."

"Then you will."

He was probably right about that. I knew he was.

Right now, though, I just couldn't feel it.

"Look," he said, "I don't know about any of this standing-up-at-the-altar shit, Elle. Weddings aren't exactly my thing. But I do know a thing or two about women and men in bed."

"You don't say."

"And I'd take you to bed over Katie in a hot minute, any day of the week."

I didn't want to be flattered by that, but... "She's not your flavor?"

"Not even close."

"You're saying that because she's with Jesse and she's unavailable anyway."

"I'm saying that because it's true."

Maybe. But even if he meant it, he was just flirting. I knew that. And just like every other time he'd done it, I knew I couldn't take it seriously.

I couldn't take *him* seriously.

I didn't want more with Ash than friendship. One tall, dark and complicated rock star was enough for me. *No more guitar players*; I'd promised myself that after the breakup with Jesse.

And Ash wasn't only a lead guitarist. He was a lead singer, which was worse.

Double the ego.

Double the drama.

Not what I needed in my life.

What I needed, probably, was an accountant. Someone logical and dependable and predictable, with not one tattoo, who couldn't play a musical instrument to save his life, who'd never been on tour, never stepped onstage, never had swarms of groupies begging to fuck him—and fucking with his head.

A normal guy, with a normal life.

Yeah. That was probably where my love life was headed, if I had any sense at all.

But a little flirting along the way... It felt good. I could admit that to myself. Ash was scorching hot, and yes, he'd had more than his share of women, but right now, he was all about me. Maybe it was only for a few minutes in the middle of the night when no one else was around to compete for his attention, but I'd take his compliments.

"Thank you for saying that. It shouldn't feel good, but it does."

"It's meant to feel good," he said, still watching me. Still flirting.

"Yeah," I said, sipping my beer. "I guess I just haven't heard enough of that kind of thing lately."

He laughed. His teeth were white against his skin in the moonlight, and his face lit up. His eyes crinkled at the corners. And, damn...

Ash just sitting around, looking all restless and angsty? Gorgeous.

But Ash laughing? Devastating.

"Shiiit," he teased. "You're shitting me, right?"

*Wish I was.* "Nope."

"Not possible. You're Elle Goddamn Delacroix. As if you don't hear it everyday. People telling you how hot you are?"

"It's different, though." I shrugged. "Different coming from a man. You know, a man..." I trailed off, not sure how to finish that. Not sure I wanted to.

"A man who wants to fuck you," he finished for me. Our eyes locked. "You must hear it from those on a daily basis too."

*I wish.*

"You'd be surprised," I confessed. "I don't exactly let men get close lately. You know, I could go entire days talking to no one at all. Have Joanie take my calls. Hole up somewhere and shut everyone out. It's kind of... pathetic."

It was true. And I'd done it, often enough; had my assistant screen the shit out of my personal calls, emails, everything.

"Really," he said, like he didn't believe me. "So it's true, then. The hottest girls sit at home alone on Friday night?"

"What can I say. You'd be surprised how lonely it is at the top." I said it casually, like it wasn't a big thing. But in reality, it was the *biggest* thing.

I knew I still had my band, my career, my family and my friends. I'd probably always have them. I still had Jesse, even, as a bandmate.

But I'd never felt more lonely, more *alone*, than when he broke up with me.

"Wouldn't surprise me at all," Ash said.

He fished out a fresh joint and lit up. He offered it to me, but I waved it away. I didn't feel like smoking up. The booze I'd drank tonight was bad enough; I was afraid, with this wedding, I was hovering on the edge of some kind of deep, ugly, bottomless depression, and drugs were hardly gonna help.

Ash took a drag, eying me.

"Joanie always puts my calls through," he said after a moment.

"Yeah," I admitted. "She does."

"And why is that?"

"Because..." I stopped there. *Because I like talking to you*, didn't seem like the right thing to say. Sounded too much like flirting back —or giving him the green light to feel me up. "Because you're my friend."

"So is Zane," he challenged. "Willing to bet you've screened his ass plenty of times."

"Maybe," I admitted. "A time or two, over the years."

"How about Jesse?" he asked. "You take all his calls these days?"

"Most of them," I mumbled into my beer.

"Uh-huh. So how come you take mine?"

"Because... You never make me feel bad about myself for being so... fucking broken."

*Because talking to you always makes me feel better.*

That was the whole truth of it, but I didn't say that either.

"How about now?" he pressed. "You sorry you let me in here with you?"

"There's hardly a door on the hot springs," I said dryly. "Couldn't exactly keep you out."

"Sure you could. You want me to leave, you just say the word."

I didn't say a thing.

And the water seemed to heat up several more degrees off the look he gave me.

*Wow...*

I wasn't even sure what to think about my male friend's sex eyes hitting me so hard between the legs.

But I definitely wasn't ignoring them like I usually did.

"So how is it that no man's told you he wants to fuck you lately?" he asked.

I considered that. Considered how far I wanted to take that

answer. But I was starting to feel a little daring here. Enjoying Ash's flirting just a little too much. Because it was making me feel something I hadn't felt in a really long time. Hadn't allowed myself to feel, maybe, since Jesse rejected me.

*Desired.*

"I don't know. Maybe they did and I just wasn't listening."

"That sounds a hell of a lot more likely," he said.

Then I decided to make a bold confession, that was definitely in the realm of TMI. "I haven't been with anyone since Jesse."

Ash stared at me. The joint stopped partway to his mouth. "No one?"

"Nope."

"But... you guys broke up in, like, March."

"April," I said.

Which meant it had been exactly nine months since I'd gotten any.

Well, actually... it had been about ten months. Because those last few weeks between Jesse and I were not good. And he'd barely touched me.

I cringed at that awful memory. The way I did every time I remembered how rough things had become between us toward the end. How quickly I went from feeling over the moon to terrified he was going to leave me.

I'd never feared losing anyone or anything so much. And I'd never been more bereaved over a loss. It was like trying to get over a death; it was that painful. And that near-impossible.

Ash was still looking at me, and suddenly I felt uncomfortable exposing my total lack of sex life to him—a male rock star. A gorgeous, sexually promiscuous rock star.

In other words, a guy who probably got laid within minutes, if not seconds, of any old time he felt like it.

"What about all the guys I see you with?" he asked. "All the fucking time. You've got, like, a dude harem swarming around you wherever you go."

"Right. They're called security guys. And roadies. And publicists, and personal trainers, and massage therapists—"

"And horny fans," he concluded, clearly not buying my excuses.

I shrugged that off. "I don't know. Guess I just never close the deal." I sipped my beer, washing down the truth of it. "I blow them off, or I get Jude or someone to do it for me."

"Huh." He seemed to be digesting that, gradually. "Well, you know you could remedy that anytime you want, right? At least you have options."

"Maybe I don't want options," I said, and the truth of it was painful.

Embarrassing.

Because even though I knew I shouldn't, even though it was fucking bullshit and it was painful and masochistic and *he* was totally fucking taken by someone else, there was a part of me that was still hanging on. A really fucking stupid part of me, that hadn't gotten the message yet. That just couldn't fucking process the fact that my chance with Jesse Mayes had passed, and that he would never again be mine.

That he never really was mine.

Because he never loved me that way.

The way I loved him.

"So..." Ash said. "You don't love him anymore, but you still want him. Is that it?"

He waited, staring at me, until I could bring myself to answer that.

"Does that make me pathetic?" I asked, my voice small in the night, as I surrendered to the fact. "Please just tell me I'm fucking pathetic. Maybe it will help me to snap out of it, once and for all."

"No, Elle," he said, his voice low and unusually serious. Actually, it was filled with compassion, and roughened by just the slightest edge of envy. "It makes you human."

# CHAPTER 3

# Ash

YEAH. She wanted him.

And if she was still this hung up on Jesse, after all this time, and after just watching him *marry* someone else, she obviously hadn't gotten whatever closure she needed out of that situation.

All you had to do was take one look at Jesse with Katie to know Elle wasn't getting one last romp with him, for old time's sake, to get him out of her system. So no closure was coming there. And if she still wasn't fucking anyone else, there had to be something holding her back from getting on with her fucking life. Because this girl could get laid in a hot minute.

For example: right here. Right now.

Any-fucking-where she wanted.

I knew female musicians on the road—even married ones—who had a steady stream of fanboys snuck up to their hotel rooms and out the back door again by their staff. Men weren't the only ones who played those games. And Elle had the power—and the looks—to do it. She could've had them lined up around the block if that was what she wanted.

But clearly, she didn't want that at all.

"You never had the breakup party, did you?" I ventured, already knowing the answer.

She cocked an eyebrow at me. "Breakup party?"

"Whenever you have a breakup, you've gotta have a party. Like an epic party. The worse the loss, the bigger the party's gotta be, to balance everything out."

Which meant Elle needed one hell of an epic breakup party.

She smiled at me, slowly, so maybe we were getting somewhere. "That's kinda ridiculous, Ash."

I shrugged. "Works. Every time. When I broke up with Summer, had the biggest breakup party ever, at Zane's place in L.A.. Woke up at some ski lodge in Alaska, I shit you not, with this hot Iranian-American couple who ran a traveling freak show. Think I picked them up at the airport. Had a new tattoo. Hangover lasted three days." I grinned at the memory. "Best breakup ever."

"I heard about that," she said, not nearly as impressed as I was with that little tale. "The Alaska part, anyway. You know Zane put you on that plane, right?"

I shrugged. "I would've done the same to him."

It was true; Elle's lead singer and I had spent the better part of the last five years in an ongoing swinging dick contest. Clash of the lead singers. He won, most of the time, since he had the bigger band and the bigger bank. Bigger everything—dick included.

But the fact was, the dude made me laugh. He rivaled my antics with women. He had a voice I'd never admit I envied like I did. If I wasn't lead singer of my own band, I'd definitely want to be in his. I could never get in bed with his inflated ego, but other than that, Zane Traynor was a hard guy to find fault with.

Unless, maybe, if you were a chick.

"Hmm," Elle said, with a tone that said *Fucking men.* "And what's the tattoo?"

"That's the part that concerns you about that story, babe?"

She leaned over and poked me in the shoulder. "You're not gonna show it to me?"

"Undercarriage. Trust me, you don't wanna see it."

She leaned back and stared at me. "Undercarriage...?"

"It's under my balls, way up my thigh." When she just kept

staring at me, her slim eyebrows rising higher on her forehead, I sighed and elaborated, "It's a prissy fucking pink flower that says *Danny 4Ever.*"

She smashed her lips together, maybe stifling a laugh. "Who's Danny?"

"No idea."

At that, she burst out laughing.

Fucking *finally.*

I'd searched my memory banks, and I was pretty fucking sure it'd been about a goddamn year since I'd heard the girl laugh—like *really* fucking laugh.

"You've got a tattoo between your legs that says *Danny 4Ever,* and you don't know who Danny is?"

"Yup."

She was silent a moment as she sipped her beer. Then she said, "You must have some idea. Like is Danny a girl? Or a guy?"

"No clue."

"Wow, Ash."

"I know, right?"

"I don't think you do know."

I narrowed my eyes at her through the smoke of my joint. "I know you think I'm a loose cannon."

"Not a loose cannon. More of a... free spirit, dancing to the beat of your own drum." Her smile faltered, then vanished. "You know... the kind that's always breaking shit along the way." As she looked at me, my heart sped up a little, doing this weird, heavy throb in my chest. Because there was something in her tone...

Like she *cared* that I was always breaking shit?

"And why do you say that?"

"Because," she said, still serious. "You don't remember who Danny is. But I'd bet you anything at all that he or she remembers *you.*"

I didn't know how to take that.

I just stared at her in the dark, the steam off the water and the smoke from my joint softening my vision. Then I looked up at the stars.

Let her words sink into me.

It was either the most romantically flattering thing anyone had ever said to me... or it was just plain sad.

Maybe it was both?

"Point taken," I murmured, and I took another drag.

"Do you have any idea at all?" she asked me. "I mean... you could be someone's Jesse Mayes."

"Huh?" I blinked at her. "The fuck does that mean?"

I liked Jesse well enough. He and I would never be best bros; we just didn't have that kind of chemistry. But we were cool.

Didn't mean I wanted to be compared to him in the relationship department. Not in Elle's mind.

"It means, do you even know how many hearts you've broken?"

"Do you?" I countered.

She didn't answer that. She didn't seem to like the thought of it, but no fucking way Elle Delacroix, platinum princess, hadn't broken a heart or two over the years. Or a hundred.

"All this talk of broken hearts is getting me down," I told her, taking another hit off my joint. Between the hot water and the weed and Elle, I was relaxed, buzzing, and decently content. But I was also hard as fuck, my cock throbbing to the point of distraction. "Let's turn this night the fuck around already."

"And how would we do that?"

"We could fuck," I said bluntly.

"Excuse me?"

As if she hadn't heard me.

"However you want," I told her, and maybe it was the pot loosening my tongue, but I fucking meant it. "Right now. Or whenever you want. It doesn't even have to mean anything. It can if you want it to. Or it can just be a friends thing."

She shook her head, looking kinda stunned, but she shouldn't have been. She knew I was hard up for her, right? "A 'friends' thing?"

"You know. Friends with benefits."

Even as I said it, I knew I was hoping for more. That I wanted more.

If I could get it.

But with her, I'd probably take *anything* I could get.

It's not that I was in love with Elle. She hadn't let me get close enough to fall in love with her. Yes, we were friends. But I'd never really gotten behind the veil she wore to shroud herself from the rest of the world. With me, she was Elle, the musician. The famous girl. The rock star. She'd never let me get near the real Elle—the girl inside all that other shit.

Every time I so much as tried to look at her that way, really look at her, really *see* her, she got conveniently scarce.

But the thing was, I knew I could probably fall for her if she let me.

Maybe that's what she was so afraid of.

I could just as easily enjoy the sex and walk away, if she really wanted me to.

Maybe.

Hard to know for sure when we hadn't even gone there yet.

"You want to get over Jesse, right?" I said. "So use me to get over him."

She was silent, so I went on.

"You can use my body. I don't mind being used. Whatever you like, I'm game."

She was staring at me, guarded, but she'd gone really still. Not-breathing still. And not just because she was scared.

Because she was thinking about my offer. I knew it when she drew a shuddery breath.

"That's a bad idea, Ash," she said softly.

"Is it?"

"Yes."

"You sure about that?"

"Yes," she said, her tone hardening.

"But how do you know unless you try?"

"It's a bad, *bad* idea, Ashley," she said emphatically.

"Or maybe it's not."

"It *is*," she insisted. "Completely. Actually, in the history of bad ideas, that may go down as the *most*—"

"Alright, alright." I raised my hands in mock surrender and blew it off. "You win. I was fucking kidding anyway."

But we both knew I wasn't.

"Right..."

"Serious. You're too skinny and too blonde for me," I told her. "And too gorgeous." I smashed out my roach on a rock and tossed it into the bush. Then I looked her in the eyes, my face carefully blank. "Who likes skinny blondes anyway?"

"Uh-huh," she said, sipping her beer. "We are really going out of style."

"Exactly. You probably couldn't get my dick up if you tried."

At that, her eyes flared. But I couldn't really read them in the dark. Had no idea if she thought that was hilarious, ridiculous, or insulting. Or if she knew it was a lie.

If she had any idea how hard I already was, just flirting with her.

She swallowed her beer and said, with a bit of bite, "That's good. Because I wouldn't want your dick up. You're way too tall, dark and egotistical for me, Ash."

But we both knew that wasn't true, either.

# CHAPTER 4

# Elle

"AM I?" he said, and he gave me such a smoldering, *Let's fuck right now* look, my pussy clenched in response.

It had been a long, long time since a man looked at me like that,

Or since I *noticed* a man looking at me like that.

But what the hell was I saying? My words were loaded with flirtation. With *challenge*. And you didn't challenge a guy like Ashley Player to fuck you.

Unless you wanted to get fucked.

He knew as well as I did that "tall, dark and egotistical" was kind of my happy place. Despite my best intentions, it was totally my happy place. Exhibit A, Jesse Mayes.

Fuck accountants.

I might as well have just spread my legs and told him to put it in.

This was the first time I'd full-on flirted back with Ash, ever, but I wasn't really prepared for the result of that flirting: his hand, slipping onto my thigh under the water as his blue-eyed gaze darkened and he ran his pierced tongue over his lip.

"I'm sorry," I blurted, "I don't know what I'm saying. I'm just kind of depressed tonight. Or something..."

His hand froze, mid-thigh.

Then he withdrew the hand and I just sat looking at him, feeling like an ass, trying to figure out what to say that didn't make me sound like a total bitch. A messed-up bitch who was so tired of apologizing for her shitty moods.

"I shouldn't have said that, Ash."

"It's okay," he said lightly.

"It's not. I mean, you are tall, dark, and..." I trailed off. "I shouldn't be flirting with you. I'm not trying to lead you on."

"Okay."

"It's just been a rough night."

"I know."

"Are we good?"

"We're good," he said. "We'll always be good."

But I wasn't so sure.

Silence fell between us. Silence filled with the sounds of the night, the rushing water of the cove lapping against the rocks and peeling away again, the babbling of the hot springs, the occasional chirp of an animal or insect in the woods. The sky was lightening over the trees; the sun would be coming up soon. And it seemed so grossly wrong, so unfair, that this day, the first day after Jesse's wedding, would start off with my heart still such a mess.

But I did not know what to say, or do, to make it better.

"You know what we need?" I looked over to find Ash watching me. "Music," he answered himself.

Then he stood up, water sluicing off his surfer's body—his lean, toned body. His sun-darkened skin... the tattoos that ran down both arms and across one pec, down the side of his torso, and down one hip, disappearing into his underwear. My gaze dropped to his package, clearly defined as the wet black fabric clung to him like a second skin.

I almost choked on my intake of breath.

He was *hard*.

And it was beyond obscene.

He might as well have been naked. I could see *everything*. Even the outline of the smooth, hard stud where he was pierced, at the head of his—

I dropped my gaze, which now landed on the inside of his thigh. Maybe I was hoping for a glimpse of that flower tattoo that said *Danny 4Ever*...

No luck.

It must've been really high up there. His briefs were definitely... brief.

I sipped my now-warm beer and averted my gaze as he climbed out of the water. It was really no big deal. I'd seen Ash's dick before. Not on purpose, but sometimes parties got wild, guys got drunk, and wearing clothes became low on their priority list.

But I'd never actually looked at it *that* way.

Mostly because even when I'd seen it, it had been hot on the tail of someone else. Namely Summer, or any number of people he'd hooked up with since they broke up.

But I was definitely looking at it—at *him*—that way now, as he bent over to dig something from inside his leather jacket and his sculpted bod shone all wet and sleek and hard in the moonlight. He fiddled around with his phone a bit, and I felt kinda guilty gawking.

I tore my eyes away again and took another sip of warm beer, my heart beating faster than it should in my chest.

He came back to the water holding a small, portable speaker in the palm of one hand. He flicked it on, and some kind of sexy dance song filled the air. I didn't know the song, but I recognized the style of the DJ and the voice; it was Calvin Harris.

Yeah. Sexy...

He set the speaker on a rock and used his sweater to dry himself off a bit as he shivered. His cock was still in my line of sight, though it was looking a little less-enthused in the frigid night air. He started to put his clothes on.

And I felt kinda... disappointed.

Fully dressed, he reached for my hand. "Come on," he said.

When I hesitated, he rolled his eyes and turned his head away.

"I won't look. Just do it fast or you're gonna freeze."

"I'm gonna freeze regardless. I was kinda hoping to stay in here until the sun at least came up."

"Still gonna freeze," he said. "That's why we're gonna dance."

Just then, the beat of the song kicked in. Ash looked down at me out of the corner of his eye and smirked.

"Welcome to your breakup party."

Okay. That got me.

I had to smile back. I totally grinned, actually.

"Always wanted one of those," I said.

I took his hand and let him haul me up out of the water. He was polite enough to make a show of looking away, though when I slipped on the rocks and bumped up against him, naked, his jaw clenched. Then I got dressed, as fast as I could, shivering all the way. I didn't look at him as I did it, so for all I knew he was helping himself to the show. But honestly, I was too cold to care.

I used the towel I'd brought to dry off, hastily, but I was still so damp that my tight jeans stuck to me and I couldn't get them all the way up over my hips to zip them. I didn't care about that either. I'd barely gotten everything on and my jacket zipped up when Ash grabbed me—and started spinning me around.

"Come on, you're gonna freeze," he urged.

"Already frozen," I complained.

But I went with it.

Mostly because Ash was a good dancer. He had a serious musician's rhythm and an athlete's body. He danced like a rock guy, which meant more jumping up and down than anything, but that worked for me. It worked for the song. It had a great, heavy, driving beat. Within seconds we had a two-person dance party going.

It felt good. Kinda freeing.

Tension-relieving.

Who needed sex?

My best guess of the song title was, "You Used To Hold Me." At least that's what I gathered from the repeated chorus line. As I moshed around in the near-dark with Ash, he sung along to it, kinda serenading me, and kept grabbing my hips to twirl me around... and I felt fucking giddy.

Before I knew it I was skipping around like an idiot.

I was fucking *giggling*.

Had I drank that much tonight?

I loved to dance, and I loved dance music. Summer—also known as DJ Summer—had worked on my solo album with me; it was mostly electronic rock with a few straight-up dance songs. Which was probably why Ash was playing this for me. He'd never struck me as much of a dance music lover.

But why the hell was I skipping and giggling in the woods in the middle of the night, with Ash?

He kept serenading me, with increasingly dramatic emphasis, like some super-hot Broadway actor, swinging me around... then dipping me low over his arm.

And I felt a rush of... something.

When he pulled me back up, plastering me—on purpose—against his chest, I told him, "You're an idiot." But I was grinning like a fool.

I couldn't remember when I'd felt this relaxed or this good about anything.

It had been that long.

Too long.

"I know," he said.

Then he kissed me.

Actually, he smashed, mouth-first, against me. And I saw it coming. It wasn't like I didn't know the instant it was about to happen. The darkening of his eyes, the lowering of his eyelids, the fading of his smile right before he did it.

But I let him do it.

I let him smear his lips over mine, hot and wet and tasting of sweet-smoky pot. I let him shove me open and slide his tongue, hot and strong, against mine.

I felt the smooth ball of his tongue piercing, and as it ran over my tongue, heat tore down my spine.

Then he started walking me up the rocky path toward the boardwalk.

And I let him.

He wrapped his arms around me, his hands wandering all over me, and he made out with me like he'd wanted this for a very long time.

And it was totally getting me hot...

Any fear I'd ever had about whether or not it would be worth crossing the line with Ash was allayed. Because no question, the man knew exactly what to do with his tongue.

I could only imagine he knew what to do with the rest of him.

And I'd seen the size of his hard-on.

Oh, yeah... This was happening.

When we reached the boardwalk, he pulled away, breathing deeply in the dark, his smoldering gaze locked on me. "You gonna let me fuck you?" he said, his voice rough with lust. "Or should I stop now?"

"Don't stop," I said, pulling him to me by his jacket. "Well... unless you don't have a condom?"

"I have a condom," he murmured, then he kissed me again, thoroughly. He kissed my face. He kissed my neck, sucking and licking, dragging the ball of his stud up my throat.

And I just let him, savoring the feeling of being kissed.

"How do you want it? Back up at my cabin, in front of the fire...?" He was kissing his way down my chest, unzipping my jacket as he went, fumbling with my sweater. "On the fucking floor...?" He was walking me backwards now, along the boardwalk, as he kissed and pawed at me.

And I felt fucking high off of all of it.

It was that reckless, *This-is-probably-a-mistake* feeling all mixed up with *Fuck-if-I-care*, and the strange thrill of knowing Jesse was up there in his cabin, right now, with Katie... and *Fuck him*. He wasn't the only one who could get laid tonight.

I grabbed Ash and stopped dead in the middle of the boardwalk.

"Here," I said.

"Here?"

"Yeah." I tugged him against me, and as our bodies connected and I felt him, hard for me, it felt so fucking good.

I was rapidly forgetting that this was a bad, bad idea.

The worst idea.

*Friends with benefits?*

Did that ever really work?

No. No, I didn't believe it ever really did.

And yet... the words kept coming out of my mouth.

"This is how I want it," I told him. "Right here."

Then I kissed him back, hard.

I fucking devoured him.

I sucked on his tongue, working mine over his, stroking his piercing... rubbing all up on it, on him, as he shoved up my sweater and slid his hand inside my bra. He felt warm in the cold night, his fingers rough with callouses as he squeezed my breast, and I moaned into his mouth. The tingle and the tightening in my nipples was the first rush of true, head-spinning arousal I'd felt in a long, long time.

Then he was working my jeans down over my hips, and my panties, and shoving his hand between my legs.

"You want it slow, Elle?" he asked as he massaged my pussy, slowly, with the palm of his hand, teasing my opening with his fingertips, just lightly. "You want it tender?" He licked his lip. "You want it rough?" Then he delved that magic tongue of his into my mouth again.

The heat and need sparked between my legs, catching fire, and I ground myself into his hand.

"Rough," I choked out between kisses.

Then he pushed me back against the railing. He spread me open and rammed a couple of fingers into me.

I gasped in shock, but I loved it.

"Like this...?" he asked, his voice low with hunger as I undid his jeans and took his cock out. He felt hot and silky in my cold hands.

"Yeah," I gasped, as he fucked me with his fingers, twisting them as he went. He rubbed his thumb over my clit. And it felt *so* good...

Desire was building in me, sharp and quick.

It had been *way* too fucking long...

I squeezed his dick; it was hard and hot. As I worked him in long, tight strokes, I felt the smooth steel ball in the head against my palm. He groaned, and I really didn't care if he came in thirty seconds flat, so long as he got me off.

I wanted it, and I wanted it hard and fast.

"Have you ever... fucked a guy... with a pierced cock?" he asked between kisses, panting for breath.

"No."

He got a wicked smile at that, a very male ego sort of smile. Then he spun me around by my hips. He pushed me forward, bending me over the railing. I heard him rip open the condom packet and felt him roll it onto his dick, his knuckles brushing against me. He held my hips in place with one hand as he lined up his cock with my opening, and I clung to the railing to steady myself.

"Fair warning. It's gonna hit your G-spot and blow your mind."

*Yes, please.*

But he didn't enter me.

"You good with that?" he asked.

Like any girl wouldn't be good with that?

"Hurry up," I forced out, bracing myself. I'd asked for it rough, and "rough" was probably subjective. "I want it fast."

But he still didn't fuck me.

"Friends, right?" he said.

"Yeah," I breathed, kinda rolling my eyes, though he couldn't see it. "Friends forever."

He smacked my ass. Guess he didn't appreciate the sarcasm, but I didn't mind the spanking, either.

"I'll take the benefits," he said, his voice rough, like it was killing him to hold back. "But I don't want it fucking with the friendship."

"No fucking with the friendship," I said. "Just fucking."

"Okay," he said. "Deal."

Then he thrust into me.

And *hell*, yeah. That feeling; hot, shocking... fucking amazing.

"Shit," he groaned. He smoothed a hand up the curve of my back, beneath my jacket. "Elle... you're so fucking gorgeous..."

"You don't need to talk," I panted out. "Don't talk."

So he didn't.

He just held my hips, tight, and fucked into me with everything he had. He was panting, grunting as he gave it to me. The boardwalk creaked beneath us. The waves crashed on the rocks below. My heart beat in my throat, behind my eyes. And my pussy throbbed, squeezing around him as he rammed into me.

My body grew hot, inside-out, warmth radiating from my core as he worked me. My entire body tingled, growing desperate for release as he rocked my hips to meet his thrusts, back and forth, pulling me onto his dick again and again... shoving me toward my climax, inch by inch. And I wanted him to push me there.

So I let loose, relaxing with an exhale, and just let myself have this. I gave into it, for just this moment.

Because I deserved this, right?

Lucky for me, my friends with benefits was a great fuck.

He knew just what to do, how to give it to me hard, without hurting me in the process. How to hold me with his strong hands. When to grind up against me to hit my clit, and when to almost pull out for a breath or two, just to make me want it more.

He even knew when to release my hips and wrap his arms around me so I could feel his heat, his strain and need and his panting breaths, against me. When I needed that feeling of comfort, of acceptance, to really let go.

And he was right about the piercing.

I could feel this crazy-hot pressure building inside as he stroked me in all the right ways. I was definitely going to come—screaming and totally losing it, like a woman who hadn't come with a man in ten long months.

Who hadn't been fucked, or held, or wanted in this way—up close and intimate—in way too fucking long.

And I realized, somewhere deep in the throes of it, on the very edge of orgasm... that this was *exactly* what I needed right now. Maybe it was what I'd needed all along.

A man who just plain wanted me.

And I didn't care what that want was all about. Dissecting it, inspecting it, rejecting it; as of right now, I was just plain *done* with outright dismissing every man who came along because he wasn't Jesse Mayes.

Jesse Mayes didn't want me.

This man did.

Ash did.

My friend.

Now, my lover.

And getting fucked in the near-dark, in the middle of the night, in the woods, from behind, with my clothes half-on... it was downright feral.

But it wasn't just sex. Not for me.

It was crazy-emotional as I trembled and panted in his arms...

I lay my head back against his shoulder. I reached up behind me and grabbed his hair in fistfuls as he kissed my neck, and I held on tight—as all the shit I'd been holding onto, kept locked down tight, came broiling to the surface. The overwhelming tension of it all. The weight of the heartbreak and loss I'd carried around for the last year of my life like a fucking anvil. The crushing *pressure*.

It all just smashed free.

And I came... gasping into the night with the release. Knowing in that instant, with crystalline clarity, that nothing would ever be the same again.

I also knew that I wasn't exactly thinking about Ash when I came—the gorgeous man embracing me, ramming up against me, inside me, as he shuddered and groaned with his own release.

I was thinking about someone else.

But not in a bad way.

Because this was a new beginning. The beginning of *really* letting Jesse go.

I knew it as I rolled on the waves of orgasm, as another man held me tight in his arms...

This was what letting go felt like.

## THANK YOU FOR READING!

Turn to the end of this book to read an excerpt from
Seth and Elle's story, the next book in the Dirty series...

*Dirty Like Seth*

*They all thought they knew him, but only she knew his heart.*

# ACKNOWLEDGMENTS

## DIRTY LIKE US

A massive, heartfelt thank you to all the reviewers and bloggers who have embraced *Dirty Like Me* (*Dirty* #1) and this new series right out of the gate. You ladies and your love of books really, seriously rock. The kind, welcoming, enthusiastic, supportive and sometimes hilarious messages I find in my inboxes throughout the day *make* my day. I could not do this without you.

A big thank you goes to Marjorie and Guinevere for beta reading—once again, quickly and on short notice. You ladies are nothing short of awesome.

My deep appreciation goes to the many reviewers, readers, and friends who are passionately, humorously, sweetly and/or weepily requesting more books from me (asap!) on a daily basis. I LOVE that you're loving my stories and that you kindly take the time to tell me so! (Believe me when I say they are coming, as fast as I can possibly write them; knowing you're out there looking forward to them is a total gift. I promise more books are on their way, featuring many of your favorite characters!)

Big love to my partner, Mr. Diamond, for always being there for every single thing, no matter how big or how small. Thank you for being the first reader of this book, and for helping me make it better; you always do. I'm so thrilled we're on this crazy-awesome journey together.

To my readers: thank you to those of you who have already read and loved *Dirty Like Me* and wanted more of Zane and Maggie. It's thrilling to me that Zane and Maggie made an impression on you in their brief appearances in the first Dirty novel.

## A DIRTY WEDDING NIGHT

First off, thank you to everyone who entered the *Name A Dirty Character* contest, which I ran shortly before publication of this book. It was such a fun idea from the outset, and with nearly 500 entries, it was an extremely difficult choice! In the end, Summer was chosen as the winning name—a huge thank-you goes out to Shellcey Germano, who entered the name Summer in the contest! Summer is a new female supporting character, first mentioned in this book (in the fourth story, *A Dirty Deal*); Summer will first make an appearance in the next book, *Dirty Like Seth*, and may also get her own book down the road, if we (and the men of the Dirty world) fall in love with her! (Update: Summer's book is *Sweet Temptation*!) Also, a special thank-you to Linda Fox and Desiree who both entered the name Skye, which was a (very) close runner-up name in the contest.

Thank you, as always, to the many bloggers and reviewers who continue to support me and my books, writing passionate reviews of my new releases simply out of a love for reading and enjoyment of my books. You amaze me and I am deeply grateful. You'll be hearing from me as soon as the next book is ready!

To the ladies in my book club, for throwing my first (awesome!) book signing parties and sharing your passion for books—including the ones I've written. Thank you for making me read to you. Scary but good. ;) To Chris, for hosting and beta reading and being so generous and cool. And to my many other girlfriends, friends and family who continue to support me in my writing and spread the word about my books to other readers—thank you.

To Guinevere, thank you for beta reading and enthusiastically supporting me and loving these stories. How cool is it that you're now an author? Congrats on getting published, lady.

To Mr. Diamond, thank you for beta reading, as always, for

helping me make it better, for sharing this dream of mine (ours!) and giving it wings. Love you. Now let's make some more books!

To my readers: THANK YOU for reading this book and for coming along on this journey with me. Your daily messages, kindness and support mean everything to me. To know that my writing has touched your lives is awe-inspiring. Thank you for reaching out to connect with me. I'm humbled by your awesomeness.

I'm so honored that you chose to read this book; my intent as a romance author is to spread love. If you've enjoyed this story collection, please consider posting a review and telling your friends about this book; your support means the world to me.

With love and gratitude,
Jaine

# PLAYLISTS

*Find links to the full playlists on Spotify and Apple Music here:*
http://jainediamond.com/dirty-like-us/
http://jainediamond.com/a-dirty-wedding-night/

## DIRTY LIKE US PLAYLIST

*Magic Carpet Ride* — Steppenwolf
*You're Crazy* — Guns N' Roses
*Let's Get It On* — Marvin Gaye
*Woman* — Wolfmother
*Howlin' For You* — The Black Keys
*40 Day Dream* — Edward Sharpe and the Magnetic Zeros
*Do You Want To* — Franz Ferdinand
*Strange Days (Thievery Corporation Remix)* — The Doors
*Can't Buy Me Love* — The Beatles
*Rebel Yell* — Billy Idol
*Whole Lotta Love* — Led Zeppelin
*Just One of Those Things (Brazilian Girls)* — Blossom Dearie

## A DIRTY WEDDING NIGHT PLAYLIST

*A DIRTY VOW*
*Every Little Thing She Does Is Magic* — The Police
*No Diggity* — Chet Faker
*Everlasting Light* — The Black Keys
*A Sky Full Of Stars* — Coldplay

*A DIRTY SECRET*
*Sex Type Thing* — Stone Temple Pilots
*Animals* — Maroon 5
*Fireside* — Arctic Monkeys
*The Trouble with Us* — Marcus Marr & Chet Faker

*A DIRTY LIE*
*Closer* — Nine Inch Nails
*Do I Wanna Know?* — Arctic Monkeys
*Hey Jude* — The Beatles
*She's Long Gone* — The Black Keys

*A DIRTY DEAL*
*Emotional Rescue* — The Rolling Stones
*Snap Out Of It* — Arctic Monkeys
*You Used to Hold Me* — Calvin Harris
*No Good* — Kaleo

*Dirty Like Seth*

*Dirty Like Seth is a reunited-friends-to-lovers redemption story, featuring a fallen hero in need of forgiveness, a superstar heroine who knows how lonely it is at the top, and a secret love that flourishes despite the odds stacked against it.*

## CHAPTER ONE

### Seth

I'd done some dangerous shit in my life. Stupid-dangerous shit.

Getting hooked on heroin.

Overdosing.

Almost dying at the age of twenty-two.

Yeah; those were definitely top three.

But this, right now, had to rank right up there on the stupid-dangerous list.

For one thing, I was trespassing on private property, on the lot outside a bar owned by a member of my former band, Dirty. The entire band was inside the bar, and while they had no idea I was here, they were about to find out. And I really wasn't sure how they were going to react.

But no doubt, they probably weren't going to roll out the red carpet for me.

For another thing, the bar was crawling with security, and the security guys who shadowed Dirty these days were mostly of the ex-military or biker variety. Which meant a whole lot of dudes who knew how to draw blood.

And last but not least, I was leaning on a motorcycle parked at the back of the parking lot behind the bar. A Harley. A bike that didn't belong to me but clearly belonged to a serious biker—one of the West Coast Kings, according to the skeletal black King of Spades insignia painted over the gas tank.

It was Jude Grayson's bike. Head of Dirty's security team. At least, I was banking on that being the case.

If it wasn't Jude's, I was banking on, at the very least, that it was the bike of someone he knew, and therefore I was not about to get murdered the instant the biker in question stepped out the back door of the building.

I was doing what I always did when I was nervous: playing guitar. But my mind was on that door. It was painted red, with a security cam on the wall above, pointing straight down. It wasn't pointed at me, but that didn't mean there wasn't some other one that was.

It was early evening and the lot was deserted. There were a few big trucks, the kind that hauled band gear and film equipment and stage shit, and several other vehicles jammed into the narrow parking spaces. But there was a high fence around the lot with a locked gate, and apparently no one in Los Angeles was stupid enough to climb that fence to get in.

No one but me.

I was halfway through Pink Floyd's "Wish You Were Here" when the red door cracked open and some dude's head popped out.

He kicked the door wide and stepped outside; he walked right over to me, winding his way through the parked cars as the heavy door swung shut behind him. And yeah, he was a biker. A baby biker. Couldn't be more than nineteen. He had an overstuffed taco in one hand, half-eaten, so I must've interrupted his dinner.

Could've been the dude with the earpiece who'd materialized on the sidewalk shortly after I'd scaled the fence; could've been someone on the security cams. But someone had tipped him off that I was out here. And since it wasn't Jude himself who'd come outside, whoever it was probably didn't recognize me.

Someone new to the team.

This kid, wearing a black leather Kings cut over his T-shirt, a badge stitched to the chest that read *Prospect*, looked more stunned with my idiocy than pissed off. I didn't know him, and whether he recognized me or not seemed beside the point. Either way, his eyes were stabbing out of his head in the direction of my ass, which was resting on the bike seat.

Maybe if I was really lucky he was also stunned by my musical skills, because his eyes kept darting from the bike to my guitar to my face.

"Do you know whose bike that is?" he said, his mouth open and full of taco meat he'd forgotten to finish chewing. Apparently, he was more concerned with my ass trespassing on the bike than with the rest of me in the lot.

I kept playing, looking him steady in the eyes, and said, "I know whose bike it is. You can tell him Todd Becker's here to see him."

The kid shut his mouth, chewed slowly for a bit, and stared at me like he was deciding whether I was dangerous, stupid, or just plain crazy. Apparently landing on the latter, he shook his head. He glanced at the plainclothes security dude on the sidewalk, who was pretending not to eavesdrop. Then he tossed me a biker-brat glare that said *Your funeral* and stalked back inside.

And for the first time today, I actually wondered if this was a giant fucking mistake.

Last thing I wanted to do was get Jude in any kind of shit.

When I first found out about the auditions for Dirty's new rhythm guitarist, I'd planned to head straight up to Vancouver to try out. But then I changed my mind. The auditions were only starting in Vancouver, but ending in L.A. the following week. And the more I thought about it, the more it made sense to wait.

Then I'd called Jude and found out he wasn't even in Vancouver. He was already in L.A.. And that sealed it for me.

I told him I was coming.

He laughed.

Truth was, I didn't think he really believed me.

But here I was.

All week, I'd hung out at the taco dive across the street. Each morning, I watched the lineup of hopefuls grow, winding down the sidewalk behind the velvet rope and around the block. Each afternoon, I watched the crowd dwindle until the last guitarist left the building. Most of the time I'd sat on the sidewalk, playing my acoustic, and even though I wasn't intentionally busking, people had tossed me cash.

That was weird.

I once had a number-one album. Now I had crumpled bills in my guitar case.

The end of each day, I'd bought three tacos and a juice. I'd given them to the old guy who lived out behind the taco place, along with all the leftover cash. Maybe that was just sponsoring an addiction, and maybe after all I'd been through with my own addiction I should've been wary of that. But the dude was seventy-six years old and living in an alley; if he wanted whiskey for breakfast, you asked me, that was his prerogative.

It was several days before I even glimpsed any members of the band.

On Thursday, just as the sun was starting to set, Dylan Cope strode out onto the sidewalk from the gated lot behind the bar—his bar—with a few other guys. The dude was crazy tall, plus his unruly auburn hair was aflame in the evening sun, so there was no mistaking him. He was smiling. Laughing.

Dirty's drummer was definitely the most easygoing of all the band members, and it's not like it had never occurred to me to appeal to his chill nature for forgiveness. Problem was, it would never be that easy. Dylan was a team player almost to a fault; the guy wouldn't change his socks without the approval of the other band members first.

Especially Elle's.

I'd seen her, too, that same evening. Elle Delacroix, Dirty's bassist. Also unmistakable with her long, platinum-blonde hair smoothed back in a high ponytail, her slim, tanned figure poured into a skimpy white dress and tall boots. She'd come outside with a small entourage—her assistant, Joanie, a stiff-looking dude in black who was probably security, and a couple of other women. I didn't even get a look at her face. She'd spoken with the guys, mainly Dylan, and after giving him a hug and a kiss on the cheek, she disappeared behind the building.

Were they dating now? I had no idea.

I wasn't exactly in the loop.

I knew Elle had dated Jesse Mayes, Dirty's lead guitarist, a while back; everyone knew that. So maybe anything was possible. But Dylan remained on the sidewalk with a bunch of guys, talking, some of them smoking, long after the SUV with tinted windows rolled away with Elle.

Today, the very last day of auditions, I'd waited across the street until the end of the day. Until every last one of the hopefuls had been dismissed and wandered away, guitar in hand. I could remember that feeling, vividly. Playing your ass off in hopes of getting noticed, of getting invited back, no idea if that was gonna happen or not.

I'd been in that position several times in my life. None more nerve-racking than when I'd first met Dirty at age nineteen. When their lead singer, Zane Traynor, took me home with him, to his grandma's garage, to meet the band. Once I met them and heard them play, I knew I had to do whatever it took so they'd let me stick around. I'd played with garage bands before. But these guys were something else. And they already had a killer guitarist in Jesse.

So I knew I had to bring something different to the mix.

I spent the next three years of my life hellbent on doing just that.

From that first informal audition, to the last show I ever played as a member of Dirty—the night they fired me from the band—I knew I had to kill it. To work my ass off to earn the chance they'd given me. I had to give them something back that they'd never seen before, never heard... something they couldn't stand to be without.

Just like I had to do now.

And to that end, I'd decided I had to be the very last person they saw today. The last person they *heard*. The very last guitarist to audition for the spot. *My* old spot.

So that no matter what came before, there was no way they could forget my performance in the onslaught of others.

*Save the best for last.*

That's what I was thinking, what I kept telling myself, as I sat here on the outside, looking in. Just waiting for Jude to come outside and *let* me in.

But I was no stranger to waiting.

I'd waited for seven long years for Dirty to come around, to ask me to rejoin the band. I'd listened to album after album, watched them tour the world, playing my songs, with guitarist after guitarist who wasn't me.

Then that day last year when I saw Zane at the beach... He asked me to come jam with him, just like he did so many years ago. And that jam turned into a meeting with him and Jesse, and that turned into a reunion show in Vancouver, at a dive bar called the Back Door, where we used to play. That was just over six months ago now. Me, up onstage with all four founding members of Dirty—Zane, Jesse, Dylan and Elle—for one song. Our biggest song. "Dirty Like Me."

Then they asked me to come back to the band.

Then Jesse's sister, Jessa, told them some ugly shit about me.

Then they fired me again.

For six months, I waited for a call that never came.

And now here I was. Poised to prove to them all how wrong they were about me, as I played my nerves out with the music. As the red door finally opened... and Jude appeared.

Big, muscular dude. Intimidating, if you didn't know him. Or maybe even if you did. Dark, almost-black hair. Black T-shirt, gnarly tats down his arms, jeans and biker boots.

And one hell of an unimpressed look on his face when he saw me.

He gestured at the plainclothes guy, who was still loitering on the sidewalk, watching me. Just a flick of his chin. *Take a walk*, that gesture said. The dude was gone, around the front of the bar and out of sight by the time Jude stepped out into the parking lot and the door slammed shut behind him.

I'd switched songs, so now I was just trying not to fuck up "The House of the Rising Sun" as Jude stalked over. He stopped two feet from his bike, from me, and looked me over like he was making sure I *hadn't* gone crazy.

"You kiddin' me?" were the first words out of his mouth. They weren't exactly hostile. More like he was mildly stunned, though not as stunned as the kid with the taco.

I stopped playing, flattening my hand over the strings to silence them. "You rode your bike here from Vancouver," I observed. "Took a few days off?"

He crossed his massive arms over his chest. "Like to do that sometimes. Hit the road. Alone. Tune out all the bullshit." He raked his dark gaze over me again. "You bringin' me bullshit?"

"Guess that depends," I said, "how you look at it."

"From where I'm looking, it looks like bullshit."

"No bullshit. This is an audition." I played a few lines from Jimi Hendrix's "Voodoo Child." Showing off, maybe. "I'm here to audition."

Jude still looked unimpressed as shit. "Auditions are closed. Invi-

tation-only. Pre-screened. And I never saw your name on the list...
*Todd Becker.*"

"So screen me now," I said, still playing, quietly, as we spoke.
"What do you wanna hear? 'Fortunate Son'...? 'Roadhouse Blues'...?"
I played a little from each song as I spoke. "'Dirty Like Me'...?"

Jude remained silent, arms crossed, dark eyes watching me as I
played. The dude was tough to read, but the Jude I knew had always
liked listening to me play.

We'd established a game, early in our friendship, where he'd toss
a song title at me and I'd play it for him. If I didn't know the song, no
matter what it was, I'd learn it, quick. It was because of Jude and this
little game of ours, in part, that I'd become as good as I had on guitar.
Because if I ever struggled to master a song he'd requested, he never
let me hear the end of it—no matter that the guy couldn't strum out a
tune to save his life. And he'd made it a favorite pastime to challenge
me with the hardest songs. In some cases, songs I never would've
learned if it weren't for him egging me on.

"You still into Metallica?" I started playing "Master of Puppets."
Not my favorite band, but back in the day, I'd mastered "Master"—
no easy task—to entertain him.

He cocked a dark eyebrow at me, so maybe we were getting
somewhere. "You remember it."

"Hard to forget. My fingers actually bled learning it."

He grunted a little at that, which was about the closest I was
gonna get to a smile right now. I knew that.

"Or how about some Rage?" I switched to "Killing In the Name"
by Rage Against the Machine, another of Jude's favorites. At least it
was, years ago.

He shook his head, which I took to mean his admiration of my
guitar skills was neither here nor there at the moment. So I did what
I knew how to do: I kept playing. My talent was the only real card I
had to play here.

Maybe it was the only card I'd ever had to play.

"Killing" was another hard song—both heavy and difficult to
master. I'd mastered it. I'd played it for him enough times, long ago,

that it was in my blood. Any song I'd ever learned was in my blood; once I'd learned it, good or bad, I'd never lost a song. Even when I was fucked out of my tree on whatever junk I was on. Which was probably how I'd lasted as long as I had with Dirty.

Yes, I'd OD'd on the tour bus and almost died. But I could always get onstage at show time and nail any song.

Jude just stood there, that impassive look on his face; a look perfected over many years working security for Dirty and riding with an outlaw motorcycle club. But since he hadn't yet told me to take a hike, I knew what he was probably thinking.

It wasn't so much that he was considering his own ass—how this might play out for him if he let me into that bar. More likely he was considering how badly *my* ass was gonna get kicked.

"You want me to dance for you, too?" I challenged, allowing a little sarcasm into my tone.

Jude remained silent until I ran out of song. Then he said, "So this is how it's gonna be, huh?"

"Looks like it."

"Looks like an idiot playing guitar in a parking lot," he said. But then he uncrossed his arms with a small, inaudible sigh. He was looking me over again, top to bottom, seeming to contemplate how quickly the band was gonna recognize me.

I knew the auditions were blind. But it's not like I was hiding who I was. Other than the assumed name, I was still me.

I'd cut off my hair as soon as I arrived in L.A.; it was fucking hot, but the truth was, I was hungry for a change. A fresh start, maybe. No one had seen me with shortish hair since I was twelve, so that was different. I also had a short beard, but I'd been rocking a beard, on and off, for the past few years, and Dirty had seen me bearded. I had aviators on, but this wasn't exactly a glasses on / glasses off Superman trick. I wasn't masquerading as Clark Kent and planning to whip out my cape later.

This was just me.

Faded Cream T-shirt, worn jeans, snakeskin boots, bandana in my back pocket. Metal bracelet with the word BADASS stamped into it, which Elle had given me when I first joined Dirty and I'd never stopped wearing.

They'd see me a mile away and know who I was.

Seth Brothers.

Former rhythm guitarist and songwriter with Dirty. Fallen star. Pariah. And still, whether Dirty liked it or not, fan favorite. No guitarist who'd come after me was loved as much as I was. No one wanted me back in this band more than the fans. I knew that much from the messages I still received on a daily basis. It was the only reason I kept a Twitter account.

It was a big part of what was keeping me here, in the face of increasingly-bad odds. I was starting to feel how bad those odds were, given Jude's hesitation to even let me in the door.

I wasn't quite sure what to do about it. I'd never expected Jude to be my problem.

"You sure you want this?" he asked me, his dark eyes locked steady on mine. "Now?"

"You once said you'd have my back, when the time came."

"I say a lot of shit," he admitted. "Not all of it smart."

"Then we have that in common."

He grunted again. "Tell you what. You play Metallica for me, you've got your audition."

"Great," I said.

Not great. The only Metallica song I knew well enough to impress anyone—maybe—was "Master of Puppets," and that did not feel like the way to go with a Dirty audition. Dirty was not a metal band.

Clearly, that wasn't Jude's problem. He turned his back on me, a non-verbal dismissal, and headed back toward the bar.

I blew out a breath; kinda felt like I'd been holding it all fucking week.

I stuffed my acoustic into its case and picked it up, along with the other case, the one that held my electric guitar—my favorite Gibson. Then I fell in behind Jude.

It wasn't exactly a red carpet, but it would do.

# ABOUT THE AUTHOR

Jaine Diamond is a Top 5 international bestselling author. She writes contemporary romance featuring badass, swoon-worthy heroes endowed with massive hearts, strong heroines armed with sweetness and sass, and explosive, page-turning chemistry.

She lives on the beautiful west coast of Canada with her real-life romantic hero and daughter, where she reads, writes and makes extensive playlists for her books while binge drinking tea.

For the most up-to-date list of Jaine's published books and reading order please go to: jainediamond.com/books

Get the Diamond Club Newsletter at jainediamond.com for new release info, insider updates, giveaways and bonus content.

Join the private readers' group to connect with Jaine and other readers: facebook.com/groups/jainediamondsVIPs

g goodreads.com/jainediamond

BB bookbub.com/authors/jaine-diamond

instagram.com/jainediamond

tiktok.com/@jainediamond

facebook.com/JaineDiamond

Made in the USA
Coppell, TX
05 December 2024

41782610R00187